# NIGHTMARE REALITY

# NIGHTMARE REALITY

## DESTINED FOR DREAMS, BOOK 2

*by*

# GINNA MORAN

*For my mom, Elaine,*
*Thanks to you, I never gave up.*

# 1

OUTSIDE OF OUR DREAM WORLD

**NADIA**

MY HANDS TREMBLE.

Hunter sits next to me on the park bench, clasping my hands. "It's not that bad." A tendril of dark brown, curly hair peeks from beneath his beanie. His hazel eyes shine, reflecting the overcast clouds. A storm brews in the distance, matching the dread swirling in my heart.

I lean into him. "It's awful. People will notice I'm not—like them." I want to say not human, but Hunter doesn't need the reminder. It's been five tough months since I discovered Hunter in Jacqueline Matthews' dream when she first arrived at the Creature Council's compound.

Jacqueline is a sin-eater, who took Hunter's soul as collateral in a deal she made with the Human Preservation Agency, an organization who hunts creatures like me on the notion that they're saving humanity from monsters. The worst part of it is Hunter's mother is a prominent member of their board and because of that, Hunter and I will never experience a normal relationship.

I sometimes believe that's just the life a nightmare inflictor must live. My father and mother's relationship was complicated, and eventually my father drove my mother crazy by inflicting so many nightmares, which led to her being murdered by an HPA agent.

I'm determined to not follow their fate.

I push the thought away. It doesn't matter if Hunter and I could never have a normal relationship, because what we've fought for is extraordinary. We know each other unlike anyone could ever know us since we met in Jacqueline's dream. Our souls connected instantly. Hunter is the only person to ever see me in a dream world as a nightmare inflictor. He's seen me turn dreams into horrifying nightmares, and yet he still accepts me for who I am and loves me regardless. He's my soul mate.

Hunter kisses my temple, drawing my attention away from my thoughts. "They won't."

I sigh, staring at the muddy snow. "They might." Winter arrived like everything else in my life—hard and fast, cold and unavoidable. My entire world changed the moment I met Hunter. I lost the safety of the compound when I forced Jacqueline to return him to his body, but I wouldn't change anything. I'd risk my life all over again so he could have his life back, and I could experience my love for Hunter outside of our dream world.

He laughs and touches my chin, running his fingers up my jaw to tuck my light blond hair behind my ears. "Alyssa will be there with you. It's only until you graduate in a few months."

I glare at him and pull away. "That's what my father said."

I still can't believe my father is making me go through with it. He casually left the student handbook for Northern Bell High School on my vanity table for me to find. I thought the tutor had been working out fine, but since I've been shunned by the Creature Council, it's cheaper to get a public education—in the real world, amid humans. *You're half human...*

The council believes my actions of saving Hunter, who they think was an ordinary human, resulted in Jacqueline's death. Unbeknownst to them, Jacqueline's body died, but she lives on in the agent who tried to kill her. Because I'm an outcast, I can't use any of the council's resources, and since my father traded his freedom for mine, he's been forced to work for the council on a reduced income so our luxuries are limited.

I wish I could tell my father the truth about Hunter, but he'd never trust Hunter with his ties to the HPA. He'd forbid me to see him because the HPA ruined our lives when they killed my mother.

Hunter puffs air through his lips, and I see his breath. "Everything will be okay. You're strong—" He pauses and kisses me before adding, "You're powerful. You're fearless."

I smile into his lips. "I'm a wimp."

"Your boyfriend is an HPA agent."

I pull away and narrow my eyes. "Not really."

He smirks. "I'm still dangerous."

I raise my eyebrows. "So am I."

I tilt my head toward the sky and laugh. He grabs my hand, pulls it to his lips, and kisses my bare knuckles. Warmth blossoms against my skin, and I lean into him until he puts his arms around me. I could stay with him forever if the world would just stop. I sometimes miss our dream world, where it was the two of us.

This empty park will have to do for now.

A car horn blares, drawing my attention over my shoulder. Alyssa parks her silver Corolla and honks twice more, flashing her high beams. I groan and lean my head on Hunter's shoulder. I hate saying goodbye.

"I have to go," I say.

"Please, stay. Just a few more minutes." Hunter kisses the top of my head.

I bury my nose in his coat, breathing in his warm sandalwood scent. "You know I can't." Tilting my face up, I meet his gold-flecked eyes. He kisses my nose, making me smile. "I'll call you as soon as I can."

I get to my feet, and Hunter reaches out and takes my hand. "Stay safe."

I smile again before I turn away and walk to the parking lot. I don't look over my shoulder, because it's hard to leave without knowing if I'll ever see him again. I'm terrified of the day we'll get caught by the HPA or the council. Either one can force us to end our relationship.

Alyssa motions for me to hurry, so I glide the rest of the way to the car. Opening the door, I slide into the front seat. The hot air from the vents warms my frozen hands, and I lean my head on the headrest.

I tap my finger on my knee. "What's up, Lys?"

Alyssa's red braid shines in the warm rays of sunshine peeking through the cloudy sky as the sun sets. "I had a vision Dmitri was on his way home early."

Alyssa, my best friend, is a seer. Two years ago, she found my father while he was on a job for the Creature Council, and he took her back to the compound where I lived at the time. After I was exiled from the compound, Alyssa left with me, and my father takes care of us both. He considers her a daughter as much as I consider her a sister.

My chest tightens. "Will we make it?"

"Maybe with seconds to spare."

## HUNTER

I should be used to Nadia leaving me by now, but I'm not. Her pale blond hair sways as she glides toward the parking lot. She only wears a gray sweatshirt and light denim jeans despite the slushy snow, and her boots don't leave a single footprint.

She never looks back when she leaves me, but I always watch her go. I can't help it. I want to follow her so badly. I want to know where she lives now outside the compound. I don't ask, though. It'd be dangerous to have that information. If the Human Preservation Agency's board were to find out about our relationship, we'd both be dead.

My cell phone rings in my jacket pocket, and I slip it out

and hold it to my ear. "Something wrong?"

"Are you on your way back?" It's Jacqueline, the sin-eater who held my soul captive in a failed attempt to gain amnesty from the HPA. If it weren't for Nadia persuading Jacqueline to return me to my body, I'd still be stuck in Jacqueline's head or worse. We have the world's most awkward relationship, but Jacqueline's grown on me over the last few months. Kind of was unavoidable after sharing the same body.

I stand up, surprised she's calling me now since my shift with the HPA ended over two hours ago. She usually doesn't bother me when she knows I'm meeting Nadia. "Leaving now, why?"

Jacqueline breathes into the phone, creating static. Her silence speaks a thousand words and without her even having to say anything, I can sense she has a lot on her mind—and it can't be good if she's calling me.

I hate to admit it, but spending so much time imprisoned in Jacqueline's mind has given me a sixth sense in recognizing her emotions. While I can't always pinpoint what she's actually thinking or planning, I know when something's off.

"Your mom is looking for you. She has a new assignment."

"What is it?"

I press the phone harder to my ear, expecting Jacqueline to explain, but I'm greeted with silence. I'd think Jacqueline hated talking to me with how cold and steely she is, but that's just her personality. Her ability to redeem bad souls exposes her to the evils people are capable of doing. She takes a person's wrongdoings onto herself and releases the soul to die in peace.

She doesn't talk much about her past, but from what I know, it haunts her in ways I couldn't ever imagine. I think it's why I'm not afraid of her like I was when she first took my soul. I understand her, so I've forgiven her. We're on the same side now as we infiltrate the HPA in hopes to change things for the better by getting people to realize humanity isn't in danger from creatures. In the end, creatures and humans want the same thing—to live life without fear.

I check my cell phone to make sure Jacqueline's still on the line. "Ja—Camille? You there?" It takes a lot of getting used to calling her Camille even though she's in the body of the former Agent Camille. After saving Nadia from being killed by the HPA agent who had trapped them in the elevator at Northern Trinity Hope Hospital while freeing me, Jacqueline body jumped into Camille to save herself. Jacqueline told me she saved Camille's soul by killing her, but I think no matter how often she tells herself that she saves people by setting their souls free, she still feels bad about it. It's why I know Jacqueline isn't some horrible person. The guilt she carries is almost palpable— even if she wouldn't do anything different.

"Yeah, sorry. I'll let you find out for yourself, but I wanted to warn you that you won't like it."

I shake the thoughts from my head. "I don't like most of the assignments."

"You really won't like this one, though. Just hurry up and get here."

"See you in thirty."

I hang up the phone, a heavy pit settling in my stomach.

I've been pretty lucky in my agent training, only having to push paperwork and follow around a few field agents, but so far nothing has made me regret staying with the HPA. Something in Jacqueline's voice tells me my luck has run out.

## NADIA

I fly behind Alyssa into the house. She jumps on the couch, her red braid smacking her cheek, and I slide into the chair across from her. I breathe through my nose to calm my heart, grinning at Alyssa when the front door's knob turns. She really was right about only having seconds to spare.

My father struts in and drops his keys on the small table by the door. His inky black hair veils his face, and he pushes it out of his eyes. His pale skin, a shade lighter than mine, contrasts his black jacket.

I smile. "You're home early."

He leans over and kisses the top of my head. "There's trouble in the city, and everyone is on alert. I came to check on you. I'm glad you girls are safe."

I knit my eyebrows together. "Is everything okay?"

He shakes his head. "The HPA is relentless. An influx of agent activity is scaring the city dwellers."

I lick my lips, swallowing the knot in my throat. It takes everything in me not to rush out the door to call Hunter. He could find out what's going on. "Does this mean no school tomorrow?" It's worth a shot. If the situation is as serious as it sounds, maybe he won't want us to leave the safety of our house.

Alyssa shifts on the couch, her eyes glassing over. "We'll be fine," she says before my father can answer my question.

My father moves away and sits on the couch next to Alyssa. He leans forward, rests his elbows on his knees, and twines his fingers together. His dark eyes shine in the lamp light as he gazes at the rug. "I don't want you to live in fear, Nadi. I was wrong for sheltering you for so long. The board doesn't control our life." He lifts his head to stare at me. "School's going to be fine. I've picked a good one. You'll be with a good friend of mine, Sandy Augustine. He was your mother's best friend growing up. I promise it's safe."

I twist my lips to the side. The name sounds familiar, but I can't find any memories of the man in my mind. "That's not what I'm worried about." While the HPA makes me nervous, I'm nowhere as afraid of them as I used to be. It helps that my boyfriend has an in with them, but I'm more afraid of putting myself in a position where I have to pretend to be human. I look at my pale fingers. "What if someone discovers what I am?"

"We'll figure it out if it happens," my father says. "There are protocols the Creature Council follows that we can, too."

Alyssa stands up. "Dmitri's right. Everything's going to be fine tomorrow."

"Until it's not."

Alyssa laughs and walks toward the kitchen, leaving me alone with my father. I get up from the chair and pad to the couch, plopping down next to him. He slings his arm over my shoulders, and I lean into him. I hardly see him anymore because the council keeps him occupied.

"I know you don't like to talk about this, but I think you need to see a volunteer tonight. You're starting to lose your color." He squeezes my arm. "I can call around if you'd like."

I meet his gaze. I hate this conversation the most. I'm aware I'm going to need to inflict a nightmare soon, and I don't need to be reminded. I raise my hand. "Dad, please, no. I can handle it. I'm not a child anymore."

He sighs. "You're waiting too long, Nadi. It's harder to find volunteers outside the compound."

I don't tell him the reason I suppress my nightmare inflictor side for as long as I can. I'm afraid of losing control again like I did with Jacqueline. I was dreams away from causing permanent damage to her sanity. I barely survived saving Hunter. I can't put myself in that situation again.

"I'll call Cian now." Cian is a longtime friend of my father. He runs The Haven, a club for supernatural creatures, within an apartment building that serves as a refuge for people with special abilities. Since I've been exiled from the compound, he gives me the addresses of people in my suburban community who want to experience what it's like for me to inflict a nightmare on them. It's easier than night stalking humans—and safer.

"Okay," he says. "Would you like me to join you?"

I grimace. "Some other time."

"You want to take my truck?"

"No, I'll walk. I could use some fresh air." Even though I finally got my license, I still don't like driving. I only drive when I have to. I prefer to move by foot.

"All right then but be careful."

I sigh. My father is being more paranoid than usual. I thought he'd gotten over his protective streak months ago when we first left the compound, but I guess nothing's really changed after all. If he didn't still have to work for the council, I bet he'd have found another sanctuary with more protection than what we have at the house.

"I'll be fine. Stop worrying. You've done a great job teaching me how to protect myself." I walk to the door and snag the spelled charm bracelet from the front table. "And I'll wear my protection bracelet."

He glides to me and kisses the top of my head. "I sometimes forget you're not a child anymore."

I hug him. "I haven't been for a while."

He looks down at me and I see how hard it is for him to let me go so I can grow as a person. I just hope he sees past the fact that I'm his daughter. I'm more than that. I'm strong and independent—and I'm not scared anymore.

"I know, Nadi. And that's why I know you'll do great in a public high school. It'll teach you what I couldn't while hiding you away at the compound."

I frown. "So, this whole thing is a test?"

"It's more of a learning opportunity."

"And if I fail?"

He chuckles. "You won't. It'll be no different than visiting The Haven or going to the store with Alyssa."

"Yeah, you're right." Except The Haven is full of people with special abilities like me and if I mess up at the store or somewhere else in public, I could avoid returning. It's different to me.

I turn away to stop from arguing because it won't matter. I'll just take it one day at a time like I've been doing and hope for the best. Until things change with the HPA, this is life—hiding and playing human. I can't wait for the day it can be something more.

Soon.

I know Hunter and Jacqueline will make it happen.

## HUNTER

I jog into the reception area of the HPA's termination facility. I haven't been here since my soul imprisonment, and I contemplate turning around and walking out. Jacqueline leans against the reception counter, whispering to Phillip, the office manager.

Her black hair twines in a bun on the back of her neck, and she wears the same black uniform I do. Her purple eyes look blue in the fluorescent lighting as she draws her eyes to me and smiles. She saunters from Phillip and nods toward the double doors that lead to the elevator.

She touches my arm, tilting her head toward mine to whisper in my ear. "Your mom has lost it."

I grin. "We already knew that."

"No, Hunter. This is different."

Dread pools in my chest. "What do you mean?"

"You'll see."

The double doors swing in, and the elevator door slides open before we can call for it. Dr. Sullivan, the woman who thinks she deserves to be called my mom, pushes her gold-framed glasses on top of her head, pushing back her short, dark brown hair. Her gray slacks and light pink blouse peek from under the white lab coat over it, which I swear she sleeps in.

She used to be a decent person—an oncologist who dedicated her life to saving people—but after the board recruited her to join the HPA, her whole personality shifted. She went from a loving mom to a workaholic, and then she let the power of becoming a board member go to her head. The HPA exposed her to all the bad things of the supernatural world—the destruction and death of humans caused by creatures. But more so, they brainwashed her into believing humanity was on the brink of devastation. She doesn't even think her trading my soul to Jacqueline was wrong. She claims she did it for the greater good.

I force myself to smile. It's necessary to fake a cordial relationship with her. I need her to trust me.

"I tried to call you, Hunter."

Rolling my shoulders, I step onto the elevator with Jacqueline on my heels. "I left my cell phone in my car while I was patrolling the perimeter."

My mom huffs. "You'll never graduate to being a field agent unless you step up."

"It won't happen again, Dr. Sullivan." I won't give her the satisfaction of calling her Mom.

I actually left the HPA issued cell phone in a lockbox I've hidden in the empty field where I usually park my car when I'm on perimeter patrol. While I doubt the board will track me because I've given them no reason to be suspicious, I don't like to carry my work phone unless I have to. I also use a prepaid phone for personal use to make it harder for the board. It's not perfect, but Nadia and I are willing to risk it to stay in contact with one another.

"It better not. We have a reputation to maintain."

Jacqueline doesn't say anything through our conversation, and when the door slides open, she exits first. I follow Dr. Sullivan out, and she leads the way to a restricted area I've never had access to. She stops in front of the door and enters a pass code before it opens.

Cold air hits my face, the temperature vastly cooler in this section. The plain cement corridor greets me with bare, recessed lighting running along the ceiling. Dr. Sullivan's black stilettos echo as she struts in front of us, and I glance at Jacqueline who stares straight ahead, stone-faced. She's not giving anything away.

I clear my throat. "What zone is this?"

Dr. Sullivan glances over her shoulder. "It's the green zone."

I scrunch my brows, trying to remember what that means.

"It's the holding area of non-threatening supers," Jacqueline whispers.

I stiffen my shoulders. Dr. Sullivan stops in front of a door with a small window. I shove my hands in my pockets and press my lips together, feigning a bored expression to mask my curiosity.

"What are we doing here?" I ask.

Dr. Sullivan touches my shoulder. "Congratulations, Hunter. You've been promoted to caretaker of the green zone with Agent Camille. The board sees great potential with you two as partners. The green zone will give you experience for field work." She adjusts her glasses from her head to her nose, and they reflect blinding light in my eyes.

I drop my gaze to the floor, the corners of my mouth twitching up. "Awesome." My voice sounds flat, but I haven't exactly been enthusiastic since reuniting with my body.

Tugging me closer to the door, she points through the window cutout before tapping her nail on the plexiglass. "The green zone is practically empty for now, so it won't be overwhelming. This specimen was caught assisting a shape shifter. He beat up an agent before being tranquilized."

I peek in the window, blinking to hide my surprise. "What is he? He looks human."

Dr. Sullivan chortles. "That's what his DNA says."

"Why are we keeping him?"

"Because I'm not fully convinced he is. He's unaffected by Serum-A127," she says.

I rub my hand across my forehead. Serum-A127 is an amnesia-inducing drug that allows the HPA scientist and doctors to manipulate the memories of humans. It's their way of cutting a human's ties to the supernatural world without having to hurt humans. "Interesting."

"He fought fiercely to protect a shifter, so we think he's working with the Creature Council. He'll be detained until we get answers."

"And then what?" I catch Jacqueline's eyes, and she shakes her head. "Never mind." I know what the answer is. We're at the termination facility after all. It's where they bring supers to murder them.

I watch the guy shift on the bed to glance at the window. He meets my stare, and I think about how one of these days it could be Nadia imprisoned, or even me, for going against the board. I stayed to protect her. But what about everyone else? I want to make a difference, and this might be my chance.

The guy's blond hair shines in the harsh lighting, his bluish-green eyes creasing in the corners from frowning. He wears plain white scrubs that are the standard attire provided by the board and looks miserable. Seeing him locked in this room reminds me of my time imprisoned in Jacqueline's mind with no one to help me until Nadia came along, and I remember how hopeless I felt. No one deserves that kind of fate. I'm going to have to figure out how to save him.

# 2

━━━━ ❧ ━━━━

## IT WON'T ALWAYS BE LIKE THIS

━━━━ ❧ ━━━━

### NADIA

THE NEAREST VOLUNTEER resides a mile away from home. I glide through the quiet neighborhood, in the middle of the street, so I don't get too close to any houses that may have someone sleeping inside. It's too easy to get distracted when I'm hungry, and I can't risk slipping up with a stranger.

Turning right onto a short cul-de-sac, I find the dark house of my volunteer nestled at the end of the street. I can sense everyone sleeping before I even touch my hand to the doorknob. It's unlocked, but probably spelled to keep humans out, and I enter a small tiled foyer. *Up the stairs, second door on the left.*

I chant the directions over and over in my mind, sensing

three sleeping people in this house, but it's only Lilyana Christianson I'm after.

I glide across the disorganized living room. A messy coffee table sits in front of a tan couch, and a few dirty dishes clutter the side table next to a recliner. A vase of dead roses decorates a short wooden bookcase near the stairs, and I pick up a dried petal off the floor and crumple it between my fingers.

*Get in and out.* Shaking the thought from my mind, I head up the stairs to an ivory carpeted hallway. Family portraits hang on the walls without any semblance of organization, leading up to the untidy linen cabinet spewing towels onto the floor. I stiffen as I pass the first door on the right and force myself to keep going. Without touching my feet to the floor, I enter the second door on the left.

A couple sleeps together on a queen-sized bed. The woman, Lilyana, rests her bare leg on top of the comforter. Strands of her messy brown hair hang from a braid, and she sleeps with an arm sprawled across her face. I glide to her bedside without looking at her partner and touch my fingers to her temples.

My stomach drops, and within seconds, I'm standing in the landscape of her dream, hovering on a dry hillside overlooking a residential neighborhood. Letting my feet touch the ground, I waste no time beginning the nightmare and want it over as quickly as possible.

The dead brush sparks and catches fire, the orange flames brilliant under my feet.

The faster I devour the dream, the less affected Lilyana will be. I'm more cautious now than I've ever been after nearly turning Jacqueline crazy from how often I invaded her dreams. My experience with Jacqueline let me see how I really affect a person's mind.

Dark smoke billows toward the cloudless sky, the hill erupting in intense flames. I trail along with them as they lick and burn the ground. Ash rains down from the smoky sky, and I smile at the first sound of screams. I'm not a terrifying monster in this nightmare, but a devastating natural disaster that's sweeping through this dream community, sparing nothing and no one.

As I glide closer, the blazing inferno surrounds me. The sunshine disappears in the haze of smoke. The burning ground crackles, yearning for the tears of its victims. Flames set my white dress ablaze, and I run my fingers through the black cloud of smoke.

The fire jumps and moves. Pieces of flaming debris fly through the air and land on the roof of a house. Within seconds, it's engulfed in flames. I suck in breath after breath of the dream world's destruction.

A woman's screams ring through the thick air, drawing me to her. I move past the burning house and find my dreamer kneeling in ash-covered grass. She clutches a half-burned photo album to her chest, hot tears branding her cheeks with black streaks of soot. She watches in horror as her house collapses with all her cherished memories, beloved possessions, and everything she owns still inside.

She chokes and spits as I draw near, gasping for breath that will never come to her. Her nightmare tastes like cinnamon and nutmeg. Wrapping my arms around her, I smile while destroying the rest of her nightmare.

I'm out of the house within seconds. My skin steams with the memory of the warm flames on this freezing cold night. I hug my jacket tighter and head toward a small shopping center outside my neighborhood. Pulling a few quarters from my pocket, I shove them into the coin slot of the old payphone hanging on the side of the building. I can't resist calling Hunter after I inflict a nightmare. It's when I think about him most and about the dreams we used to share.

I dial his number, one of the few I've memorized, and watch my breath fog the air as I breathe through my mouth. It rings four times before I hang up. I'll call again in five minutes, so he has time to get somewhere safe if he's able to talk.

Rubbing my hands over my arms, I lean my back on the stucco wall and watch the parking lot. Most people are home sleeping this time of night, though the rumble of an engine draws my attention to the street. Bright headlights illuminate the road, and I duck into the shadows, the closed market lit up just enough that a passerby could see me if I don't hide.

A black SUV slows to a stop at the stop sign and then continues driving straight down the road. I release a breath and stroll back to the payphone. Dialing Hunter's number again, I turn to face the street, listening to it ring.

"Agent Hunter."

I clear my throat. "It's me."

Hunter breathes into the phone. "Can we meet?" His low voice wraps me in warmth, fighting the winter night, though he sounds weird—different. Nervous even.

My heart hammers. "Is something wrong?"

"Yeah. I need to see you."

I hold my shaking hand to my chest and say, "Meet me at the bus stop on Sunrise and Silverwood near Canyon Road."

The line drops without Hunter saying a word, and I hang up the receiver. Covering my face with my hands, I inhale a few deep breaths through my nose, wishing Hunter would have given me at least a clue as to what's wrong. Right now, all I can think about is the worst has happened. That the board discovered the truth about him and Jacqueline, and he's been waiting for my call.

Dread swirls in my stomach, my feet heavy as I force them to take each step without gliding, though I want nothing more than to fly through the night.

*Alyssa would've seen something,* I think to myself. *It's going to be okay.*

It's all I can hope for.

## HUNTER

I wasn't expecting Nadia to call me so soon, but I'm glad she did. I don't think I could've waited a few days to tell her about my new assignment.

I park my BMW wagon at the bus stop where I'm meeting Nadia and shut off the engine. Leaning against my car, I pull my beanie down lower on my forehead, stopping snowflakes from landing on my face. I wish spring were here already, but winter has barely started.

The empty field stretches toward a residential neighborhood across from me. Nerves settle over me, thinking I might be closer to Nadia's house than I've ever been, since we usually put a lot more planning into meeting each other.

A white figure catches my attention, zooming through the field, and Nadia blinks into view. Her pale blond hair cascades from a high ponytail. Wearing a puffy white jacket and jeans, she's eerily beautiful, like an apparition in the snow. She smiles when she sees me, and I stand up straighter and open my arms for her to fall into.

I kiss her and embrace her for a moment, wishing I could meet her somewhere normal instead of abandoned places in the middle of the night. "I'm glad you called."

"Is Jacqueline—are you—?"

"We're fine. It's okay," I say, worry washing over me. Of course that's what she'd assume when I told her something was wrong.

She pulls away. "Oh, thank God. I was scared."

"I'm sorry, Nadia. I didn't mean—"

Cutting my apology off with a sweet kiss, she slides her hands around my neck, pressing into me. "As long as you're safe, I'm fine. And I'm happy we could meet despite whatever it is. I missed you."

Holding her for a long moment, feeling her breathe her

cool breath on my neck, I soak in everything about her into my soul, the memory of how our souls used to touch in the dream world consuming my thoughts. "It won't always be like this."

She pouts her always kissable bottom lip, but pulls too far back away for me to do so. "And if it is, we'll manage."

Guiding her to my car, I slide into the backseat after her and touch her chin so she looks into my eyes. A flash of sorrow softens her features. I hate seeing her eyes glass over like this so much so that I hesitate to tell her why I wanted to meet her. I don't want to worry her. The only thing I want to ignite from her is happiness, love...desire. All the good stuff that stirs within me every time I see her.

"I'm willing to leave the HPA for you. Just tell me and I will," I say, blowing a breath of air through my lips.

She crinkles her nose. "And then what? I can't run away and neither can you. It wouldn't be easy. The HPA would hunt you down."

"I can protect us."

She closes her eyes for a second. "I want to, but no, Hunter. I can't."

I keep my face expressionless. "The offer will always be here."

Wrapping her arms around me, she clings to me before shifting onto my lap, still holding my neck. She slides her cold fingers into my jacket, resting them on my warm shoulders. I haven't seen her wear gloves once, but I don't mention it. She never complains about the weather.

"I only have a few minutes," she says, pressing her forehead to mine.

"It's the middle of the night. No one will miss us."

Her eyes shine with tears, and one slips onto her cheek. "Hunter..." Her voice trails off.

I swallow and stare into her indigo blue eyes, so vibrant I know she must've come from a volunteer's house. A blip of jealousy warms my insides, wishing I could see her in a dream again as the beautiful nightmare inflictor she is.

"Nadia, I—" I don't want to mess up this moment with my HPA problems. If I wait a while longer, she'll have to leave and then I won't have to tell her. *But you have to tell her.*

I press my lips together.

She frowns even more, her forehead furrowing. "You're thinking about not telling me why you wanted to meet here."

I nod. "It might upset you, and I hate doing that."

"You're not who upsets me. Is it the board?"

I nod again.

"Just tell me."

I sigh, tilting my head toward the roof. "They've assigned me as a caretaker of the green zone at the termination facility."

"That's bad." She doesn't ask but says it. "You don't have to—" Taking a deep breath, she pauses for a moment. "You don't have to kill people, right?"

I meet her eyes. "No, at least I don't think so. I wouldn't."

"So, everything's still okay?" Her indigo eyes shine. "For a second I thought you wanted to run away because, well, you're not a murderer." A few strands of her pale blond hair fall from her ponytail, and she tucks them behind her ear. "I don't think this is the end of the world. You can manage. I know you can."

I twist my lips to the side, wishing I could think like her. It feels like the world may end at any second for me. "There's more," I finally say.

She grimaces, her hands trembling under my jacket. "Just tell me, Hunter."

"I saw a prisoner in my zone, and he appears to be human. The board is getting out of control. They're starting to take anyone who they suspect has ties to the council and the supernatural world when they used to just concentrate on creatures."

"So much for fighting for humanity if they're just taking anyone." She leans her forehead to mine, like she prefers to be close enough to touch but not have to see my eyes clearly.

"They look at the bigger picture. Keeping one person is nothing to them—not if they can use them to save more humans."

"What made them suspect?"

"He was caught defending a shifter, and he's resistant to the board's memory altering drugs."

Nadia eases back to look at me. "He must not be one-hundred percent human."

I frown. "That's what the board thinks, too."

Nadia stares off into space with a million questions furrowing her brows. She sucks in her bottom lip and looks so fragile that I'm afraid if I say anything more, she'll shatter into a million pieces like a dropped porcelain doll.

After a silent minute, she releases a breath. "What will happen to him?"

I look away. I can't form the words to tell her that he's basically on death row. Depending on the circumstance and what kind of creature it is, the HPA will hold a creature prisoner and try to extract usable information from them—anything they don't know or they want to find out about to help their agents do a more efficient job at catching or killing any creatures who are a threat.

Then, other times, the HPA scientists will perform experiments to discover things like weaknesses, strengths, if they can breakdown a creatures genetic makeup and recreate it—a lot of different things. Creatures who fight or pose an immediate threat are usually eliminated on the streets by an agent or in the black zone of the termination facility.

Nadia shifts on my lap and pulls her hands out from my jacket. She touches my cheeks with her cool fingers. "Hunter?"

I meet her gaze but don't say anything.

"They're going to kill him, aren't they?"

I shrug. "Probably."

## NADIA

My chest tightens. Maybe we should run away after all. While Hunter isn't murdering anyone, he'll have to sit around and watch the board do it for him. Every person who arrives in his section will be another face to haunt him. He's been through enough already. He'd never admit it, but this may be enough to break him.

Hunter rubs his finger over my damp cheek. "I won't let them hurt him."

Pressing my lips together for a moment, I force myself to open my mouth to ask the question on my mind. "It could put you at risk. What do they do with traitors?"

He doesn't answer.

I slide from his lap and out of his car. "I have to tell my father. Maybe he can save him."

Hopping out after me, he grabs my hand, begging me to close the distance between us. "Will you tell him about me?"

This is so complicated. I can't tell my father about Hunter. If my father found out I've been lying to him and risking my life seeing Hunter, he would do something crazy like send me to a faraway sanctuary. Even if I don't deserve my father's trust, I don't want to lose it. My father would do anything to protect me, including making sure I'd never see Hunter again, and it's hard enough being with Hunter as it is. It's why only Alyssa and Jacqueline know I've been seeing Hunter since helping him back to his body.

I shake my head, clenching my hands into fists. "He won't understand, but we have to do something without risking our relationship. Maybe Alyssa will know what to do."

He hugs me. "We'll figure this out."

"I have to go," I say, hating the words so much, because I never want to leave.

"Stay with me a while longer."

I kiss him. He asks me this every time, and every time, I have to deny him. If I stay, I'll never leave. I'll let him convince me to run away with him. "I'll call you soon."

Gliding away, I don't give him a chance to stop me. I cross the street and walk into the empty field that backs up to my neighborhood. The charmed bracelet my father gave me lies on the ground where I dropped it, and I wrap the string around my wrist. To Hunter, it'll look like I disappear, but he just won't be able to focus on me. I don't look back to watch him drive away.

## HUNTER

I hate we're in this position in the first place. We shouldn't have to worry about when we'll see each other again. It sucks. But Nadia's worth it. I wouldn't trade this for an easy life if it meant I couldn't be with her.

I move to the driver's side and get in, leaning back. I don't feel like going home yet. Cracking the window, I let in freezing air because it helps clear my head. In a few hours, I'll have to look the prisoner in the eyes. It's not like I can tell him I'm on his side, either. It'd be too risky.

Sighing, my breath fogs the air. I pull my jacket tighter, now colder and lonelier without Nadia here.

I pull my cell from my center console and glance at a missed call from my brother on my HPA cell phone. I've been avoiding Mason for weeks since I heard my mom talking to another doctor about bringing Mason on as an intern at the facility. He'd be in a similar position as I was when my mom traded my soul to Jacqueline. I'd hate to have to look him in the face all the time. It's been easy not seeing him since I moved in with my aunt. I had to move because I couldn't stand to be in the same house as my mom.

Mason is one of the few people who know the truth about what my mom did to me, but it's like he doesn't believe it. He plays everything off as a coincidence, and he even had the nerve to say that it was possible I'd been dreaming in a coma despite the fact I was never in one and my body was brain-dead without my soul.

I contemplate not calling him back, but I've ignored the last five messages he left me. I have to pretend his beliefs don't bother me and that I believe in the HPA's ideologies so he doesn't suspect otherwise and bring up his suspicions with our mom.

Pressing Return Call, I listen to the phone ringing through my car speakers. I beg for it to go to voicemail, but after the third ring, Mason picks up.

"You're the hardest person to get a hold of, man," Mason says. "I figured the middle of the night was the only time you weren't hung up on something."

"Sorry, Mase. Been busy. Got promoted today." Heading out of the suburban neighborhood, I merge onto the highway. It's twenty minutes from the city and about thirty from my place.

"Mom told me, congrats. Maybe you can show me your zone sometime." Mason breathes in to the phone.

I stare out the windshield, trying to come up with an excuse to not let him. "Maybe in a few weeks once I'm adjusted to the new routine."

"Sure, Hunter. I miss hanging out with you."

I clear my throat. "Hey, Mason, I gotta go. My shift starts earlier than I'm used to." I change the subject so he can't confront me about how I don't make time for him. The truth is I don't want to. I've changed too much to have the relationship we used to have before Jacqueline showed me the real world through her eyes.

"Well, call me the next time you're free, and we can hang out."

I nod even though he can't see me through the line. "Sure. Maybe in a few days."

Hanging up the phone, I push my guilt to the back of my mind. I wish my relationship with my brother were different, and I could tell him what I know, but he's in too deep with my mom and the HPA. I know it wouldn't go over well. He'd think I was crazy and a traitor.

Well, I *am* a traitor to the HPA. I just hope they never find out.

## NADIA

I open the front door and find my father and Alyssa on the couch. Alyssa was asleep when I left, and my father had gone out for what I thought was the rest of the night. I hope they haven't been waiting long.

I tuck the loose strands of hair that fell from my ponytail behind my ear and slide into the armchair, crossing my legs.

"What's wrong?"

"The son of an enchantress was taken by the HPA earlier today," my father says.

I blink a few times to hide what I know. That explains why Hunter thought the prisoner was human. Men can't be enchantresses, because power only runs in the women. The only thing that makes a son of an enchantress different from humans is that his enchantress blood will protect him from being manipulated, whether it is by the magic of another creature or science. He can also pass down the enchantress ability to his female children.

"That's terrible," I say after a few seconds. "Is there anything you can do?"

My father straightens his shoulders. "Not without orders from the council."

"Why are you telling me this?" I ask.

"Because it's no longer safe to go to the city. The boy shouldn't have been taken. He wouldn't register as a creature. And honestly, I'm not even sure it's safe where we are in the suburbs. So tomorrow, I want you both to go straight to school and straight home. Don't stop anywhere."

My mouth drops open. "I thought you didn't want us to live in fear?" While I wasn't looking forward to school, I don't want my freedom stripped from me. How will I meet with Hunter? "This isn't fair."

Alyssa looks from me to my father. "Yeah, Dmitri. You know we can take care of ourselves. I don't see anything bad happening to us."

My father sighs. "It won't be forever. Just give things a few days to settle."

I stand and turn toward the hallway. Arguing won't make a difference. Alyssa gets up, and we leave my father looking sullen on the couch and head to my room. Alyssa opens the door and saunters to my bed before plopping down. I close the door, meeting her serious eyes.

She pats the bed next to her. "I saw something."

I twist my lips to the side. It's been a while since Alyssa wanted to share a vision with me. She doesn't tell me about them unless they're important or it's something I can try to change. While her visions are based on the decisions people make and aren't always set in stone, there's a possibility that what she sees will come true. "Why didn't you say anything?"

"Because I saw the taken boy with Hunter." Alyssa stares at me, and I hold my serious expression even though I know she'll see right through me. She's been so supportive of my relationship with Hunter, I'm nervous she'll eventually tell me it's not going to work out. It's one of my greatest fears, because I want nothing more than for it to work.

I slide out of my jacket. "What?"

Her eyes widen. "You know."

I can't keep anything from Alyssa. "I just saw Hunter, and he told me."

"What are you planning to do?"

Twining my fingers together, I shift in my spot. "I don't

know. I was hoping you could help me."

"I'm a seer, Nadia. I can only predict the outcome of your decisions. You know that."

I pull the elastic band from my hair and pale blond tresses fall over my shoulder. "He's in serious trouble, Lys. They have him at the termination facility. It's where—"

Alyssa's eyes glass over and she shudders. Raising her hand, she cuts me off. "The boy will die."

# 3



# THE RIGHT THING

## NADIA

I PRESS THE phone to my ear. "It's bad, Hunter. Please promise me you'll be careful. If they suspect anything, get out." I can't bring myself to warn Hunter about Alyssa's vision. He probably already knows.

He clears his throat, like his words are hard to say. "How will I find you? I won't leave without you."

I play with the payphone cord. "Hopefully we'll never have to worry about that, but if it does come down to it, I'll find you."

Groaning into the line, he says, "I still think we need a

plan. Can we meet later today? My shift starts in thirty minutes, but I should be home by this afternoon." The sound of running water partially muffles his voice.

Alyssa honks her horn.

I glance at her over my shoulder. "I'll call you if I can, but I have to go."

"Nadia?"

"Yeah?"

"You're going to be fine today."

I smile. "I love you, Hunter."

Hanging up the phone, I glance at the gray sky once and dash to the car. Alyssa reverses before I have a chance to buckle my seatbelt and merges onto the busy street. She flips down her sun visor and watches me in her peripheral vision.

I tap my fingers on the dashboard. "Let's go to the mall instead of school."

Alyssa laughs, hitting her throttle to pass up a slow car. "We'll get caught."

"It'd be worth it."

"Then we'll be grounded past the few days Dmitri wants us to stay home."

I sigh. My father has as many rules as the compound, but I don't miss feeling like an outcast. I'd never want to go back. I hated it there. The council, especially Mr. Soto—the head council member—treated me like a monster every time my father left to do the council's bidding. They constantly reminded me that the only reason I was under their protection was because they needed my father, and now, he's bound to always serve them all because of me. My father swears he's fine with it, but I can see it every time he leaves that he wishes he could stay. I hope it's not like this for him forever.

I tuck my hair behind my ear. "At least we have the same lunch period. It's so lame we don't have any classes together."

She reaches over and touches my knee. "It's only for a few months and then high school will be behind us."

Alyssa pulls into a parking lot marked for students next to a towering, three-story brick building. A digital sign on top of a pole displays upcoming events for Northern Bell High School. My boots crunch on a mixture of mud, slushy snow, and salt when I step from the car. I shove my bare hands into my pockets, regretting not wearing the gloves my father bought me a few weeks ago. I should try harder to blend in.

Pressing my lips together, I snatch my satchel from the backseat, slinging it over my shoulder. Alyssa slides her backpack on and runs her fingers through her coppery red hair to pull it free. Her green eyes sparkle in the morning light. She looks ethereal against the contrast of the dreary parking lot.

Alyssa hooks her arm with mine and drags me to the front entrance. I force a smile every time a random student looks in our direction in an attempt to look friendly. Imaginary wasps swarm in my stomach when we reach the double doors, and a boy with sandy blond hair and chocolate brown eyes holds one side open for us.

"We have to check in with the office for our lockers," Alyssa says.

"Do we have to?"

She rolls her eyes. "Oh, come on. It's not so bad."

"Yet," I say, adjusting my satchel. "Just lead the way. I want to get it over with."

## HUNTER

"Are you sure you can handle this?" Dr. Sullivan asks. She hands me a tray with a dry piece of chicken, a cup of peas, a piece of toast, and an apple. "I know it might be hard since..." Her voice trails off.

I clench my jaw. "So I'm basically supposed to play nice and hope he talks?"

"Can you manage?"

I clear my throat to stop from laughing. She's so delusional it makes it easy to fake my way around here. Nodding, I say, "I'll be fine."

With a small smile, she squeezes my shoulder. "I know. It's just part of my job to ask." She slides a clipboard under her arm. "Agent Camille will relieve you at three, so have your paperwork done by then. The cameras are recording, and you must watch the monitor at all times."

"Got it."

Dr. Sullivan nods once and heads toward the elevator. I hope this will be the last time I see her for a while. I've been pretty good at avoiding her until now, and I'd like to keep it that way. She enters the elevator, and I wave as the door slides closed.

Setting the tray on the desk, I glare at the monitor. The guy paces the room, his hands hooked to the back of his head. I wait for him to sit on the edge of the bed before picking up the tray and making my way down the corridor. He won't be happy to see me, and I don't blame him.

The first thing I need to do is to get up the nerve to meet the prisoner face-to-face. I haven't had to actually converse with prisoners—or any creatures—while working. It's a little unnerving because he's going to think I'm his enemy, and I can't blow my cover to tell him otherwise. My plan is to treat today like any other day and try to show him without being obvious that I'm unlike the other agents, doctors, and scientists he's met here. While he'll never trust me, maybe he'll see that my intentions are good, and I don't want to hurt him.

The board wasn't clear on how they want me to handle things, but like everything else, they'll let me know if I do something they disapprove of. They won't make me be mean or anything, because some agents go the friendly route, but they'll analyze everything I do and scrutinize me more if I am. I just hope I'm doing the right thing for the prisoner and everything works out in our favor.

## NADIA

I somehow managed to survive the majority of my day without embarrassing myself or scaring any students.

"We have one more class together," Evangeline Thompson says before handing me my schedule. She's a girl from my third period Economics class with stick straight, coffee brown hair with red streaks. Her deep golden skin brings out her hazel eyes, which remind me of Hunter's, and she wears white, thick-framed glasses. Swinging her arms at her sides, her hands hide in her sleeves as she strolls next to me.

I grin. "Perfect. Does it happen to be next?"

She scrunches her forehead. "No, but you'll be fine. Mr. Augustine, the librarian, is nice."

I frown. "What?" I didn't realize my father's friend was the librarian, and I had a class period with him.

"You're the librarian's aide. Didn't you choose it?"

I unfold my schedule and glance at it. I don't want to admit my father was the one who picked out my elective. There's been so much going on in my mind that I didn't even make the connection. "It slipped my mind. I was too busy worrying about starting here in the first place."

Evie bobs her head. "I couldn't imagine having to change schools the last semester of senior year."

I lift and drop my shoulders. "It's not as bad as I expected."

Stopping in front of a stairwell, Evie taps the small sign that says the library is in the basement. "My class is upstairs, so I'll see you later."

She waves over her shoulder, and I peer around the crowded hallway. I wonder how Alyssa's doing and where her next class is. I should've paid more attention to her schedule in case I need her.

The bell rings, and I take one step at a time down to the basement. It's quiet and cooler underground. The lighting shines harsher without natural light filtering in through the windows. I pass four empty classrooms, all with the lights off, and find the double doors for the library at the end of the hall.

I push the door open and enter the library, the warm, musty air smelling of books. A man leans on his elbows, reading at the wraparound counter that separates off a cluttered office. His bald head gleams with sweat, and his dark, thick eyebrows almost touch in the middle. Now that I see him, Mr. Augustine looks vaguely familiar.

I clear my throat, drawing his attention to me. He straightens his back, smiling, and pushes his sleeves up to his elbows.

Coming around the counter, he offers his hand out to me. "Nadia! It's so good to see you. How do you like Northern Bell?"

I tense while shaking his hand because of his nicety. I'm not used to being welcomed so easily. "It's a nice campus."

"It is, isn't it? Has a great library, too." He chuckles and waves his hand out at the packed bookshelves.

"My father told me you two are long time friends, but I don't remember you," I blurt.

Silence falls between us, and he smiles again. Turning toward the wraparound counter, he stares into space for a minute caught in a memory.

"You were friends with my mother?" I add, trying to drag out the conversation.

He rubs his head with his hand, blinking his eyes. "Oh, yes. And it's been a very long time since I've seen you or your dad. The last time I saw you was…"

I frown. "Was when?"

He blinks a few more times. "Oh, dear. I'm sorry. I'm a little nervous. I was surprised when Dmitri called me. I couldn't believe he moved you from the compound after what happened to your—"

He doesn't have to say it, because the sudden sadness in his eyes tells me everything. Mr. Augustine hasn't seen my father since my mother's death. I'm sure I knew him once as well, but it was so long ago.

"He didn't really have a choice." I twine my fingers together. "I was outcast for helping someone."

"Sounds like something that would've happened to your mom. She was always so kind and empathetic. She had the biggest heart. You know, we graduated from this very school twenty-two years ago? Were friends until, well—" He shakes his head and smiles again. "Never mind. The past is the past, and I have a million things to do around here."

## HUNTER

I tap on the door.

"Why do you even bother knocking?" The door muffles the guy's voice, but I can still hear the anger in his tone.

I consider turning around and heading back to my desk. "Hey, man, if you don't want to eat, that's fine. I'll come back in a few hours."

"Wait."

I punch in my pass code, unlocking the door. Setting the

tray of food on the small table against the wall outside the room, I rest my hand on my taser and push the door open. I half expect the guy to attack me, because that's what I'd do if I was him, but instead, I find him sitting on the edge of his small cot.

He looks up with his brows knitted together. "I didn't realize the HPA trained agents so young."

I grab his tray of food and enter the room to set it on his desk. "You say that like I'm a kid. I'm probably only a few years younger than you."

He twists his lips to the side. "You're allowed to talk to me?"

"Why wouldn't I be?"

"No one else has."

"It's possible they didn't want to."

He stands. "Why are you?"

I touch my taser in its holster. "Oh, I don't know, maybe because I'm not your enemy. I like to think that I'm a nice guy."

The guy paces in a circle, keeping his distance from me. He obviously doesn't believe me, but why should he? He knows how the HPA works and probably knows his time is limited.

"If you were a nice guy, you'd let me out of here."

I sigh. "It's complicated."

"But I'm not a creature. I have no power." He picks up a folding chair and swings it at the wall, surprising me.

I scramble back into the hallway, half holding the door to

slam it shut if he charges. "You were protecting one, though. If you need anything, just yell for me. My name is Hunter."

Setting the chair down, he steps closer, his hands raised in a non-threatening way. "Can you bring me a magazine or something?"

I shift on my feet. "Sure thing, man."

"You can call me Camden, but don't expect me to say much more."

I shrug. "Whatever."

I shut the door and lock it. This is a lot harder than I expected. He reminds me of myself when I was imprisoned in Jacqueline's mind, except this time, no one's here to fight for him. I want to help him without giving myself away, but I need him to be willing to cooperate. He won't until he really believes I want to help him. I need Nadia's help, too. I can't do it without her. She can find creatures brave enough to face the HPA, and we can break Camden out. Before we do so, I need to figure out how to escape the HPA myself and convince Nadia to come with me. I'm just afraid she won't. And then where would that leave me?

## NADIA

I put the last of the pile of returned books in their homes on the shelf. It's like Mr. Augustine waited a month to even glance at the stack. Wheeling the squeaky cart toward the wraparound counter, I freeze before leaving the aisle. A tingling sensation rolls over me, igniting hunger in my stomach, and I grip the nearest bookshelf.

This can't be happening.

Not now.

Not here.

I sense someone falling asleep nearby. My nightmare inflictor side threatens to take over, forcing its way out even though I just inflicted a nightmare last night. It's not that I need to inflict a nightmare, but I won't be waking up the sleeper, either. I don't want to.

Peeking around the shelf, I watch as a boy with short red hair sits at a long table, his arms folded on a book, his head bobbing a few times as he fights off sleep.

But he's not fighting hard enough and neither am I.

The silent room does nothing to help the situation. I hold my breath, sweat prickling my hairline. I don't have to intrude his dreams. I don't. And he doesn't deserve to be inflicted with horrifying nightmares, but then, he shouldn't be sleeping in the library. *Keep telling yourself that...*

Gliding forward, slow and steady, I circle the room. He falls asleep at the table near the door, making it so easy to invade his head and leave without anyone knowing.

I run my finger along his table, my stomach on fire and my mouth watering with anticipation. My predatory side rips free from me, turning me into a midnight stalker right in the middle of the day. I slide up next to him, my hand hovering inches away from his temple.

A door slams.

Stumbling back, I hit my shoulder on the end of a bookshelf.

Mr. Augustine throws a hard cover book at the boy. It lands with a thud on the table, startling him awake. The boy bolts upright and falls off his chair, crashing to the ground. I scramble farther into the aisle, hugging myself. The boy moans, rubbing his eyes, and pushes onto his knees. Grabbing onto the table, he pulls himself to his feet.

My heart races, my chest feeling like it's about to explode. My whole body shakes and tears blur my vision. To calm myself, I dig my nails into the wall, scratching the old paint. I find my footing and step toward the exit. I need to run. I need to get out of here.

I stop at the door when Mr. Augustine picks up the book and hugs it to his chest. "This isn't your bedroom."

The boy clears his throat. "I didn't mean—"

Mr. Augustine waves the book in the air. "Go see the nurse if you need more sleep."

The boy picks up his backpack off the floor and slings it over his shoulder. Shuffling to the door, he pushes past me without making eye contact. I glance at the floor, too embarrassed to meet Mr. Augustine's gaze, and too embarrassed to admit I was seconds away from inflicting a nightmare on an unsuspecting victim my first day of public high school.

My father was right about my lack of control and how the only way to stay in control is to inflict nightmares regularly. I just hate it so much.

Mr. Augustine closes the distance between us and touches

my shoulder. "Are you all right? Your father warned me you came into your ability."

I swipe a tear from my watery eyes. "I'm so, so sorry." Squeezing my eyes shut, I pull myself together.

"Don't even worry about it. I'm well aware of what to expect and how to help you. I learned a lot from your mother. We didn't keep secrets from each other. Both our lives were quite complicated, and we leaned on each other a lot." It's not unheard of for people to discover the supernatural world, but it is unlikely. My mother and father must've trusted Mr. Augustine to let him into our world.

The bell rings, but I consider staying. I want to know everything about my mother. What she was like growing up, how she told him, what he thinks about everything...if she had any regrets.

"I'd love to know more about her," I say. A few students come through the door, and I know my chance to talk is up.

"There will be plenty of time for that tomorrow, Nadia. My door is always open if you need anything." He saunters to the counter and grabs my satchel before returning to me.

I sling the strap over my shoulder, sad I have to leave. Apart from the stupid sleeping boy, assisting Mr. Augustine has been the highlight of my whole educational career—even more so than the tutors back at the compound. I'm almost excited to return tomorrow. I guess high school isn't so bad after all.

"Thank you." I turn to leave.

He holds the door open for me. "It's no problem at all. Do

try to be more careful. I can't run around throwing books at students all day long, even though it would be quite entertaining."

I smile. "I wish you could, though."

# 4

## WORTH THE RISK

### HUNTER

"I BROUGHT WHAT you wanted. Get him to talk?" Jacqueline asks, plopping down in the chair next to me. She leans over and stares into the monitor.

I lace my fingers behind my head. "His name is Camden. He refused to say anything else. I'm hoping if I give him what he asked for, he will though. It's been pretty boring otherwise."

Jacqueline pulls a magazine from her bag and sets it on the desk. "What'd you expect? This isn't field work."

She studies my face for a moment, tapping her fingers on the desk. I'll take a thousand boring days than have to work in the field, facing creatures, because I'd expose myself as a traitor faster when the board notices I'm not bringing in anyone.

"I just expected to be a little more productive." Standing up, I turn toward the corridor leading to the cells. "I'm going to try to talk to him one more time before I go. Oh, and Dr. Sullivan left you a note. You can take an extended lunch since it's pretty calm in here."

Jacqueline lifts an eyebrow. "You read my note?"

I shrug. "Told you I was bored."

She rolls her eyes and throws a pen at me as I stroll toward the cells. When I reach the first door, I punch in my pass code and peek in. Camden sits at the empty desk, staring at his hands. He jerks his head up, hearing the door beep as I step in.

I wave the magazine. "I wanted to give you this before I left. My partner is taking over."

Camden gets up but doesn't come any closer. "Is this a trick?"

"Just being nice," I say.

He takes the magazine from me and moves to sit on his cot. "You know, I've never met an agent who was nice just to be nice."

"So, you've come across other agents before?" I ask because it's what the board would expect. It's not really a question that'll reveal any information about Camden personally, but it'll keep the board off my back before I can talk to Nadia.

Camden leans back and stares at the ceiling without answering. He's shutting down, and I sense he won't be answering any other questions I have for him today.

"All right. I get it. See you tomorrow, man." I exit without looking back. It's a lot harder to leave, because I'm worried something will happen to Camden when I'm gone before I can help him. The board does things fast and without warning.

Heading back to the viewing room, I stop at the desk near Jacqueline. "Maybe you'll have better luck with him."

She smiles. "I'll try my best."

Every conversation I have with Jacqueline under the HPA's watch has a different meaning. She knows our goal is to get him to trust us to be able to help him. It'd be ideal to do it without the HPA ever knowing so we can continue to help others, but being discovered is a risk we both have to take. We'd risk a lot to see a change happen with the HPA. This is just the start.

## NADIA

Alyssa pulls the car into the garage. "I told you school would be fine."

I roll my eyes. "It almost wasn't."

Things would've gone wrong quickly if Mr. Augustine didn't intervene. I hate to even think about how close I was to inflicting a nightmare, how unpredictable and unstable I am. I should've tried harder to resist.

I follow Alyssa into the house, looking at the empty spot my father usually parks his truck. The warmth of the heater hugs me the second I enter the kitchen. Heading to the living room, I notice the answering machine's light blinking. Dad always leaves messages instead of notes.

I push the button and listen.

"Nadi, Alyssa. It's going to be a late night for me. If you need to inflict a nightmare, Nadia, take Alyssa with you. I'll be home as soon as I can."

The line drops, and I bring my gaze up to look at Alyssa. She twirls her car keys, grinning. I smile back. She knows me so well. I've been anxious to meet with Hunter to tell him about Alyssa seeing the boy die. I don't know how much Hunter can take if he has to pretend to be okay with the board killing people. A person can only take so much.

"Think I have time, Lys?" I ask.

Alyssa sucks in her bottom lip. "Why don't you have him meet here?"

I glance at the front door like my father will burst in any second. "You sure? I don't want to risk my dad co—"

"As long as he's gone before dark, he'll be okay. You deserve to have a little normal date at home. I know you two worry about him knowing where you live, but I've already seen him here. It'll be fine."

Alyssa's words are enough to push me toward the door. I've always wanted to bring Hunter here, especially now with winter ruining our outside dates together. Gliding out the front door, I head to the usual store I call Hunter from without asking Alyssa for a ride. I pop a few quarters into the payphone and let it ring a few times before hanging up.

Keeping my back to the wall, I peer around the empty parking lot. After a minute, I dial Hunter's number again.

"Can you meet me?" he asks, picking up after the first ring without waiting for me to say anything.

I smile at the sound of his voice. "I was hoping you'd come to my house."

The line goes silent for a moment apart from his breathing. "You're not worried about your dad? Or me?"

I shrug even though he can't see me. "Alyssa says it's fine. I have some important things to tell you. Think you can bring Jacqueline, too? She needs to hear it as well."

He clears his throat. "I'll try."

I swallow, a battle between excitement and worry raging inside me, twisting my stomach in knots. Inviting Hunter and Jacqueline to my house poses a risk, but, some things are worth the risk. Especially if one of those things is Hunter.

"Thanks, Hunter. My house is on Sage Street in the community behind the field near the bus stop we met at last night. I'll wait for you outside."

"See you soon."

The line clicks off, and I release a long breath. I can't just stand around waiting for the council to figure things out about the enchantress's son. I can't let them allow the HPA to take more people—not if Hunter and Jacqueline can help. We can make a difference.

## HUNTER

Something in Nadia's voice leaves me on edge. I haven't had a chance to tell her I found out Camden's name, but I hope the tiny bit of information can help us. Nadia can find out everything I'd need to know about Camden, and I could use that information to help him. If I can somehow get that personal information to him without the board knowing, he'd know I was a good guy and on his side.

Tugging my work phone from my pocket, I call Jacqueline. She picks up after the first ring and says, "Want to get a bite to eat? I don't know what to do with myself with a long lunch hour."

I breathe into the phone. "I have an idea. I just pulled up. Come on out."

I hang up and wait a few minutes. Jacqueline struts from the lobby of the termination facility, her black hair shining from her severe bun. She slides on dark sunglasses over her bluish-purple eyes, looking like the perfect agent in her wrinkle-free uniform, holding herself with a natural confidence I haven't mastered.

She hops in and smile without a word.

I lock the doors and idle my car for a minute. "Nadia wants us to go over to her house."

Jacqueline stares out the windshield. "Did something happen? Does Dmitri know?"

I shrug. "Dmitri's gone until tonight."

She taps her chin with her index finger. Unsaid thoughts swirl through her mind, and I stare at her in my peripheral vision. "I have a bad feeling," she says after a minute. "After watching Camden all day, I don't think we can save people alone."

I furrow my brows. "What are you saying? This is the reason why we stayed."

Jacqueline shakes her head and strands of black hair fall from her bun into her face. "I stayed to try to change things. I wanted to shift ideologies within the HPA, but now I'm worried about every creature who gets captured. I feel like that's all I'm doing."

I run my hand through my hair. "You sound like you don't want to save anyone."

She slams her fists on the dashboard. "Are you kidding me? You have no right to accuse me of not wanting to save people. I want to save everyone! You don't know how hard being at the termination facility has been on me. So much evil swirls through a lot of the people we work with, constantly reminding me how cruel people are. I feel like I'm going to break at any second."

Reaching over, I touch her knee. "I didn't realize this was how you felt. You're so together most of the time."

She flicks my hand, so I move it. "Because we have to be."

Exhaling a long breath, I say, "It's okay to leave and put this all behind you, Jackie."

She cringes at the sound of her real name. "You don't understand, Hunter. I can't. I need to do this. I need to be here. It's the right thing for me to do. It's the *only* thing for me to do." The words spill from her mouth.

Curling her fingers into her palms, she stiffens and leans away from me, resting her head on the window. She's said everything she's willing to say and no matter how much I'd like to understand what she's going through, I don't think I ever can.

I clear my throat and glance at her. "Well, I'm here for you."

Shifting again, she meets my gaze. "You know, after everything, I'll never understand why."

It's taken me a while to understand it myself. The truth is that ever since I found out that Jacqueline saved Nadia's life, I don't look at her the same. She's not a monster. She's just another person trying to survive in a world that wants her dead. "Because you're not the worst person in the world."

Jacqueline smiles. "I guess I'm not."

## NADIA

For a split second, it feels like everything around me freezes when Hunter's BMW comes into view. Jacqueline gets out first and waves, and I glide to the street, hugging her, before meeting Hunter's gaze. He closes the space between us, and I wrap my arms around him. Leaning down, he kisses me, tasting of mint, and I nuzzle into his neck, making him chuckle.

"You're here," I whisper. "I almost can't believe it."

"Me either." He holds me tighter. "You sure your dad isn't going to show up any minute?"

Tilting my head up, I peer into his hazel eyes, feeling the worry radiating from him through his tense muscles. "I don't think so, but I don't really care right now. I'll protect you."

He laughs and kisses the top of my head. "My angel. Always watching out for me."

"I'm glad you two are here," Alyssa says, pulling my gaze from Hunter. She hugs herself, hugging her knee-length coat tighter around her. Shifting on her black lace-up boots to look between us, she smiles, playing with her red hair still in a braided bun as perfect as it was this morning.

Alyssa waves Jacqueline forward, tugging her inside ahead of us. "I've missed you. How are you holding up?" I hear Alyssa ask from the open door.

I drag Hunter with me, and he shifts nervously, peering around my quaint living room. I wonder how different it is from his aunt's house.

"It's been fine. Still trying to decide what to do," Jacqueline says, looking at Hunter.

I puff air through my lips. "That's why I wanted you to come here."

"I saw the boy die," Alyssa blurts.

Hunter turns to me. "Camden?"

My eyes widen. "You know his name? That's great. We can use that."

"How do you think we can save him?" Jacqueline asks, interrupting, wringing her hands together. "It'd be a huge risk for Hunter or me to try."

Hunter drapes his arms over my shoulders and rests his chin on the nape of my neck, holding me from behind. His chest presses into my back, making me want to spin to face him. "I'm not afraid to risk it."

Jacqueline glares at the both of us. "Well, you should be.

You can't save him alone. What were you considering doing? Leaving his cell open and hoping no one noticed?"

Hunter breathes in my ear, tickling my cheek with strands of my hair. "If he knew how to get out, he might make it."

"He might," Jacqueline says, "but you won't."

I stiffen and turn in Hunter's arms. "You need to listen to Jacqueline. You'll be in over your head. I want you alive, you know."

"I think we're all in over our heads. We need help from someone who knows what we're dealing with." Jacqueline crosses her arms and bounces from foot to foot. "Word has it that there's been a scientific breakthrough in the HPA that could be game changing. It's why the board has increased agent activity. It's going to get a lot worse."

Hunter's brows furrow. "No one told me."

Jacqueline glances at the floor. "I overheard Dr. Sullivan."

I shift my gaze to Alyssa, who's quietly listening to everything Jacqueline and Hunter say. She meets my eyes, and we stare at each other for a minute. I know what she's thinking without her having to say it, because I'm thinking it, too. If we seek any outside help, it'll be from my father. He's the strongest and bravest person I know. He can help us make a difference.

I take a deep breath and say, "We can't keep this a secret. People need to know so they can prepare if the HPA does gain more power." I look at Hunter. "We need to tell my father. There's really no other way."

Alyssa presses her lips together. "He'll ask how we know."

Jacqueline touches my arm. "You can tell him about me and keep Hunter out of it."

It's like Jacqueline read my mind. My father wouldn't understand how much I love Hunter. He'd have a hard time trusting him, and if my father can't trust Hunter, then what? Things wouldn't get done. Telling him about Jacqueline makes more sense. He knew her when she was at the compound.

Hunter frowns. "You don't have to keep me out of it. Dmitri will find out about me eventually."

I touch his chin so he looks at me. "I'll tell him when the time is right, okay?"

His hazel eyes shine with an intensity that sends my heart racing. "What if it's never the right time? I can't change the world if I don't do anything."

I twist my lips to the side. "Just trust me."

He leans down and kisses me softly before saying, "I already do."

## HUNTER

"Good," Nadia says, pressing into me. Any argument I had for telling Dmitri about my existence slips from my mind feeling her cool body through her sweater.

"I can come back later after my shift." Jacqueline moves across the room to sit on the couch, leaning her elbows on her knees. "It'll give me time to put a few things together for him about the termination facility. I'm sure he'll want to take something with him to the council."

Nadia sucks in a breath but doesn't say anything.

Alyssa plops down next to Jacqueline. "It'll take a lot more than knowing the way around."

"I'm sure my dad can figure it out." Nadia's voice quivers at the idea of her father going to the termination facility, even if it'll be on his terms, because I'm a little nervous by the idea, too.

My cell phone rings, cutting off our conversation. I curse under my breath, because it's my work phone. Fear slithers through my veins, knowing it's someone from the HPA calling me, reminding me that the HPA will always be breathing down my neck as long as I wear this uniform.

I clear my throat. "It's my work phone."

"You brought your work phone here?" Fear laces Nadia's words.

My eyebrows pinch together. "I had to because of my promotion."

"I have mine with me, too, Nadia," Jacqueline says.

Alyssa stands up. "You have to answer it."

Jacqueline gets off the couch and strolls next to me, leaning in close as I press the phone to my ear. The edges of my vision shadow, and I force the words from my mouth. "Agent Hunter speaking."

"I know you're off, but I need a favor," Dr. Sullivan says without greeting me.

"Sure," I say.

"Pick up Agent Camille. I need you both to meet Agent Rosaline in the city in the parking lot next to the city library.

She needs an escort to the termination facility."

Before I respond, the call drops.

I shift my gaze from Nadia to Jacqueline. "That was Dr. Sullivan. She needs us to escort Agent Rosaline from the city to the termination facility."

Before Jacqueline has a chance to respond, her phone rings and she holds it up to show me Dr. Sullivan is calling her now. She presses it to her ear and plops onto the armchair. "Agent Camille," she says, crossing her eyes at me. "I'm at lunch. Yes, no problem. See you later." She hangs up and slides her phone into her weaponry belt. Jacqueline turns to Nadia and Alyssa. "We have to go. I'll get you what you need after my shift tonight. Let me know when I can meet with Dmitri."

Nadia sits on the edge of her couch, playing with a loose thread on her purple sweater. "You're taking people to their deaths." I don't know why her words surprise me. It's not a question. Her sad eyes line with tears, and Alyssa touches her knee.

I cross the room and bend down to hug her. "I can't disobey orders unless I'm ready to run away."

She sighs. "I know. I just hate that you have to do this."

Jacqueline struts up next to me and rests her hand on my shoulder, looking between Nadia and Alyssa. "We'd save them if we could, but you have to look at the bigger picture. Revealing our motives now will destroy what we've been working toward. I've thought about this a lot, and I'll remain at the HPA and give creatures what they need to fight against the HPA for as long as I can. Becoming Camille was my second chance. I'm not going to waste it to save a few creatures when I can save more."

"She's right, Nadia. Imagine the things we can do with their knowledge of the HPA," Alyssa says.

Nadia closes her eyes for a second. "You two don't have to lecture me. I'm well aware of sacrificing things for the greater good."

Pushing to her feet, she glides to the front door and steps outside. Jacqueline shrugs at Alyssa, and I get up to go after Nadia.

Freezing air hits me as I step on the porch. Nadia sits on a small wooden bench stationed below the front window. I sit next her, sliding my arm around her back. She leans her head on me, and I kiss her hair. "You okay?"

She sighs. "Yeah, I don't know why that bothered me so much."

"It bothered me, too. Jacqueline sounded like my mom for a minute. Those were almost the exact same words my mom used to justify trading my soul."

She swivels, bumping her knees into mine. "How do you do it?"

"What do you mean?" I ask, knitting my brows together.

"How do you show up to work and look your mother in the eyes?"

I shrug. "I do it for us—for anyone I might be able to save." Which is the truth. It's the only way I can. If I didn't have Nadia, if it was just me alone in this life after all I've been through, I wouldn't do it. I'd have abandoned my mom the second I could've.

A whisper of a smile plays on Nadia's lips, but as quickly as it comes, it disappears into a thin line before she puffs out her bottom lip. "Promise me if it gets to be too much, you'll leave, Hunter. I can't stand you being there, having to deal with that regardless of you doing it for us. You're important to me, you know."

"I promise," I say, leaning in to kiss the serious expression from her lips. I'd promise her to leave this second if she asked. Her intensity heats the cold dread sliding into my jacket from the chill in the air. "There are only two things that'll make me leave before I change things for the better. One, if they find out I'm not loyal to them, or two, you ask me to."

She nods and kisses me again. "I'll only ask if I know I can run away with you, too."

## NADIA

My front door opens, and Jacqueline steps out with Alyssa behind her. Wrapping my arms around Hunter, I hug him tighter because I know he has to go. I imagine pushing all my strength into him, so he has it to deal with what is to come.

"Call me later?" he asks.

"As soon as I can." I hold his hand until my fingers slip from his as he walks away with Jacqueline to his car.

The icy air sinks into my bones, and I shiver, feeling cold for the first time in weather that never usually bothers me. I stare at the ground instead of watching him walk away. After a moment, Alyssa grabs my hand and pulls me inside.

"I'll call my dad and find out when he'll be home," I say.

Alyssa nods and walks toward the kitchen, leaving me alone. I grab the phone from the side table next to the couch. Dialing my father's cell phone number, I listen as it goes straight to voicemail. "Hi, Dad. It's me. Call me when you get this. I just wanted to see if you knew when you'd be home. Love you." I hang up and set the phone back on its charger.

Alyssa bolts from the kitchen and looks at me. "I had a strange vision."

"What about?"

"I saw you in the meeting hall at the compound."

I raise an eyebrow. "Yeah, that isn't happening."

"That's why I thought it was strange."

"Anything else to it?"

She shakes her head. "No. You weren't wearing that outfit, so it could be well into the future which means that it could change."

The farther out Alyssa's visions are, the higher chance they're just glimpses of possibilities of what could happen. It's the ones that look like they take place the same day that are more concrete and worrisome.

"Let me know if it does," I say.

Alyssa crosses her arms. "I always do."

I smirk. "Not always."

She laughs. "Fine, I'll let you know from now on."

"Good. I hate surprises."

## HUNTER

Agent Rosaline leans against a white van when I pull into the crowded lot of the public library. I don't park but instead pull up behind the van and idle the engine of my BMW. Jacqueline gets out first and greets Agent Rosaline.

I come up next to them and cross my arms.

"Thanks for meeting me on such short notice. Rob's staying behind to patrol the area to make sure it's clear. Can one of you ride with me?" Agent Rosaline's brown hair, shorter than mine, sticks to her head with sweat. She's just over five feet and tougher than me, but she lets her partner walk all over her.

Jacqueline side glances me, because she's thinking the same thing I am. Agent Rob, while great at what he does, isn't a team player. More than once Agent Rosaline has been left doing his cleanup, but she's never said anything. Together, they're the number one team for field agents and have over thirty creature captures to their names.

"How many?" Jacqueline asks.

Agent Rosaline unlocks the back of the van and opens the door. Three bodies slump on the seats with bags over their heads. They've been bound for transportation. I glance at each person's clothing, but there's nothing identifying. By the sheer size of what I think is a man, he could be an ogre or a cyclops— or he could just be tall. It's hard to tell when the creature next to him looks child-sized.

"Species?" I ask.

"TBD," she says. "I'm alive and uninjured, so I don't think any of them are a threat...at the moment."

Jacqueline peers into the van. "I can't tell."

I don't know if she's lying or if she really can't tell. Until I can watch them interact and move and see them without bags over their heads, I can't guess either. I take one more look before Agent Rosaline slams the door.

She turns back to us. "Ready?"

I nod. "Want me to lead or follow?"

"Lead."

Jacqueline struts to the passenger's side door and gives me a pointed look before opening it and stepping in. She knows I can't read her thoughts, and I can't even correctly guess what she's thinking half the time, but I know something's on her mind.

The drive to the termination facility is uneventful and when we meet Dr. Sullivan at the side entrance, she dismisses me. I stop by the green zone with Jacqueline to check up on Camden, but he won't even look at me.

He just sits with his back to wall, looking ready to die.

## NADIA

It's well past midnight, and my father isn't home yet. He hasn't called either, which is unlike him. What if the council has him and isn't letting him come home? What if they're enforcing my punishment for getting Jacqueline's body killed? Not only was I exiled, but the council cut me off from all of their resources and sanctuaries—what if they consider my relationship with my father part of that consequence?

Alyssa strolls in from the kitchen and plops down next to me. "I'm sure he's okay, Nadia."

I swipe a tear from my cheek. "He always calls back, Lys."

She touches my knee. "He might still call."

Pushing to my feet, I tuck my hands into the pockets of my sweater. "I'm going to run to the payphone to call Hunter. If my father does call, tell him I'm with a volunteer."

"Be careful," Alyssa says.

The dark, cloudless sky sparkles with glittering stars. It's eerily quiet apart from the sound of my own breathing. Each breath I take fogs the air, and I glide just over the snowy ground, not leaving behind footprints.

The convenience store shines with dim lights, creating shadows across the parking lot. I pop in change and dial Hunter's number. He picks up without making me hang up to call back.

"Hello?" Hunter says.

"My father isn't home yet," I say without greeting. "Things are going to have to wait."

His breath creates static through the line. "You okay?"

I sniffle. "I'm worried. It's unlike him to change plans without telling me."

"Want me to meet you?"

I don't say anything for a second. I'd want nothing more than to see Hunter right now, but until I know where my father is, I don't want to stay away from the house long. It'd be too risky for Hunter to meet me there because of the chance of my father showing up. I lick my dry lips and say, "Tomorrow."

"Hey, Nadia," Hunter says.

"Yeah?"

"I love you."

A smile plays on my lips. "Love you, too. Tell Jacqueline I'll call her as soon as I hear from my dad."

I hang up the phone and stare at the empty parking lot. It's going to be a long night.

# 5

# HOPELESS

### HUNTER

I WATCH CAMDEN in the monitor. He sits at the desk and flips through the magazine I gave him from for the millionth time. I'm as bored as he is, but at least my shift ends. Who knows how long he has here. Hopefully long enough to get him out.

The elevator door dings open, and I swing my gaze from the monitor to Dr. Sullivan and Mason. I clench my jaw to hide my surprise. This scene is all too familiar. It's exactly how I was, following my mom like a good son, when I was an intern.

"Hey, bro. Dr. Sullivan." I don't move to get to my feet.

Instead, I turn back to my monitor. "What're you doing here?"

"Just giving Mason a tour of the different zones," Dr. Sullivan says.

I move my mouse without clicking anything. "What for?"

Dr. Sullivan sets her clipboard on the corner of my desk. "He's going to start his internship next month. I wanted to get a tour in before it picks up around here."

"Oh, well, have at it." I wave around the bare room. It's all cold cement and harsh lighting besides the lonely desk with the video feed of the cells.

"So, this is what keeps you busy," Mason says.

I turn to look at him. "Yeah, pretty much. The HPA is my life." I don't know what else to say, so I glance back at the monitor.

Dr. Sullivan saunters up behind me and puts her hands on my shoulders. I stiffen under her touch, but she doesn't notice. Leaning down, she peers at the monitor from over my shoulder. "Why don't you and Agent Camille come over for dinner sometime? She can take the evening off. While I like to hear how devoted you are to the board, it's okay to have a life outside these walls."

The last thing I want to do is have dinner with my mom and brother. "Sounds good," I lie. I'll make an excuse to not show up like always.

"Good. I look forward to it. I miss my family," she says.

*I'm sure all these creatures miss their families, too,* I think.

"Can I see the cells?" Mason asks, interrupting.

I shrug and point to the corridor. "Only one is occupied and with nothing special."

Dr. Sullivan smiles. "That'll change, Hunter. And soon."

I turn my eyes back to the monitor. I can't stop the dread from clouding my mind as her words sink in. Saving Camden will be hard enough. I'm going to need the strength to save all those people who get locked in a cell. It's the only way to balance the evil of the HPA. It's the only way to set things right.

## NADIA

"You look anxious," Evie says, standing near my locker as I watch Alyssa stroll to her next class.

I lift and drop my shoulders. "I have a lot on my mind," I say, tossing my books in my locker. I don't say anything else because I don't know what to say. My father never came home, and I don't know where he is.

Evie stands quietly next to me, watching me look into my hanging mirror. I'm paler than yesterday since I never visited a volunteer. I couldn't bring myself to do it. I can still go a few more days without standing out too much, though my father would never allow it.

Sighing, I peek at Evie in my mirror. I'm afraid Alyssa's vision about me running to the council will come true. I need to see if they're keeping my father from me. It's best to keep Evie separate from my dramatic life—it's safer, too.

Evie touches my shoulder, realizing I'm done talking. "I'm here if you ever want to talk. Maybe we can hang out after school or something. Go to the city for some window shopping on Ninth Street. It always helps my mood."

I smile because I'm not used to this sort of nicety from anyone besides Alyssa and Hunter—Jacqueline isn't even this nice. "Thanks, but I can't." Disappointment sweeps across Evie's face, and I almost give in and agree to go with her, but instead I say, "My dad will be home sometime today and doesn't like me to go to the city. He's overprotective." *I hope he comes home today…*

She nods. "He sounds like my mom. It's a good thing my dad let me live with him." She shifts her bag from one shoulder to the other. "We'll go some other time."

The bell rings and the halls clear, but we don't move from my locker. It's nice having a friend who doesn't know the truth. I can pretend to be normal for once. "Yeah, definitely. He goes out of town a lot." We head to the stairs to go to our different classes.

Evie smiles. "Awesome, just let me know. I'll see you later."

The late bell rings as I turn to walk to the library. I pound down the steps to the basement to meet Mr. Augustine. I hope he's not too angry about my tardiness. When I reach the library, I'm surprised to see a sign taped to the door declaring that the library is closed until Monday and for students to go to the computer lab in room 34A.

I frown, shifting on my feet. I'm not sure if that means me as well, so I try the door and crack it open. Soft music plays from a portable stereo, and Mr. Augustine stands on top of a table. He peers over mountains of books sprawled all over the floor and smiles, waving me in when he sees me.

"Nadia!" His voice bellows through the quiet room, and I close the door behind me. "You're just in time. I figured now was the perfect time to spruce up the place."

Mr. Augustine climbs onto a chair and jumps from it to the ground. His thick eyebrows dance like two fuzzy caterpillars over his coffee brown eyes, and his bald head shines with sweat. He wears a burgundy dress shirt with the sleeves rolled to his elbows, and half the shirt tucks into his black slacks. I smirk, noticing he's not wearing his shoes.

He holds up his foot, showing off his black and red striped socks, and chortles. "It's casual Friday."

I crack a smile. "It's only Thursday."

Pulling a salmon pink handkerchief from his back pocket, he wipes his glistening head. "Well, then, looks like I get to relax tomorrow, too." He plops down on the chair and pushes a giant scroll of paper with barcodes on it out of his way before reaching over and grabbing a portable scanner. "Ever use one of these?"

I tuck my pale blond hair behind my ear. "What's it for? I'm sure I can learn."

He hands me the scanner. "I've decided to finally go digital. I figured since I have your help, I'd make life easier."

Mr. Augustine shows me how to use the scanner and puts me to work scanning every barcode he stickers on the back of each book. I lose myself in my work and the worry and stress I've been carrying since last night melts away.

*Things Fall Apart, Don Quixote, The Inferno, The Tale of Genji*...there are so many books I haven't read, but I'd like to one day. *One day*. All my plans are for a future I'm not sure will be there. I push the thought away and keep scanning.

"Oh, your mother loved this one!" Mr. Augustine hands me a copy of *Love in the Time of Cholera*.

I flip through the well-read pages. "Can I borrow it?"

He chuckles and waves his arms around. "This is a library."

I laugh at myself and set the book aside. It's strange talking with Mr. Augustine, because he's the only person I know who grew up with my mother. I have my own memories, but they're clouded by pain and sorrow. Mr. Augustine's memories are full of life and happiness, only the good things. A ping of jealousy knocks me in the chest. I'll never have what he has.

I stretch my legs. "Tell me more about her. What was she like?"

Mr. Augustine sets the barcode stickers down and turns to me. "Emily was very outspoken. You couldn't miss her when she entered a room because she talked to everyone." He chuckles at some memory I can't see unfold in his mind. "She was always smiling."

I sit up straighter. I do remember that about my mother. She smiled even as she died. It's the one thing that'll always haunt me.

"And when she laughed," he adds, "she cried!" A deep bellow of a laugh erupts from him, and he clutches his stomach. "Full on tears, every single time, which made her always laugh harder because she couldn't stop. That's how you knew something was really funny to her. If there weren't tears, she was faking it."

I smile as he fans his face, his eyes watering just like I imagine my mother's did when she laughed. I wish I could see her do it, laugh like Mr. Augustine does when he remembers. I'll have to ask my father about it. See if he made her laugh like Mr. Augustine.

The bell rings, and I sigh. I wish I could finish my day here, laughing and hearing more stories about my mother. Mr. Augustine helps me to my feet, and I grab my book bag from the wraparound counter. When I reach the door, I wave to Mr. Augustine and his laughter follows me into the cool corridor.

Alyssa sits at the bottom of the stairs, surprising me. Her gaze lifts from the floor and she glances up at me but doesn't say anything. I sit next to her on the bottom step and stretch my legs out.

"What's wrong," I say.

"I had another vision." Alyssa rubs her temples, the words coming so quietly that I strain to hear them.

"Well, what did you see?"

"Tears frozen to your cheeks."

I frown. "That's even weirder than this morning's."

She fiddles with the hem of her sweater dress. "I have a really bad feeling."

"Think it's my dad?"

She shrugs. "Possibly. Could be Hunter. I know the vision

happens today because you're wearing the same outfit."

My chest tightens, the hairs on my arms standing on end at the thought that something today will make me cry. I don't know what I'd do if something were to happen to either Hunter or my father. It'd be like everything I lost was for nothing. *Don't say that. You'd do everything the same.*

"I need to call Hunter, Lys," I say.

She hugs me. "I'm sure they're both fine. I haven't seen anyone die."

"I just need to make sure."

## HUNTER

The elevator dings, and Jacqueline steps out to relieve me from my post for the day. I glance at the monitors, watching as Camden does pushups for a second.

I push away from the desk and stand up. "Any news regarding the supers?"

Jacqueline shakes her head. "Still in processing. On my way in, Dr. Sullivan mentioned we might get some transfers today."

I twist my lips to the side. "All right. Call me if we do, and good luck with that one," I say motioning to the monitor. "He wouldn't even look at me today."

I head toward the elevator without saying anything else. It's best to keep our conversation work related and short because the board is always watching. The cells aren't the only rooms with cameras. I bet they're analyzing every small gesture and word between Jacqueline and me.

I drive home in silence, watching the world pass me by.

Just when I'm about to pull onto my street, my prepaid cell rings. I answer it immediately instead of waiting for Nadia to call back.

"It's me," she says.

I smile at the sound of her voice and pull over and park in the parking lot of a grocery store. "I'm glad you called. Want to meet?"

She breathes into the phone without answering.

"Nadia? What's wrong?"

She sighs. "I'm just glad to hear your voice. Alyssa had a vision, and I was worried about you."

My chest tightens, and I grip the steering wheel. "Hear from Dmitri?"

"No." Her voice sounds out barely above a whisper.

"You sound shaken. Let me come to you."

The line remains silent for a minute apart from her breathing. I don't say anything, either. Whatever Alyssa saw must've gotten to Nadia—I hope it wasn't about me. I'm not ready to face the HPA's wrath.

"Can you meet me on the corner of Northern Bell Road and Sacada Lane?"

"I'll be there in thirty."

## NADIA

"Cover for me if my dad's home? Hunter's picking me up." I peer around the crowded, snow-covered front lawn of Northern Bell. Hunter will be parked far enough away that no one should notice him.

Alyssa follows my gaze. "Maybe you shouldn't go."

"I won't stay out long." I touch Alyssa's shoulder. "We'll be careful."

She presses her lips into a thin line but doesn't argue. Pulling her trench coat tighter around her, she walks down the stairs and toward the campus parking lot. I slip back inside the building and head to my locker to grab my books.

"You're not leaving with Alyssa?" Evie asks, coming up next to me.

I don't know why I'm surprised to see her, but I guess it's because I'm still getting used to the idea of having friends besides Alyssa. She smiles, moving her bag from one shoulder to the other, and then decides to drop it at her feet.

"No, I'm meeting my—" I frown, because I told her I couldn't hang out with her after school earlier and now I'm meeting Hunter. I look over my shoulder nervously, almost expecting my father to be standing behind me. "My boyfriend."

She smirks and wags her eyebrows without mentioning our earlier conversation about the city. "Does he go here?"

I shake my head. "No, he graduated already. I never get to see him, and Alyssa's going to cover for me for a few so I can."

She nods in understanding. I shrug, sliding my book bag over my shoulder and glance at the front entrance. Hunter should be here any minute. Evie follows my gaze and picks up her tote bag off the floor. She takes a step forward.

"I'll walk you out," she says. "Can I meet him?"

*Really? No. That's insane.* I never thought about having to introduce Hunter to anyone that he hasn't already met. It's a strange concept, but Evie isn't a part of our world. She's human and has no ties to the council. "Sure, I guess." I regret agreeing, but what else am I supposed to do? I don't want to risk killing my first normal friendship before it has even begun.

Freezing air smacks my face as we exit the building. Evie strolls next to me, and I lead her toward the sidewalk and away from the circular drive where students wait for their rides. Hunter's BMW is parked exactly where I told him to.

He leans against the door with his arms crossed. Snow dusts his dark chocolate curls and his hazel eyes crease in the corners as he smiles. His dark blue jacket hangs open over his HPA uniform, and I cringe. If non-humans see him dressed like this, we might have a problem. At least he's not showing off his collection of weapons.

Hugging him, I whisper, "Close your jacket."

Hurrying, he zips up his jacket and looks at Evie standing behind me. "You made a friend."

I roll my eyes. I can't help it. "Don't be so surprised." I step next to Evie. "Evie, this is Hunter."

He offers her his strong hand, and she beams a giant, per-fectly straight smile. Jealousy sneaks up on me, watching as Evie bats her long eyelashes. Strands of her red streaked hair fall in her face and instead of letting go of Hunter's hand, she blows the hair out of her face.

Hunter tugs his hand away. "Nice meeting you, Evie." He turns his gaze to me and winks. "Ready to get out of here, babe?"

*Babe?* Hunter's never called me a pet name, and I grimace. "Yeah, I guess." I turn toward Evie and say, "I'll see you tomorrow."

She quickly hugs me, and I stiffen, then she presses her lips to my ear. "Does he have a brother?"

I pull away and take Hunter's hand. "Yeah. I'll talk to you tomorrow."

Evie grins and flips her straight brown and red hair over her shoulder before sauntering toward the school parking lot. She shakes her hips a little too hard, but Hunter doesn't even give her a second glance before he kisses me and leads me around the car.

When he gets in and starts the engine, I shift in my seat to look at him. "Babe? Really? What was that all about?"

He puts the car in drive and shrugs. "It just came out."

"Whatever," I say with a laugh.

He shakes his head and pulls onto the highway. "Where do you want to go?"

I pucker my bottom lip. I'm way too nervous to risk going anywhere again. I just want to be with Hunter and not think about what kind of trouble is stalking us. Adjusting the vent away from me, I lean my head back.

I tap my finger on his knee. "There's a park by my house. Should be pretty abandoned."

He grabs my hand and brings it to his lips. "I like abandoned."

My heartbeat quickens, my stomach tingling with anticipation. His desire for me is so palpable that it makes me shiver just thinking about it.

"Me too," I whisper.

He kisses the top of my hand again, his mouth lingering. I bite my lip, enjoying his hot breath on my cool skin. Goosebumps prickle over my arms. I slip my hand from his and drop it back to his leg where I trail my fingers over his pants.

He grips the steering wheel and sidelong glances at me. His breathing comes faster, and I smile when he does. He looks in his rearview mirror and then pulls off the highway and into the nearly empty lot of a strip mall. He parks in the corner and grabs his sunshade from behind the seat and covers the windshield. His side windows are tinted dark enough that someone would have to press their face to the glass to see us inside.

He unbuckles his seatbelt and shifts in his seat, wrapping his arm around my shoulders to pull me closer. He kisses me deeply, hungrily. His tongue slips through my lips and my heart thuds against my ribcage.

I break away and look at the backseat. He studies my eyes for a moment, and I don't draw my eyes away from him. I've never felt so much love and longing in my life, and I want to know Hunter like I've never known anyone before. I've waited forever to be here with him, like this, without worry or fear hanging over my head. This moment feels so perfect, so right, and I know in my heart that I'm ready to go to the next level. I've risked my life for Hunter, and I'm ready to risk my soul for him, too.

He leans over and kisses my cheek, moving to my lips, and then tilts his head back to look into my eyes again. "You sure?" he asks.

I've never been more certain of anything. I smile and nod, and then say, "I love you."

## HUNTER

I trail my hand over Nadia's bare stomach one more time before she slips her shirt back over her head. I'll never forget the way she looked, so vulnerable yet so powerful, as she laid beneath me. Her alabaster skin is as smooth as it looks, and I lean over and kiss the blush crawling from her chest to her neck.

She runs her fingers along my bare arm, and I shiver. "I wish we could always be together," she says before pressing her lips to my shoulder blade.

I kiss her temple. "Soon, I promise."

Sadness clouds her eyes, and she sits up, curling her knees to her chest. She doesn't say it, but I can see the thought cross her mind. She doesn't believe it'll ever happen. She doesn't believe there is a future for us. I've known it since the first time she told me goodbye in the dream world before I got my body back.

Nadia thinks she's a monster and undeserving of happiness. She thinks her love for me will turn me crazy and get me killed like it did her mom. She told me when a nightmare inflictor loves a person, they lose control and inflict nightmares on them. Dmitri did it to her mom and after experiencing so many, she lost touch with reality to the point that when an HPA agent broke into their home, her mom did nothing while the agent murdered her because she didn't believe it was real.

But I don't believe it.

I wish Nadia didn't, either.

I reach over and touch her chin. "Please, believe me."

She attempts to smile, but a tear falls onto her cheek and she frowns. "I want to, Hunter. I do."

I know she does. She wants to believe me with everything she has, but she can't. I don't know if she ever will, even when we can finally rid ourselves of the board and the council, of everything holding us back.

I lean over and hug her tightly. "I know it's not easy. It's hard for me to see all the possibilities we have when everything seems so bad, too. But I know it can't be forever. We'll change things."

She stares out the window as the sun starts to sink into the horizon. "You should take me home." With those words I know there's no convincing her. She's already lost to her dark thoughts and grief. No matter how much I want to make her happy again this moment, I can't.

I feel hopeless.

We're hopeless.

# 6

## NIGHTMARE REALITY

### NADIA

ALYSSA SITS ON the bench at the bus stop across from the field that connects to our neighborhood. Hunter pulls next to the curb, and Alyssa rushes to the back door and jumps in before I have a chance to roll down the window.

Fear and uncertainty mar her usual bright, happy eyes, and dread seeps into my bones. She slams the door and leans between the seats, shivering. I wonder how long she's been waiting in the falling snow. Hunter turns up the heat as high as it goes, and I adjust the vents to give her additional heat.

Her blue lips quiver. "Take us home."

"What about Nadia's dad?"

"He isn't there. Just take us home."

With furrowed brows, Hunter nods and drives around the field and into our small neighborhood. He doesn't say it, but it's taking all of his willpower to return to my house. So many things could go wrong—we could get caught by my father or someone part of the creature community. Hunter could accidentally lead the HPA to my doorstep, and the way he risked going there with Jacqueline yesterday has probably used up our good luck for a year. His uncertainty and reluctance are tangible.

His arms stiffen, like two metal poles, as he grips the steering wheel. I touch his leg, but he doesn't relax. He probably feels the way I did when I stood in the elevator that led to the basement of Northern Trinity Hope Hospital where his body was being kept a few months ago.

The driveway leading to my open, empty garage is clear of snow. Alyssa's wasted no time since she left school to prepare for Hunter.

"Park in the garage so no one sees your car," Alyssa says.

I didn't think Hunter could stiffen any more, but he does. He drives into the garage and shuts off the engine but doesn't get out. Unbuckling his seatbelt, he swivels to peer at Alyssa. "I don't like this. I can't escape as quickly as I could if I were parked on the street."

Alyssa sighs. "You won't need to escape. Trust me."

I touch his scruffy cheek. "If you can't trust her, then trust me. Even if my father came home, he's not going to kill you. He's not a monster, just an overprotective dad."

Hunter grimaces.

Alyssa hops out of the car and pulls Hunter's door open and waves for him to hurry up and get out. I'm already closing the garage door and entering the house when he finally gets up the nerve to follow us.

He hovers in the mudroom, and I smile and lace my fingers through his, pulling him into the kitchen. He never left the living room the last time he was here, and I'm excited he gets to see the rest of my house. Glancing around, he takes in the white painted cabinetry, the marble counter tops, and the wooden island with pots and pans on a rack above it. His boots squeak as he shuffles across the tan, ceramic tiles, and he stops before the swinging door leading to the living room.

Alyssa pushes past us and leaves us alone in the kitchen. I turn to Hunter and stand on my tiptoes to kiss him. My kiss only takes a second to relax him before he kisses me back. His shoulders slump, and I slide my arms around his waist, hugging him against me, letting him breathe into my hair. Our lips meet again, softly caressing together, and I consider never breaking apart. He won't if I don't do it first.

I try to pull away, and he moans into my mouth, begging me for one more kiss. Smiling, I relent and kiss him three more times, just quick, teasing brushes that make him chuckle.

I gaze into his hazel eyes. "I need to find out what Alyssa saw. Help yourself to anything in the fridge. The bathroom is in the hall."

Hunter bobs his head, squeezing my hips, pressing his body into mine. Thoughts of this afternoon cross my mind, sending warmth blossoming up my chest to heat my neck. My blush doesn't go unnoticed. Hunter raises his hand, brushing my hair from my shoulder to drink me in with his intense gaze.

He holds me a minute longer and finally lets go, a smile playing on his lips. I suck in my bottom lip between my teeth, my eyes crinkling in the corners. I glide backward until my back hits the door. Reluctantly, I push through the door and head into the living room where Alyssa hovers at the answering machine. She lifts her emerald eyes to stare at me and tears rim her dark lashes.

The moment of love and desire vanishes, my heart falling into my stomach, the air knocking out of me. Alyssa doesn't have to say anything. I know something is wrong.

I don't step forward. My knees shake, weak with fear, and I grip the back of the couch to steady myself. Alyssa's fingers tremble as she hits the play button on the answering machine and a familiar, gruff voice echoes through the tense air.

"Dmitri, it's Javier. Where are you? Give me a call back."

I release a breath and relax. The head of the Creature Council, Mr. Soto, calls our house phone if he can't reach my father by his cell phone. It's nothing out of the ordinary.

The machine beeps and Mr. Soto's voice rings out again. "Dmitri, Javier again. You were supposed to meet me at the meeting hall an hour ago. Where are you? Call me back. It's urgent."

I swallow. Mr. Soto sounds nervous. It's unlike him to sound anything but confident and self-assured or annoyed and angry. He just sounds worried.

The machine beeps again. "Dmitri, my friend, Javier Soto came by The Haven just now. He's looking for you. I tried your cell, but it's off. Call me when you get this." I can hear Cian breathing into the phone. He doesn't hang up. After a minute his voice blares through the speakers again. "Nadia? Alyssa? This is Cian. If Dmitri isn't home by nightfall, call me, all right? Or if he's just avoiding the council, call me and let me know that as well so I can cover for him. I thought he was only joking when he said he was leav—"

I dig my nails into the palms of my hands when the message cuts off. I don't know what he meant about my father joking, but my father would never leave without me.

A phone rings from the kitchen, and I glide to the door and crack it open. Hunter sits at the table, leaning on his elbows, with his cell phone to his ear. A lump forms in my throat as I hold my breath and study his face. His face gives away no emotions, steeling to whoever is calling him. I can't tell who he's talking to or what it's about. For all I know, it's nothing.

"Thanks for letting me know," he finally says. He hangs up his phone and rubs his hand across his forehead before slamming his fist on the table, startling me.

I gasp, my heart racing at the frustration and anger rushing from him. Glancing up, he meets my gaze through the crack in the door. He presses his mouth into a tight line, his eyes crinkling in the corners.

"Hunter?" My voice comes barely above a whisper. "Who was that?"

His hard façade breaks, his eyes clouding with so much emotion, they shine in the kitchen light. "Nadia, I'm sorry."

With those three words, my heart squeezes, collapsing into itself, making it hard to breathe, to think, to feel anything except agony pouring through me. My stomach heaves, and I clutch my knees, breath hard to come by. I'm drowning in a sea of all the horrible reasons he'd need to apologize. Without him having to say so, I know it has to do with my father.

## HUNTER

Rushing to Nadia, I attempt to take her into my arms to pull her to me, but she stiffens. A wildness in her eyes stops me from touching her out all.

I can't believe I have to tell her that her dad was picked up by an HPA agent in the city yesterday. I can't believe I have to tell her I was the one who escorted him to the termination facility—the place he's surely never going to leave alive. How am I supposed to tell her I had the opportunity to save him, but I didn't pay enough attention to the supers in the back of Rosaline's van or I just shrugged and watched her close the door instead of asking her to remove the bags so I could look at the prisoners?

She's going to hate me for this.

She'll blame me for her dad's death.

I'll lose her forever.

"Is he dead?" Nadia's nearly inaudible voice rings in my ears. Her pale fingers grip the doorframe, and it's hard for me to hold her gaze. The color seeps from her irises by the second, and her hair already seems a few shades lighter. She's becoming the beautiful nightmare inflictor I dream about.

She reaches out and shakes my shoulder. "Hunter? Answer me. Is he dead?"

My throat burns, the words staying buried deep within me. How can my life go from incredible to gut-wrenching in a matter of hours? I wish I could turn back the clock to the moment I picked up Nadia. I want to stay in that moment forever.

"Hunter!" Anger swiftly rolls over Nadia's frightened expression, and she pushes me back into the kitchen, grabbing a handful of my jacket. Her nails scratch my chest, and I wince as all the love she has for me drains away, leaving nothing but an empty shell beneath her fair skin.

I cover her hands in mine. "No," I finally manage to say. "He's still alive."

She drops her hands to her sides, her chest heaving and her shoulders shaking as relief washes over her. She blinks away her tears, wiping her pale blond hair from her face. Breathing deeply, she brings her gaze back to mine. A dark shadow crosses over her light gray irises, and she purses her lips.

Then she slaps me.

My cheek stings, but I don't move. I can't.

"You jerk! Why didn't you just tell me? I was so scared."

I open my mouth to say something, anything. "He's at the termination facility. He was one of the creatures I picked up yesterday. I had no idea, I—"

Releasing a deep sob, Nadia squeezes her eyes closed. "So, he's basically dead. Hunter, how could you? You should've done something. I knew you being there was a bad—"

"I didn't know. Even if I did, I couldn't have. It'd have blown my cover. You know what we're trying to do."

"He's my father!" She lifts her hand again, her eyes wild, and I grab it and bring it to my lips and kiss her knuckles.

"I didn't know. I—"

Yanking away, she stumbles back, and turns to leave. "I need to tell Alyssa."

"Nadia, wait." My chest tightens as I think about what I'm going to say next.

"What?"

I pull her back to me, wrapping my arms around her. "Your dad isn't dead yet, and they didn't send him to the black zone immediately. There's still a chance. Jacqueline saw him in the gray zone."

"The gray zone?" I didn't think she could get any paler, but the rest of her color washes from her, and she looks like a beautiful apparition, hovering against the tan wall.

"Ninety percent of supers—people—in the gray zone get sent to the black zone where they'll be euthan—murdered." I cringe as I stumble over my words. I've grown use to the HPA terminology that I sound heartless.

Nadia puckers her bottom lip. "What happens to the other ten percent?"

I release a breath. "Five percent get sent to the green zone and the others get sent to a testing facility to be experimented on. Most don't live long there either."

"You have to save him, Hunter. I can't lose him."

My heart aches for Nadia because the one thing she asks me to do—needs me to do—is the one thing I don't think I can do. I stare into her teary, beautiful gray eyes. I want to lie to her and tell her I'll have him home by morning, but I can't.

"Nadia," I whisper. I kiss her forehead and then drop my gaze to the tiled floor. "I don't know how."

## NADIA

My world crumbles around me. It feels like it did the day after my mother died once the shock and fear faded away. I always knew this day would come, and the HPA would kidnap my father and leave me an orphan. I didn't think it'd be so soon.

But I don't understand how. My father is the strongest, bravest, fiercest fighter the Creature Council has. It's why he was chosen to face the world outside the compound and eliminate the threats that try to annihilate the council members as they hide behind the protection of spells in the compound.

He's never gotten close to being captured before. Ever. My only guess is that something went wrong and surprised him. I wish I knew what happened—what changed. I wonder if he's scared, if he's thinking of me, or if he's already accepted his fate.

*Don't think like that. Dad won't give up that easily. He won't go down without a fight…*

Black fog swirls around the edges of my vision, my chest throbbing with each shallow breath I take. The room grows smaller and smaller, and every time I look at Hunter, I'm reminded of the HPA.

I grip his jacket and unzip it to show off his uniform. Pushing him back, I wave my arm from his head to his boots. "What good was all this if you're going to stand around and watch the HPA murder everyone I know and love? It makes you no different!"

Instead of rushing to the living room, I push past him and out the back door.

Dark, foreboding clouds churn above me, stealing any chance of sunshine cutting through the persistence winter. Snow falls from the sky to blur the world in white, keeping the ice in my blood from thawing.

I drop to my knees and bury my hands into the powdery snow. Lying down, I roll to my back and watch as snow dusts over me. If I stay here long enough, I could disappear in its pure, freezing whiteness and just fade away. I'll no longer feel sorrow and pain. My soul will be frozen and nothing could hurt me again.

But I won't feel love and happiness either.

I'll feel nothing.

## HUNTER

A gentle hand touches my shoulder. I turn and gaze down at Alyssa. Her fiery red hair spills over her shoulders, and she's changed out of her sweater dress and into track pants and a long sleeved T-shirt. Tear stains streak her cheeks, her usually vibrant green eyes dulled from the redness of crying.

"It's not your fault," she says. "You should go to her."

I clench my teeth for a moment. "She hates me."

"That's not true. She loves you. She needs you."

"The last person she needs is me. Maybe you should talk to her, Alyssa. You're her best friend. Help her."

Alyssa sniffles, sorrow puffing the skin under her eyes. "I can barely keep myself together."

I rub my hand over my face. "You saw him die, didn't you?"

She shakes her head. "No, but it doesn't mean I won't. It scares me. I hate this. It's these visions that make it hard for me to function." Blinking her eyes a few more times, she crosses her arms and glances out the bay window at the falling snow. "Just go to her and be there for her. Tell her we'll figure this out."

Alyssa leaves me standing in the empty kitchen, and I get up the nerve to face Nadia, meandering to the open back door. Fresh snow piles on the uncovered patio, and I zip up my jacket. Everything sparkles white with untouched snow, and I scan the yard for signs of Nadia. If it weren't for her black coat, I'd have looked right past her.

Her hair and face blend in with the snow. She stares at the cloudy sky and doesn't blink her gray eyes. She looks like an innocent, crying angel statue with tears frozen on her eyelashes and cheeks, haunting and ethereal just like her dream world persona. It reminds me of the first time I met her and how she set Jacqueline's nightmare ablaze. But where her eyes held fire before, they now darken with grief, empty and cold like the world around us.

I crouch down and run my bare fingers over her frozen cheeks. She stares right through me, nestling fear deep in my bones. This is what she looked like after being trapped by the nightmare catcher that nearly killed her. I wonder if a broken heart could kill a nightmare inflictor. I wonder if I'd survive if Nadia wasn't here anymore.

"Nadia," I whisper. My ears buzz with the sound of the wind picking up. I barely even hear myself speak out loud. "Nadia, please. Please, look at me."

Her icy gray eyes pierce into my soul. "I feel like no matter how hard we try, things will never be how they're supposed to be," she whispers. "Every time things start to look up, they take a turn for the worse. You know Alyssa never mentions us having a happy ending. What if we're doomed to live a nightmare reality?"

Pulling her from the ground and into my arms, I cup her chin and kiss her deeply, fiercely, determined to warm her with my love and hope and faith in us. Faith that even if the world is against us, if we stand together, we'll make it out okay in the end.

Pulling away even though she clutches me to her, trying to keep me close, I stare into her eyes. "You're wrong, Nadia. You know that's not true, and Alyssa can't tell us how it'll be in the end because she doesn't see it. Things are always changing, but you're my constant. I know we're going to get through this."

"I don't think I can," she whispers.

"I'm not giving up on us so easily. I need you." I run my hand over her snow covered hair, dusting the snow away while pushing it from her bluing cheeks. "I'm not going to let them kill your dad. I'll die trying to save him. I'll give up everything so he can live."

Her bottom lip puckers, her unblinking eyes drawing to mine. "They'll kill you," she whispers. "I can't survive that, either."

"You don't know that."

But she's right. There's no way I could get Nadia's father out of the termination facility without giving myself away. But I'm willing to risk it. I can't stand seeing Nadia like this. I know she'd do it for me. She *did* do it for me.

"I do, Hunter. I'm scared of losing you, too."

I lift Nadia into my arms and stand from the frozen ground. She buries her frozen face into my shoulder without another word.

"You won't lose me. I promise," I say.

Now, if I could only keep that promise.

# 7

# BEAUTIFUL NIGHTMARE INFLICTOR

## HUNTER

I TURN ON Nadia's shower and watch steam fog the mirror. Nadia perches on the toilet lid and doesn't say anything as I slip off her wet clothes and pile them on the floor. Her pale, ice cold skin, stings my warm fingers. Shivering, I brush them over her bare side and help her into the shower.

My heartbeat races at how beautiful she looks and how I want to pick her up in my arms and take her back to her room. She grips my hand, not letting me go, and my sleeve soaks up the warm water, but I don't pull away.

Water drips down her cheeks, blending with her tears. Her white hair sticks to the sides of her face, her bottom lip quivering. I lean in and rub my free hand under her chin and graze her lips with my fingers. She opens her eyes and looks at me, desire pushing her sadness away, but I don't move. Not now. Not like this.

"Hunter..." Her voice trails off. The way she says my name sends goosebumps down my arms.

I swallow the lump in my throat. "Let me help you dry off," I finally say after a moment.

Nadia just stands under the running water until I turn it off and wrap a towel around her. I lift her into my arms, carrying her back into her room, her face nuzzling my neck.

She shrugs into jeans and a sweater and falls back on her bed, patting the spot next to her. "Stay with me, please."

I nod and climb onto her bed. She pulls off my wet shirt and presses her body against me without a word. We just lay together, unmoving, until darkness closes around us.

## NADIA

Hunter's breathing slows, igniting hunger deep in my soul. I'm worn out and exhausted and can't find the will to keep him awake. The last two days have drained me, and I need to inflict a nightmare. His dreams call to me, begging me to enter his head. Tears burn my cheeks, spilling onto the pillow. If I become his worst nightmare, it could change our relationship. It could change Hunter. He could go mad like my mother.

I'm out of control.

"Hunter, please, don't fall asleep." My hoarse voice barely sounds through the quiet room.

"It's fine," he whispers. "I'm not afraid of you."

"What if it's not?"

"Nadia, trust me."

"Hunter, I—" I stiffen, snapping my mouth shut, sensing Hunter falling asleep completely next to me.

I moan, sliding my fingers up his arms to cup his face. Leaning over his sleeping body, I press my lips to his, catching a hint of mocha and whipped cream, a part of me screaming for him to wake up but the darker part of me begging for him to stay asleep. In his sleep, he shifts, hugging me to him. His sweet and irresistible lips taste how I imagine his dreams do.

Kissing him harder, devouring the taste of his dreams trickling to me, I graze my fingers to touch his temples, shifting me from reality and into his dream.

Warm sun caresses my cool, porcelain skin, and I glide over white sand. Crystalline waves crash against my flowing, white dress. I expect the turquoise ocean to darken with my touch, but it just laps at my legs like I'm not the nightmare inflictor come to destroy this breathtaking dream world.

Lowering my feet into the wet sand, I sink into the beach when the wave pulls itself back into the peaceful ocean. My wet dress clings to my balmy skin, everything around me feeling so utterly real, just like Hunter used to feel inside Jacqueline's nightmare.

My soul recognizes his and refuses to hurt him. I'm in complete control over my nightmare inflicting side, my hunger just a dull ache in the pit of my stomach.

I saunter away from the tranquil waves until the wet sand dries. It looks like a million tiny crystals glittering in the sun. Bending over, I trail my fingers through it, mesmerized that I have no effect on it.

"Nadia?"

My heartbeat skips, and I twirl on the balls of my feet in the direction Hunter's voice came from. He sits on a dark blue beach blanket with an ice chest positioned on the corner and a magazine open on his lap.

His dark, curly hair sticks to his forehead, his hazel eyes appearing bluer with the ocean reflecting in them. I trail my gaze from his muscular chest to his well-toned abs glistening in the sunlight. I imagine grazing my fingers over them, turning this dream into a fantasy.

Smiling, he jumps to his feet. "I could feel your presence." He jogs closer, eliciting fear to build in my chest. This isn't right. This isn't what it's supposed to be like. He shouldn't be able to see me within his own dream.

I hold up my hands. "Stop! Don't come any closer." My voice echoes over the soft roar of the waves. "I could hurt you."

He skids to a stop, kicking up sand against my wet dress. It speckles the white fabric in splotches of cream, and I absently dust it off like it matters. Narrowing my eyes, I study Hunter's face. He looks like he does in the real world, but also just like I remember him in Jacqueline's dream. Is he really aware of the dream, of what's happening, or is it just a dream he'll forget upon waking? Will I remember?

Hunter brushes sand from his hair. "It's only a dream, Nadia. You can't really hurt me."

I frown. "What? I don't understand. You shouldn't know anything. You shouldn't be able to see me."

"Being imprisoned in Jacqueline's mind, learning to control myself in her dreams, taught me how to control my own." He takes another step closer, and I stumble back and fall onto the sand. "I can't believe you're really here."

I crab walk backwards. "I can't believe you can see me."

"Why? I've seen you in a dream world before. I can feel your soul. It's just as amazing as I remember."

"Why didn't you tell me?" My voice rings high pitched and squeaky, and my heart pounds so hard against my ribcage that the sound resonates like a drum in my ears, making it hard to focus on Hunter. "I need to leave."

Hunter reaches for my hand. "Nadia, please, wait. You just got here. We have all night."

Before he can touch me, I scream.

## HUNTER

I cringe as Nadia's screams echo through the air. I can't believe she's in my dream and not a figment of my imagination. She shakes her head with her eyes squeezed shut. Her white hair catches a breeze, making her look like the beautiful nightmare inflictor I thought I'd never see again.

I knew being in Jacqueline's head had changed me, changed something in my soul, but I never guessed this was how it changed me. I learned to control my dream world from constantly being inside Jacqueline's with Nadia, but I never brought it up because dreams and nightmare inflicting are such taboo things for Nadia. I knew she hated talking about her nightmare inflictor side, so I never mentioned it. I didn't think it mattered.

But I can see now that it does matter. It matters a lot. Nadia is flipping out like the first time she realized I wasn't a dream person and couldn't turn me into a cloud of dust like everything else in the dreams she destroys and devours.

It's strange, though.

I can feel her presence, her very essence, and I can sense all of her emotions more so than when we were together in Jacqueline's dreams. She's not only confused, but she's also frightened, angry, sad, and even somewhat happy. But, what I feel the most is her love for me. It's hotter and more intense than every other feeling radiating from her. It's unconditional and irrevocable. It's all for me.

Wrapping my arms around her, I pull her onto my lap, cutting her scream off with a kiss. She relaxes, the tension easing away from her, her fear morphing to undeniable desire and fear, a different kind of hunger than I've ever felt. She sinks into me, combing her fingers through my hair, straddling me, pushing me back into the sand. In this moment, my world is complete. I have everything I need in this dream and want to stay here with Nadia forever. Stay in my head where nothing can hurt us. Because here, we control everything. Here, all we need is each other to survive.

Thunder claps in the distance and lightning strikes the sand. The world shifts, and Nadia pulls back and touches my lips with her fingers. She disappears before I can beg her to stay, and I feel so empty when she leaves.

My paradise world starts to crumble, but not because of Nadia. She had nothing to do with the destruction of my dream. I'm willing it to end. I don't want to dream anymore now that she's gone. Without her in my dream, it's a true nightmare, and I'd rather be awake.

## NADIA

I lean my back on my bedroom door, my heart racing and my hands trembling. I'm falling apart. I've wished with every fiber of my soul that I could go back in time and share a dream world with Hunter again without him being trapped in another person's head, but now that I have, it's really strange.

Unlike all my other dreamers, Hunter remained in control of his dream. It was like I was just a spectator, probably how he felt in Jacqueline's dream, and it scared me. How unexpected it went, how out of control I felt, and I'm still starving. I should be grateful I wasn't able to inflict a nightmare on Hunter. I should be ecstatic he'll never see me as a monster. But, I'm terrified. What if this was a one-time thing? What if Hunter doesn't remember any of it and hates me for losing control and invading his mind? I wonder if my father has ever dealt with this before.

I slide to the floor, my heart aching, and pull my knees to my chest.

My father isn't coming home.

I have no one else to turn to.

A sob shakes my shoulders, an animalistic groan erupting from my throat. Tears spill onto my cheeks, blurring my vision. I cover my eyes and cry into my hands. Everything aches. My head, my stomach, my heart. I don't know if I can survive the paralyzing pain any longer. Each breath I take burns my lungs. I feel like if I could just stop breathing, everything would be okay.

I hold my breath and close my eyes.

I try to disappear.

"Nadia?" Alyssa shuffles from her room and wraps her arms around me. I sink against her, letting her rubs circles on my back until the sobs turn into hiccups and sputter out with each deep breath I force into my lungs.

"What do we do, Lys? Haven't we been through enough?" My voice cracks, and I swallow the hard lump in my throat.

"First, we'll call Cian and let him know, and then you need some sustenance." She shifts and stares at me. Her emerald eyes glass over and she blinks. "Second, I'll call the council. Dmitri is one of their best enforcers. They'll help us."

I nod, feeling slightly better. It's not the best plan, but it's a start. I'll do whatever it takes to get my father away from the HPA. "What would I do without you?"

The memory of Hunter's dream pushes thoughts of the council away, and I consider telling her what happened, but before I open my mouth, my bedroom door swings open and

Hunter's shadow casts over us.

He hovers in the doorway, his bare chest rising and falling as he breathes, and he looks down on us. "It's getting late. The last thing we need is for people to wonder where I am."

"You're right," Alyssa says.

She raises her hand to Hunter, and he pulls her to her feet before turning to me and grabbing mine. My heart thuds in overdrive when he squeezes my fingers and holds my gaze. A million thoughts cloud his hazel eyes as he looks to me for answers I don't have.

Alyssa touches my shoulder. "I'll call Cian." Turning, she struts to the living room, leaving us alone.

Hunter doesn't say anything. He slides his muscular arms around my waist and pulls me close. I hook my hands around his neck, running them over his shoulders before sinking into him and resting my cheek on his chest. I feel so small and safe in his arms. I don't want to pull away.

He kisses my forehead. "What you did..." His voice trails off, and my stomach flips. I was hoping he wouldn't bring up me invading his dream, but we can't just pretend it didn't happen.

I tilt my head to look him in the eyes. "I'm so, so sorry, Hunter. You fell asleep, and I lost control. I shouldn't have done it. It was wrong."

He offers a small smile, reaching up to tuck my hair behind my ear. "You didn't let me finish. What you did was amazing. I've dreamed of you every night since I was released from

Jacqueline, and I didn't think we'd ever get to share a dream like that again."

I squeeze my eyes shut. "I didn't either, but it doesn't make it right. I intended to inflict a nightmare on you. I couldn't resist. Just because I couldn't, doesn't make it any better."

"Don't think like that. I told you it was okay. I'm not your victim. You know I'd do anything for you."

Shaking my head, I say, "Not that. You don't know what it's really like. You know I can turn a person crazy. That's what happens to my victims."

"People make mistakes. And all your supposed victims? They're volunteers. It's what makes you different. You're a good person, Nadia, no matter what you think. Just because you say you're a monster, doesn't mean you are. I've seen what true monsters look like, and they're nothing like you." He cups my chin so I have to look at him. "You know I'd never love a monster."

I sigh. I can't argue with him. I don't want to. He'll never understand, but that's okay. He doesn't have to. I'd never want him to either. I force my mouth to smile even though all I want to do is cry, and then I stand on my tiptoes and kiss him.

Pulling away, he grabs his damp clothes from my dresser and shrugs on his shirt and jacket. My heart hurts looking at his HPA uniform, and I draw my eyes to the floor. He zips his jacket up and runs his fingers through his messy, curly hair. Taking my hand, he guides me toward the door to the garage.

Icy air hits us in a cold wave. He opens the door and kisses me once more. "Call me as soon as you can. I'm going to head over to the termination facility to meet Jacqueline before I head home. I'll check on your dad, too."

My breath catches. "You can see him? Can you talk to him?"

He shrugs. "I don't know, but I'll try."

Turning his back to me, he gets into his car. For the first time, it's me who watches him drive away.

# THE ONE WHO NEEDS PROTECTING

## HUNTER

THE TERMINATION FACILITY is empty this time of night. Only a few agents monitor the premises and no one questions what I'm doing here. The evening shift, apart from the caretakers, ends at nine and most people leave by then. The supers are monitored on camera in the offsite security office but are basically left to fend for themselves between midnight and seven.

Jacqueline doesn't smile at me when I step from the elevator. She glances from the monitor to me and back to the monitor, running her fingers over her tight bun.

I stroll up behind her and set a greasy paper bag of take-out on the desk.

"Did you get my message?" she asks.

I haven't checked my phone since she first told me about Nadia's father. She leans back in her chair to look at me, and I shake my head. Sighing, she points at the monitor. Camden is no longer our only charge.

"We've had two transfers from the gray zone," she says. "Because they didn't fight or resist the scientists during testing, they were deemed safe enough to bring over. The gray zone is impacted, and the scientists want more time for testing."

I steel my expression. The red light on the camera positioned in the corner blinks and reminds me we're being watched. I can't show even an ounce of emotion in regards to the people being held captive.

"What are they?" I watch Jacqueline tap her fingers on the keyboard. She brings her eyes to mine, her gaze saying a thousand words, and I know that one of the new transfers is Dmitri.

"Not sure. The test results haven't come in." The corner of Jacqueline's lip twitches as she lies for the camera. She can identify more creatures than any other person here because she is a creature. She knows the supernatural world.

I shift my eyes from hers to the monitor and study the screen without being able to see anything distinguishing through the blurry video feed. Stepping back, I shove my hands in my pockets. "Mind if I look?" I jerk my head toward the corridor leading to the cells.

"Fine, but you have to pass out these then." Jacqueline kicks the case of water bottles next to her. "And I'm going to start eating without you."

## NADIA

After Hunter's dream left me still in need of a nightmare, I arranged for another volunteer. He offered to come over after I told him about the HPA taking my father, but I declined. I want to try the council first.

Alyssa waits in the car, and I open the unlocked door of my dreamer's house. I slip into his bedroom and into his dream without hesitation.

Opening my eyes in his dream world, I take a step forward. The floor boards creak as I climb the wooden stairs of the abandoned house. The scent of burning wood drifts to my nostrils, and I glance at the trail of branded footprints I leave as I move through the dark house.

I run my fingers along the wall in a circular pattern, setting the walls ablaze. A moan erupts from the last door on the right. I grin as I taste the dreamer's fear, strolling closer, drawing out the dreamer's anxious anticipation. I catch sight of my reflection in the crookedly hung mirror on the wall.

My eyes widen, and I pause to take in my appearance. I'm a woman with limp brown hair, dark circles under my eyes, and cracked lips. A torn veil hangs behind me, clipped into my hair. A gaping wound in my stomach drips blood down the front of my wedding dress, and I turn away, noticing my innards.

I scratch my nails on the door, causing the dreamer to scream.

"Leave me alone, Diana," he says. "Please, leave me alone."

Turning the doorknob, I smile, hearing the quiver in his voice. I suck in breath after breath of tangy, citrusy fear and slam my hands on the door to shove it open. It bangs against the wall, startling the man.

I rush the room in a swirl of red and white, my fingers cupping the dreamer's face before a scream can rip from his throat. He explodes in a cloud of delectable dust. The nightmare crumbles around me, and I leave his mind and glide from the house and to Alyssa's car parked in the empty driveway.

She pulls away without saying anything, and I flip down the visor to gaze at my reflection in the mirror. Color flushes my face, my pale hair golden once more. I feel alive and like myself again. Flicking the visor back up, I lean in my seat, ignoring the monster peeking through my deep blue eyes. I stare off into the star-speckled sky instead.

## HUNTER

I knock on Camden's door first. Every move I make must be calculated so I don't look suspicious. He doesn't respond, even though I know he's awake, so I knock once more before punching in my pass code and pushing the door open a crack.

"Hey, man, I brought you some water," I say, setting the bottle on the desk.

Camden narrows his eyes. "It's not your shift."

"What's your point?"

He glares. "Nothing. Thanks for the water." Turning his back on me, I realize he's done talking.

An idea hits me, thinking about how to get him to open up

for me and only me. The HPA wanted me to try to make friends with him to get the answers they want, and I want to let him know I'm on his side without flat out telling him. The perfect way to do so is to come randomly when he doesn't expect me. I could do it for everyone. The board will be pleased with my effort, and I can figure out a way to save as many people as I can.

"You're welcome. See you in a few hours."

Stepping back, I lock the door behind me. I shuffle down the corridor to the next cell and peek in the glass window. A young girl, with red hair the same color as Alyssa's, sits on the desk chair with her legs curled under her. Tears stream from her green eyes, and she doesn't look older than ten.

Rage buries deep into my bones. The HPA is insane. This girl is a kid. What are they even thinking? Digging my nails into the palms of my hands, I suck in a slow breath between my clenched teeth.

I knock.

"Come in," a small voice says.

I punch in my pass code and crack the door open. "Would you like some water?" I ask through the crack.

"Do you have any milk?" she asks.

I push the door open wider and watch as the girl rubs her hand over her wet cheek. She stiffens in her chair, so I don't move any closer. She's scared enough as it is. I wish I could scoop her up and run out of here with her. I wonder how Jacqueline handles all this. She seems more put together than I feel.

I shake my head. "Sorry, all I have is water right now. I can bring you some milk in the morning if you'd like."

Her bottom lip trembles and tugs at my heart. "I have to stay the night?"

I nod. Nothing I say will make her feel better. I change the topic. "What's your name?"

"Ella," she says in a soft voice. "What's yours?"

"I'm Hunter." I set the water bottle on the ground. "If you need anything, just call for me. I'll be back in the morning with some milk, okay? I have to go now."

She sniffles. "Okay."

I shut the door before I lose my resolve. My life as an HPA agent has gone from tolerable, to bad, to freakin' awful in what feels like seconds. I don't know what I was thinking. I can't do this anymore.

*But the girl, Ella, she needs you.* The thought pounds in my mind. I shuffle to the next door, because as much as I want to, I can't just quit and run away. Nadia isn't the only one relying on me anymore. She's not the one who needs protecting right now.

Ignoring the pit in my stomach, I bang on the next door. A body lies covered on the cot and doesn't move. I enter in my pass code and crack the door. Inky black hair spills from under the sheet and a sinewy, pale arm hangs off the bed with its knuckles grazing the floor.

"You want some water?" I ask.

The figure sits up, the sheet falling away, and I freeze. I haven't seen Dmitri in person since I was in Jacqueline's mind, and he's much more intimidating now. Nadia's dad swings his feet off the bed and stands up, looming a good six inches taller than me. His obsidian eyes narrow as they train on my weaponry belt.

He shakes his head. "No, thank you, but you can leave it by the door."

I nearly jump out of my skin at the sound of his voice, even though he didn't threaten me or anything. I'm not sure if it's because he's my girlfriend's dad or scary as hell, or both, but I reflexively step back, furrowing my brows. I had expected him to charge at me and rip my head off, fighting like the one time I saw him subdue an agent from the safety of Jacqueline's mind prison, but he just stands there and studies me.

I set the bottle down. "I'm Hunter by the way. If you need anything, just call for me and I'll come back as soon as I can."

He steps closer. "Actually, I do need something now."

I press my lips in a line. "I can't guarantee you'll get it."

Frowning, he says, "I only want to know where the little red-haired girl is. Is she okay?"

My chest tightens. "She's next door." I glance at the wall dividing them and lower my voice. "Don't tell anyone I told you this, but these walls are thin, and if you want to talk to her, I bet she could hear you."

He nods and turns away from me. I shut and lock the door, heading back to the front desk where Jacqueline finishes up the burger I brought her. I need to get out of here now. I need to tell Nadia that I saw her father and he's safe.

At least for now.

## NADIA

"I couldn't get a hold of any council members, but Roxanne mentioned the compound is having a mandatory meeting in an hour."

"This late?" It's unlike the council to interrupt their beauty sleep to meet with the community. It must be really important.

Alyssa glances at me in her peripheral vision. "Weird, huh? I think we should go."

I tap my fingers on the dashboard. "I'm not allowed, re-member? They'll never let me through the gates."

She turns left at the end of the block. "I have an idea. Should be simple enough."

I shift in my seat to study her face. I expect her to tell me her plan, but she just stares at the road. Alyssa merges on the highway and hits the throttle, racing past the flow of light traf-fic, heading north. We pass the city, brightly lit and alive in the dark, and keep traveling until civilization thins out.

"Can we stop at a payphone? I want to call Hunter before we get there. Maybe he can give us some information we can take to the council." A chill runs down my back thinking about facing Mr. Soto and his disapproving glower.

Alyssa crosses over three lanes and speeds off the highway. It's the last exit with a gas station for miles.

We pull into a gas station with one lonely payphone. Grabbing change from the cup holder, I jump out of the car. I punch in Hunter's number and let it ring a few times before hanging up. I cross my arms and eye Alyssa, who's staring right back at me, before dialing Hunter's number again.

It rings and rings, and I hang up again.

I walk over to Alyssa, and she rolls down her window. Leaning over, I say, "He's not picking up. Do you think everything's okay?"

She nods. "He's fine. I had a vision he and Jacqueline met us in daylight."

I blow a relieved breath through my lips. "Let me try one more time." Jogging to the payphone, I feed it more change before pounding Hunter's cell number again. It rings and rings, and when I'm about to give up, the line clicks and a weird static noise buzzes through the speaker.

"I'll see you tomorrow." Hunter's voice sounds muffled, like his phone is in his pocket, and I press the receiver to my ear to try to hear more.

"Later, Agent Hunter. Tomorrow should be fun. It's sure picking up around here." It's a feminine voice and not Jacqueline's. He must still be at the termination facility.

The line beeps, and I add the last of my change. I hear a car door slam, and then the rumble of an engine. The line goes quiet. I wonder if it disconnected, but I hold the phone to my ear to wait for the dial tone.

"Nadia? You still there?" Hunter's voice wraps me in love and warmth. "Sorry about that. I was leaving the facility."

I skip over the small talk and blurt, "Did you see my father? Is he—" I sigh. I can't ask the question.

Hunter clears his throat. "He's alive and okay. They trans-ferred him to my zone, because he didn't pose a threat and the gray zone is overcrowded."

I grip the cord. "Thank God. Did you talk to him?"

"Mmmhmm. He was surprisingly nice. If I were him, I'd have tried to take me out. He was worried, though."

"What else do you expect from him?"

"No, he's worried about—about—" He clears his throat. "Nadia, it's really messed up. There's a kid in the room next to his. Her name is Ella. I'm pretty sure she's the reason your dad ended up with the HPA. He was trying to protect her."

My stomach ties in knots. I'm going to be sick. That poor girl must be scared out of her mind. "Oh, Hunter." I can't find my voice to say anything else. The only thing worse than this situation is...*shut up! Don't think about it.*

"I know," he says. "I want to meet you. Maybe in the morning? How about the park near your house? I'll bring Jacqueline."

I nod even though he can't see me. "Yeah, sure. I'll see you then." Alyssa honks the horn, and I look over my shoulder at her. "I love you, Hunter."

Hanging up, I meet Alyssa's eyes. She waves for me to hur-ry. I run and hop in the car, hanging onto the grab handle as she speeds to the compound. Alyssa parks the car, and I hop out. Before I have time to compose myself, I find myself strolling through a dark forest alone and a tiny bit frightened.

# 9

## ALWAYS ANOTHER WAY

### NADIA

THE CHAIN-LINK FENCE buzzes with power. I stand a few feet away, leaning on the sturdy trunk of an oak tree. The scent of frozen dirt and dead leaves swirl around me in a freezing breeze. Tiny icicles hang from the branches and glitter like a thousand stars in the pale moonlight.

A dark silhouette moves on the other side of the fence. The gate swings open, and Alyssa stomps through the snow to me. She dangles a small talisman from her fingers. "Sorry it took so long. I had to wait for Roxanne to leave before I could snatch it."

If we had come during daylight hours, the talisman would've been hanging on a tree for the forest nymphs to access the forest with. At nightfall, it's locked away so people can't sneak off after dark. It's not like anyone really wants to. Alyssa and I are no longer here.

I hesitate for a second before entering the premises. I toss the talisman back to Alyssa, and she enters and hangs it on a tree for someone to find tomorrow. Hopefully the council will let me speak before throwing me out.

We walk together, arms hooked at the elbow, and cross the green stretch of field. Magic prevents snow from falling within the fences, and the temperature feels at least ten degrees warmer. I almost miss this place. I don't miss the council, though.

"We should sit in the back and see what the meeting is about before making our presences known." I pull my hood up and tuck my hair into it so people don't recognize my pale blond tresses.

Alyssa slows her pace. "Good idea." She guides me to the main building and up the steps. "The lobby will be empty, so no one's going to see us. They're all inside."

Dragging my feet, I force my legs to move. I stare at the tiled floor as Alyssa drags me to the elevator. When we're finally in it, she hits the button for the basement. The doors open, showing off a small lobby with a desk, a few chairs, and another set of double doors.

I meet Alyssa's gaze. "Let's get this over with."

Mr. Soto's deep voice echoes over the small auditorium. "I

received news that the HPA has increased their agent activity in the city so much that the city dwellers are leaving."

The crowd gasps.

"Settle down. We're increasing security measures and won't be escorting anyone to the city for a while. Our highly trained delivery staff will bring everything we need." Mr. Soto turns and looks at the three other council members. They stare at the crowd but don't show any emotion.

A shifter raises his hand. "What are you going to do about those taken?"

Mr. Soto clears his throat. "I'm sorry, but they're already gone. The HPA doesn't keep prisoners."

A woman cries out, and a man wraps his arms around her.

I give Alyssa a sidelong glance. Mr. Soto has no idea what the HPA is up to, and he's just making blind assumptions. Veronica Sanders, the HPA scientist turned council member, wrings her hands together. She knows the truth. I can see it in her eyes. That means Mr. Soto is purposely lying. But why?

I gather all my courage and stand. Alyssa squeezes my hand, and I grip it until her fingers slip from mine when I glide to the center aisle and up to the small stage. The crowd continues to mumble, and it takes me pulling off my hood to get their attention.

Mr. Soto jumps to his feet. "Ms. Petrov, you have a lot of nerve showing up here. We made it clear you've been banned from the premises. How did you get in?"

I turn to the crowd and meet Alyssa's gaze. "You need better security."

"Clive, escort Ms. Petrov off the premises. If your father wasn't an important member of our team, I'd guarantee your punishment would be much more severe. A girl died because of you. If you return, Ms. Petrov, I won't be so nice about it."

A tall, well-built man reaches for my arm, and I glide out of his reach. He huffs and cracks his neck and comes after me again, but I'm faster and keep evading him.

"Wait, please. I need your help. It's important," I say. "Please, we can help each other."

"Clive!"

"Javier, give the girl a chance," Thierry Stevens, the elf council member says, his smooth voice cutting through the murmur of the crowd. "She's made some bad choices. It's not like she released an army of agents upon us."

Mr. Soto raises his hands in the air. "Fine, speak. You have three minutes."

The crowd hushes, and all eyes turn to me. I didn't prepare a speech or anything and just wanted to ask if they'd help me get my father back, but I know the answer to that already. They only take care of themselves.

*Just try. Do it for Dad.*

I link my fingers together. "I've lived outside the compound for months now, and I know what the real world is like and how it works."

"What's your point, Nadia?" Veronica says, interrupting.

"My point is that I know the HPA, and what you've told

everyone is wrong."

A roar of voices erupts in the crowd, and it takes Mr. Soto screaming to quiet everyone down.

"Ms. Petrov! I won't stand here and listen as you sully our good word."

"You mean your lies?" Alyssa asks from the back of the room.

"Ms. Callaghan!"

"Then tell them the truth!" I yell. "The HPA doesn't kill people the moment they get them. They do keep prisoners. They have facilities all over the country filled with creatures, and you're not doing a dang thing about it. They took my father, and he's still alive. I came here for your help."

"Dmitri," Veronica whispers. "No."

"So, please, you have to help me."

Mr. Soto looks at me with grim eyes. For once, he isn't looking at me in distaste but in pity. "I'm sorry, Nadia. There's no way your father is alive."

Anger boils in my veins. "But he is! And so is a guy named Camden and a little girl named Ella. We need to help them."

Mr. Soto takes a seat at the table next to Veronica and the two other silent council members. He rubs a hand over his deeply wrinkled face. "No, we can't. It's too risky. We need to worry about the people in this room. We have too much to lose."

"You're a bunch of cowards," I say through gritted teeth. Angry tears spill from my eyes. I hate that this crowded room of people are witnessing me mourn my father. I hate all of them. The council disappoints me once again. What good are leaders who choose not to lead? Who choose to stay hidden? Who choose that a life is not worth the risk?

"Ms. Petrov!" Mr. Soto bellows.

"It's true!" I look at the audience. "It'll only get worse. The HPA will get to you, too. It's only a matter of time."

Mr. Soto pounds his fists on the desk. "This meeting is over. Everyone go back to your living quarters." He turns to glare at me. "Nadia, you stay here. I'm not finished with you."

Crossing my arms, I straighten my shoulders. Alyssa pushes through the crowd and comes up next to me. With her by my side, I gather the courage I need to face the council. No one I know of has ever stood up to the council like this. Most people who don't like what the council does keep to themselves—like Cian. He runs The Haven for those people the council won't help. Unlike me, he's a silent rebel. I'm not.

I've faced the council two other times. Once before I met Hunter when Mr. Soto thought it was acceptable to allow an enchantress to peek in on me while I was inflicting a nightmare and the other was when I forced Jacqueline to leave the compound to release Hunter.

This is different though. They don't control me anymore. I don't live by their rules.

Silence wraps around me when the last few people exit the auditorium. The sound of my heartbeat rings in my ears. My palms sweat as I bring my gaze to the four council members.

The only one who hasn't said a word is the enchantress, Ana Midnight. Her long black hair twists up in a bun, and her electric blue eyes sparkle in the bright stage lights.

Mr. Soto struts from the table and stands in front of me and Alyssa. The old man lifts his hand and points in my face. "I should wring your neck for causing the community to doubt us." Spittle flies from his mouth, and I reflexively step back. He immediately closes the distance. "Do you know what happens when people don't think we can take care of them? They panic. Start questioning everything we do—open us to attacks not only from the HPA but from creatures waiting for us to grow weak. I won't allow it!"

I squeeze my eyes shut as his deep voice cuts through me. "I just wanted your help. My father is a prisoner at the HPA's termination facility. We can get him back. I know it."

Veronica Sanders clears her throat. "How are you so sure?"

A million lies swirl through my mind, and I open my mouth to give a half truth when Alyssa says, "Have you forgotten I'm a seer?"

"Everyone here knows how reliable your ability is," Mr. Soto says. "I can come up with a bunch of what-if scenarios, too. We need real evidence—and even then, we can't use our resources to save one person."

Anger burns my cheeks. "Are you kidding me? It's not just my father!" My voice echoes through the air, and I push past Mr. Soto and face the other council members. "It's like you don't even care the HPA is taking control."

Ana looks at Thierry and then to Veronica before meeting my eyes. "I care. I care a lot. The matriarchs of the Enchantress Sisterhood see what you see and are concerned as well."

"Will they help me?" I ask. Hope gives me the strength to keep myself together.

"What would you need?"

"People. I want to invade the termination facility," I say.

Thierry widens his eyes. "That's a death sentence, Nadia. No one gets out of there. No one."

"Well, I'm going to change that," I say.

Mr. Soto clears his throat behind me. "Not with our help." He glares past me at Ana. "You will not call the sisterhood, understand? If you do, I'll take that as your resignation from the council."

Ana drops her gaze to the table and nods. "Yes, Javier. I apologize for overstepping my bounds. I was just trying to help Dmitri."

"Dmitri is already lost to us. Take a moment to mourn him and move on. All of you."

I turn and glower at Mr. Soto. "You're a horrible man. You're no better than the board."

He points to the door. "Get out! If I see either of you again, you'll wish I were the board."

Alyssa grabs my arm and pulls me toward the door. Tears spill from my eyes and a hatred so consuming sinks into my bones as I glance at Mr. Soto and the rest of the council once more before I slam the door. I was wrong when I said Mr. Soto was no better than the board, because he's a million times worse.

"Don't lose hope, Nadia," Alyssa says. "There's always another way."

I sniffle. "Let's just get out of here. I don't want to ever see this compound again."

## HUNTER

I stare at my ceiling.

I can't sleep.

I don't want to dream without Nadia.

Shifting on my bed, I turn to my side. Ella's tear-stained face haunts me. I would trade my body and soul's freedom for hers if I could. I'd gladly spend the rest of my life inside someone else's head and not think twice about it.

I don't know what I'll do if they deem her unnecessary. I'll fight to keep her safe. I'll drench myself in the blood of my coworkers so she can be safe. I'll drive my blade into my own mother's icy heart to protect a child, a real innocent.

No person, especially a kid, should experience the wrath of the HPA. It's that wrath that fuels me. It's the reason I know I'll get out alive in the end.

My cell phone vibrates on my nightstand, pulling me from my thoughts. I stretch before picking it up. "Hello?" My voice sounds hoarse and low, like I've strained my vocal cords from yelling.

"I need you. The council won't help and I feel so lost." It's Nadia. Her voice sounds so small and defeated. My heart aches because I can't reach through the line and hold her.

"It's risky," I say, even though I'm already sliding on my pants. I shove my boots on and grab my keys from my computer desk.

She breathes into the phone. "I don't care. Please, just come over."

I shuffle down the hall and listen to the hum of the TV in the living room. My aunt must've left it on when she went to bed. I click it off and head into the garage. My breath fogs the icy air, and I climb into my car. After opening the garage door with my remote, I start my engine. Fresh salt covers the streets as I drive through the night. Before I have time to argue with myself over how dangerous it is going back to Nadia's house with everything that's going on, I'm already pulling into her open garage.

She meets me at my door, only wearing a baggy shirt, and I hug her cold body to me. I pick her up in my arms. She wraps her bare legs around my waist, letting me carry her back inside.

"Alyssa's asleep," she whispers into my ear.

I shuffle down the hall to her bedroom. "I'm glad you called."

I kiss her lips as she shuts the door, and we move together as one to her untouched bed. My hands run through her blond hair, sliding down her back to hook on the hem of her T-shirt. My lips move eagerly from hers and to her neck, brushing her jawline, exploring her skin with my lips. She helps me pull off my hoodie, tossing it onto her nightstand. Her cool fingers slide under my shirt, touching my stomach, grazing up to my chest while tugging my shirt up as she maps my skin with her hands. Pulling my shirt off completely, she pushes me back, trailing her lips down my chest and to my stomach. She fumbles with the button on my pants, smiling, her breathing against my skin driving me crazy in a good way.

I tug her shirt over her head and unhook her bra. She doesn't move, just pressing her soft fingers into the skin on my stomach, staying so still apart from our chests heaving in sync. Licking my lips, I drink in the sight of her porcelain skin glowing in the soft, iridescent sliver of moonlight shining through the window. Every time I gaze at her, she gets more beautiful. My heart bangs around my chest in an attempt to close the space between us.

Straddling my hips, she bends down and kisses me again, flicking her tongue over mine. I run my hands up her smooth sides and pull her down, pressing her against me, feeling every inch of her almost like our souls touching through our skin. Desire and love rush over me, and I moan against her mouth begging for more kisses.

"I love you," I whisper. "More than anything in this world."

She smiles into my lips and pulls back to look into my eyes. "In this universe. You're my soul mate."

Her indigo eyes shine in the veil of moonlight, a beautiful, fierce expression crossing her face, reminding me that she's the girl of my dreams, of my reality. My everything. She's not the weak girl I talked to on the phone just an hour ago—Nadia's confident and powerful. She's absolutely beautiful.

In this moment, as she lets me into her world completely, I know we can make it through anything. We're better together. Always together.

## NADIA

I rest my head on Hunter's bare shoulder with my arm sprawled across his chest, tracing my finger along the curve of his taut muscles. I don't want to ever leave my room again as long as he's here with me. I don't have to think about anything except how much I love him and how perfect life is without everyone else in it.

Guilt pangs in my chest. My life wouldn't be perfect without everyone I love in it, though. I'm used to my father being away, but it kills me that he can't come home, or that he might not ever get to. What if something happens to Alyssa? I can't survive on my love for Hunter alone as much as I wish I could.

I run my fingers over Hunter's side. "You can sleep. It's okay. I can go sit in the kitchen or something."

He grabs my hand. "No, stay."

I sink into him, and he kisses my forehead. I don't have enough energy to argue with him over how risky it is for me to be here if he sleeps. Just because I can't control his dreams, doesn't mean that I won't affect his sanity. The mind is fragile and so much can go wrong if we're not careful.

"Only if you're sure."

He kisses my head again. "Stay."

## HUNTER

I sit on a wooden bench in a tunnel made of wisteria trees. Bright sunshine trickles through the lavender and white flowers, casting shadows over the thick green grass. I sink my bare feet into the grass and dust falling petals from my lap.

I feel her presence before I see her.

Nadia shimmers into view a few feet away, spinning on the balls of her feet with her head tilted toward the cascading wisteria trees. Her white hair matches her white, eyelet lace dress with a sweetheart neckline that accentuates the sharp bones in her shoulders. She reaches up and touches the blooming flowers, and they drift to the ground around us like a rain shower of fragrant blossoms.

She smiles, meeting my eyes. "This place—it's amazing."

"It's the wallpaper on my aunt's computer," I say.

She laughs and glides to me, easing onto the bench next to me as if she'll break it. As much as I want to, I don't touch her. It's how it used to be in Jacqueline's dream world where I let Nadia make all the moves.

She shifts on the bench to look at me. "I still can't believe this. It's so strange." Reaching out her hand, she runs it just over my cheek without touching me. "I'm scared I'll destroy it any second."

"Don't be afraid. It's just a dream."

She gingerly rests her fingers on my chin and closes her eyes. Whatever she's expecting to happen doesn't, and after a long moment, her eyes flutter open, and she cracks a heart-melting smile.

"My father would be shocked by my inability to inflict a nightmare on you." She covers her mouth, her eyes wide, and then her gaze drops to the floor.

"Don't give up on him, Nadia. When this is all over, we'll come clean, and he really will be shocked."

Nodding, she takes my hand in hers. She pulls me to my feet and tugs me to walk with her. "You're right. I need to stay positive. He'd want me to." She runs her fingers along the blooming flowers, and they fall around us.

We reach the end of the tunnel, and I stop and kiss her once. "Come on. Let me show you what else my dreams are made of."

# 10

## TOO MANY CLOSE CALLS

### NADIA

THE WORLD SHAKES under our feet, and Hunter grips my hand. The sudden urge to leave overwhelms me. I tug away and stare around the beautiful forest, wide-eyed, as a storm of falling leaves pelts us.

"I have to go," I say. "Something's happening in the real world."

Before Hunter has a chance to say anything, I yank myself from his dream, blinking a few times as sunlight drifts in through my half open curtain. Jumping out of bed, I stand and throw some clothes on to pull myself together.

A knock on the door reverberates through me.

"Nadia? Open up. Is everything okay?" Alyssa bangs again.

Rushing to the door, I open it a crack and peek at her. "I'm fine. What's up?"

"I've been knocking for like ten minutes. I almost broke down the door," she says, standing on her tiptoes to glance into my room. "Someone's here to see you."

My mouth dries, panic seizing my chest. It was a mistake to ask Hunter to come here. No one can know about him. It isn't safe. He can't help my father if anyone besides the four of us knows that he's not loyal to the HPA.

"Uh, yeah, okay. Who is it anyway?"

"Sandy Augustine."

"Mr. Augustine? Why is he here?"

She shrugs. "I don't know. That's why you should come meet him."

Hunter moans on my bed behind me, and Alyssa's gaze flicks to my room. She narrows her eyes, her eyebrows scrunching together, and presses her hand to the door, forcing me to step back so she can see past me.

Her hand flies to her mouth. "Are you crazy?"

I cringe. "Maybe? Yeah, okay. I know it was stupid, but I needed him."

She shoves me into my room and closes the door behind us. "We were going to meet this morning. You couldn't wait a few hours? We just left the compound after basically flipping off the council. What if they decided to come here?"

I rub my hand over my eyes and groan. "I didn't even think of that."

Hunter sits up on my bed, causing Alyssa to spin to face the door. "Of course you didn't. If you did, he wouldn't be sitting there on your bed naked."

Heat claws up my neck and into my face. Reaching down, I grab Hunter's clothes and toss them to him. His eyes shift from Alyssa's and back to my eyes, and then he pulls his pants on and climbs out of bed.

"I'll leave now. Sorry, Alyssa. Don't blame all this on Nadia. I didn't have to say yes."

Alyssa turns toward him and glares. "You shouldn't have said yes!"

"Lys..." I touch my hand to her shoulder. "I'm sorry."

Hunter steps closer to try to walk around us. Alyssa presses her palm to his chest and pushes him back. He raises his eyebrows, turns, and sits on my computer chair, staring between us.

"You can't leave. A family friend is sitting in our living room. I'd rather not have to explain you. You're going to wait here, *quietly*, until I say so. You got it?"

He nods. "Yes, ma'am."

Alyssa sighs, and I shrug, grinning at Hunter behind Alyssa's back. I still don't regret inviting him over. The smile he offers me in return proves he doesn't either. Alyssa drags me into the hallway and to the living room. Mr. Augustine perches on the edge of the couch with a mug of steaming coffee in his hand. He looks up and smiles, something different in his eyes than his usual happy self.

I slide into the chair across from him. "What are you doing here, Mr. Augustine?"

"I heard about Dmitri, Nadia. I'm so sorry," he says. The light that usually shines in his eyes shrouds in sadness.

I cross my legs. "He's going to be fine."

His thick, dark eyebrows pinch together. "You know he was taken by some dangerous people, right?"

"The HPA doesn't kill everyone. My father's going to be fine, trust me." I comb my fingers through my hair and lean my elbows on my knees. "I'm coming up with a plan. I've dealt with the HPA before."

His eyes widen. "You're going to get yourself killed."

"He's my father, Mr. Augustine. I'm not going to leave him there to die. He'd fight for me."

He sets his coffee down. "He wouldn't want you to fight for him, Nadia."

"He'll get over his pride."

"It's not pride. It's fear. The last thing Dmitri would want is for you both to die." Mr. Augustine leans back on the couch. "Your father would also still want you to live your life and not put everything on hold for crazy, poorly thought out plans."

I glare. "I think you should leave."

He shakes his head. "No. I'm going to watch out for you girls like I think your father would want me to. Now get dressed. You're going to live your life."

I laugh, exasperated. "I'm not going to school."

Alyssa touches my shoulder, and I stiffen. "He's right, Nadia. If it's too hard, we can just leave."

I turn my head up to look at her. "I thought you were on my side."

She frowns. "I am, but you need time to think. You know how rash decisions turn out."

I release an angry breath and get to my feet. "Fine, whatever. But I'll find my own ride."

## HUNTER

Nadia storms into the room, her blond hair swirling and her indigo eyes wild. She throws herself on the bed next to me, screaming into the pillow. Resting my hand on her lower back, I rub small circles through her shirt until she slumps deeper into her pillow.

"I wish I could stay with you all day, but I have to go. My shift starts in an hour and I need to pick up some milk," I say.

Nadia rolls over to look at me, her blond hair veiling her face. She pushes away the strands over her mouth. "Milk?"

I run my index finger along her cheek and pull the rest of her hair from her face. "I promised Ella I would bring her milk."

She grimaces. "That poor girl. She must be so terrified."

"I'll do my best to see that she isn't."

Nadia sits up and kisses me, climbing onto my lap to look me straight on. "I thought I couldn't love you anymore than I do, but you're seriously the best person I know."

I kiss her one more time before I stand, carrying her with me to set her on her feet. Glancing into her vanity mirror, I comb my fingers through my messy hair. I wish I had a tooth brush and deodorant, and I make a point to remember to pick some up at the store.

Nadia slides her arms around my waist, hugging me, making it incredibly impossible for me to leave. "Mind doing me a favor?"

"Anything."

"Drop me off at school?"

I raise an eyebrow. "School?"

She rolls her eyes. "Don't ask. I'm just glad it's Friday."

## NADIA

I leave the house with Hunter way earlier than I would've with Alyssa, but I'm angry she took Mr. Augustine's side. Who does he think he is? My father's replacement? Even if he was my mother's best friend years ago and knew me as a child, I've only spent all of two hours with him since, and he can't just drop in and tell me what he thinks is best for me. I force myself to comply with his suggestion but only because I might really need him. It's best not to cut ties without thinking things over.

All I have to do is make it through today. I'll have a clearer head. I can devise a better plan. It's not like I can storm the facility on a rescue mission. I'm neither powerful nor brave, and I'd just end up in the cell next to my father, or worse.

"I'll just be a second," Hunter says.

"Can you pick up a newspaper? My father likes to read

them."

Hunter nods and runs into the convenience store. I hunker down in the seat even though the tinted windows make it too dark for anyone to see me. I still can't shake my uneasy feeling.

The stereo rings, startling me, and I mess with the volume dial to try and turn the annoying sound down. Just when I think Hunter's phone went to voicemail, a voice booms through the speakers.

"Agent Hunter?" It's a woman, and she sounds irritated. "Agent Hunter, can you hear me?"

I cover my mouth with my hand, afraid to even breathe. Whoever is on the line is from the HPA. They're probably wondering where Hunter is.

Fear slides down my spine when the phone doesn't click off after a minute of no response. I wave at the store at Hunter in line, but instead of understanding that I'm begging him to come back, he returns my wave.

"Agent Hunter, are you injured? Do you need assistance?"

My heart sputters and then beats in overdrive, trying to crash through my chest and into the windshield. Flinging open the door, I stumble from the car and trip on the curb. I catch my fall, scraping my hands on the frozen sidewalk.

If the HPA thinks Hunter is hurt, they'll track his phone and send someone to investigate. They'll catch us together, and we'll both be dead.

"Na—"

I slam into Hunter before he calls my name and slap my

hand over his mouth. "There's someone on the line. I accidentally picked up. Hurry!"

He rushes to his car and swings open the door. "Agent Hunter speaking."

He motions for me to get in, and I reluctantly slide onto the front seat and stiffen when he reverses.

"What took you so long? I almost sent a team searching for you," the woman says. She sounds less authoritative and more...loving? I'm not sure if it's love, but it's more than business.

"Relax, no need to overreact, Dr. Sullivan. I'm fine. I was picking up a few things at the store before my shift." Hunter eyes me in his peripheral vision.

Dr. Sullivan? This woman isn't just anyone; she's his mother. She's the woman who gave him over to Jacqueline as collateral. She was willing to send him to his death for the sake of her corrupt and distorted ideologies. She's basically the worst woman in the world in my eyes.

The woman breathes into the phone. "How is that going? Maybe I'll stop by this afternoon. We could have dinner. Your brother misses you...I miss you."

I grimace. She sounds so sincere it's hard to believe she's faking it. With the way Hunter describes her, I thought she couldn't care less about anything in the world apart from her precious HPA.

"Is that the reason you called me?" Hunter doesn't hide the annoyance in his voice.

"Can't a mother call her son just to chat?"

He clears his throat. "Not when your mom is on the board at the Human Preservation Agency." He turns onto the street where Northern Bell High is and turns off onto a side street and parks along the curb.

She sighs. "Well, this isn't business. I wanted to invite you to dinner tonight."

"I'm busy tonight. Maybe some other time."

"Oh, okay." The line goes quiet for a minute. "Maybe next week then. I really do miss you."

"Hey, I have to go," Hunter says. "I'll see you around." He clicks off the phone without acknowledging her affection.

I step out of the car, now too afraid to talk inside. That was a little too risky for my liking. Hunter follows me out and steps back, tilting his head to the side.

I can't stop shaking. "We've been having a lot of close calls lately. Maybe we should—" My voice falters. I can't say what I'm thinking even if it would be the safest thing to do. How can I tell Hunter we should take a step back and keep some distance between us until things settle down? It's the right thing to do, but the thought of even going a few hours without Hunter is painful.

"Don't say it," Hunter says.

Tears rim my eyes. "I'm just really scared."

Hunter touches my cheek. "We'll be more careful."

I nod. "We don't have a choice."

He kisses me, pulling me into his arms. It takes every

ounce of strength in me to step back and walk away. I feel his eyes on my back, but I don't turn to look. I can't stand that I'm walking into high school, the last place on earth I want to be, and that I have to pretend that everything is normal. That I'm normal.

## HUNTER

I watch Nadia carefully take one step after another, leaving footprints in the snow, as she strolls down the street to her school. I get back in my car and drive to the corner, watching her meet her friend Evie on the stairs, and together they disappear through the double doors. The school is pretty vacant this early in the morning, and I drive away before the buses of students start showing up.

I remember the conflicted look in Nadia's eyes when she said we had too many close calls. I'm glad she didn't say what was really on her mind, because I can't keep myself away from her. She's the only good thing in my life—the only thing that isn't scrutinized by a board of malicious, controlling monsters. I can't lose her.

# 11



## WHAT OUR LIVES SHOULD BE LIKE

### HUNTER

THE EMPTY PARKING lot greets me when I park in my assigned space outside of the main entrance to the termination facility. Turning off my engine, I wait a few seconds before grabbing the bag with the carton of milk and the newspaper. I need to focus on the task at hand and get Ella, Camden, and Dmitri to trust me. I can't tell them I'm on their side, but I can show them.

I need to take my mind off Nadia, too.

Every time I close my eyes, even if it's just to blink, I see her shimmering, white hair from the dream world, the curves of her smooth hips, her pouty bottom lip as she sucks it between her teeth... I want my time to fly by so I can see her again, invite her into my dreams so our souls can be alone without worry.

That's what our lives should be like.

I enter my pass code at the door and wave at Phillip, the office manager, and stride to the elevator and hit the button for my floor. When the doors ding open, the dark, quiet air slithers around me. The red blinking light on the camera overhead reminds me that I'm never really alone.

I touch a few keys on the keyboard and the monitors light up, showing the cells. It looks like Camden is asleep, and possibly Ella too, but it's hard to see her on the monitor. Dmitri sits at the desk, staring at nothing in particular. He doesn't sleep, but he'll need to invade a nightmare eventually or he'll weaken, and then it'll be harder for him to defend himself if he has to. Maybe I can move him into the room with Camden. I'm sure the guy will get over it. Having a nightmare isn't the worst thing that can happen to him here.

I scan the desk and notice the note Jacqueline left me.

*We've been ordered to interact more with the prisoners. The board wants to know what the supers are capable of and any other imperative information that will lead us to others.*

I glare at the paper. I can't let them get the answers they want, but I can't look like I'm not trying, either.

I swear under my breath.

*Pull yourself together.*

Scooping up the milk and newspaper, I head down the corridor to the cells. It'll be another thirty minutes until someone brings up breakfast, but I can't wait. I'll check on my charges every chance I can. I want them to get to know me.

I enter the pass code for Ella's cell and peek in to see her curled up in a ball on the floor next to the bed, half under it. No wonder it was hard to see her on the monitor with the cot obscuring her. I set the small carton of milk near the door and close it, punching in my pass code to lock it.

I walk the ten feet it takes to get to Dmitri's door and knock. Through the small window, I watch him push to his feet and move toward the wall. He crosses his arms and leans his back against the concrete.

"Come in," he says like he has a choice.

I unlock the door and crack it open, sticking my head in to peer at him. "Do you read the newspaper? I have an extra."

His thin lips disappear when he presses them together. "Is that a trick question?"

I can't blame him for being suspicious. I extend my arm through the crack and wave the paper back and forth. "Just offering you a paper."

After a long moment of silence, Dmitri says, "Sure, I'll take it."

I open the door wider and with one hand on my taser and the other outstretched to Dmitri, I enter the cell. He smirks and watches me cross the room and takes the paper from my outstretched hand. Most agents would've left it on the floor.

"You're brave. I like that," he says. "The black-haired agent won't even look me in the eyes."

I wonder if Jacqueline worries he'll recognize her and blow her cover before she's ready. Dmitri knew her in her old body, but he also thinks she's dead. If only Nadia had a chance to tell him about her, things would be a lot easier for us.

I drop my arm to my side. "It's not that I'm brave, I'm just not afraid of you."

The corners of his mouth pull down, and he nods his head, appreciating my honesty. He doesn't have to tell me, because I see it on his face.

He glides closer without touching his feet to the floor, and my heart aches as a vision of Nadia gliding across her room to me flashes in my mind. She looks nothing like her dad, but her mannerisms are the same. Where she is pure light, he's dark. His hair is blacker than a crow's feather and his skin is a gaunt, flat white. His eyes shine like black obsidians, and with the way they sink into his face, he looks dangerous, like a creature that can devour me. It's probably why they sent him to the gray zone first.

I don't flinch when he stops a foot in front of me. "Cool trick," I say to break his intimidating gaze.

He chuckles. "You're not like the other agents."

I glance at the camera and back to Dmitri, leaning closer to him. "Don't tell them. That could get me locked up in the cell next to you."

Dmitri studies my stare for a minute, not sure whether or not to believe me, and I don't show any emotion otherwise. He glides back to the desk, picks up the paper, and spreads it open.

Striding to the door, I peer at him from over my shoulder. "I'll have breakfast here soon."

"I don't eat," Dmitri calls.

I cringe, stepping into the hall. The board will be fascinated by that.

"You can give my plate to the girl next door," he adds.

I shut the door and lock it behind me. I hope I didn't mess everything up. The last thing I need is to have the board breathing even harder down my neck for more information about Dmitri.

I need to stop them. I need to protect Nadia by protecting her dad.

## NADIA

"Can I meet his brother? Maybe we can double date?" Evie asks, strolling next to me with her arm hooked through mine.

It feels like it has been years since I introduced her to Hunter. I regret doing so, because it's all she's talked about since I saw her in third period.

"I don't know. They don't live together. I think Mason lives kind of far," I say. I want her to drop the subject. She's the last person I want to be involved in my outside-of-school life. It isn't safe for her.

She pouts her bottom lip. "That sucks." Her thin brows furrow, and she swipes red and brown strands of hair out of her face. Staring at the tiled floor for a few seconds, she sighs and gives me a sidelong glance. "Oh! Does he drive?"

She's not giving up as easily as I hoped. "No, I don't think so. Hunter's never mentioned it." It's a flat out lie, but she won't know any better. "He's a grade younger than us."

She sighs. "Dang. I bet he's hot, too."

I shrug. "I've only met him once. I can't really remember." *Sort of met him.* More like just talked to him on the phone and was in the same vicinity as Mason.

She bumps my shoulder. "You're saying that to make me feel better."

"Nadia?"

Alyssa leans against her locker, her emerald eyes puffy and red, and she looks like she's been crying. It physically hurts me to see her like this, and I clutch the ache in my chest. I should be angry with her, but seeing her so down pushes the fury away.

"Hi, Lys. You remember Evie?" I stop in my tracks, forcing Evie to stop with me. "She was just walking me to the library."

Alyssa nods. "Can I join you?"

I shrug. "Sure."

Evie tugs her arm from mine. "It looks like you two need to talk," she whispers in my ear. "I'll just catch you last period."

I smile, showing my appreciation, and Evie saunters down the hallway and to the stairs. She disappears from view, and I turn and hug Alyssa. She leans against me and releases a small cry in my ear, her shoulders shaking. I hold her until she pulls back and looks into my eyes.

"I'm sorry about this morning. I'm just so worried." She pushes her red braid over her shoulder. "I don't want anything to happen to you."

I tug her with me toward the library. "I wish I knew how to fix things. Why are the council members such jerks? My father has dedicated his life to them, and this is what he gets?"

She brings her finger to my lips. "Not so loud."

My shoulders stiffen. "People should know. All they do is use."

Pressing her lips to my ear, she says, "I'm talking about the humans. Just because creatures are integrated among them, doesn't mean they're uninformed bystanders. You never know who you can trust."

I glance behind me. Alyssa is right. I'm much too careless. If I get caught by the HPA, it'll be my own fault. I should know better than anyone that I'm not invincible.

Alyssa follows me down the stairs to the basement and into the library where Mr. Augustine places books in tall, unsteady piles. He smiles when he sees us and locks the door behind us, so no one else can enter the library. It's convenient that it's closed for inventory.

"I'm so glad to see you both here," he says, waving his hands with a flourish. He sets down the scroll of barcode stickers and pulls out two chairs at the table. "I couldn't stop thinking about you all day. I went about this morning all wrong. I only wanted to show you that you're not alone."

"I appreciate it. I was just overwhelmed," I say.

He pulls a mauve handkerchief from his back pocket and rubs it over his eyes. "As you should be. This entire situation is troubling."

"Tell me about it," Alyssa says. "It's like the HPA has built an impenetrable army and the council wants to pretend nothing is happening."

"We need our own army," I say.

Mr. Augustine shifts in his seat. "I'll do everything I can in my mortal power to help you. The HPA won't hurt me. This wouldn't be the first time I've encountered them."

My mouth falls open. "You're joking, right?"

He chortles, clutching his stomach. "I wish I were. Did you know before Dmitri went to work with the council he was a lone vigilante in the city to stop whatever agent tried to stir things up?"

"It's why the council wanted him," Alyssa says.

I glance between them. I guess I knew that, but it never clicked in my head. It's how he knows so many creatures and knows his way around practically everywhere. It's also why the HPA stalked and killed my mother. The agent who murdered her wanted to make a point.

"I don't understand. Did you help my father or something?" I ask. I can't see Mr. Augustine with his well-manicured hands and mauve handkerchief even touching a weapon. He's better suited to the library where the most exciting things that happen are in books.

He barks a laugh, tilting his head back. "Can you imagine? Sandy and Dmitri, the protectors of all things non-human." He bellows another laugh at his own imagination, and I smirk at

Alyssa. "Heavens no, but I did tackle an agent who laid their hands on your mother."

Now that I can see him doing. He seems to have loved my mother as much as I did. "You're lucky they didn't kill you."

His eyes widen, and he raises his hands. "I know!"

I laugh. I can't help it. And it feels good to do so. "So what happened?"

"They experimented on you, didn't they?" Alyssa asks, leaning on her elbows.

He lifts and drops his shoulders. "I have no idea. I don't actually recall protecting Emily. I only know because she told me. Emily swore I was missing for three days after her attack, and then I just showed up like nothing ever happened. Whatever they did, I lost a week's worth of memories. It was like the time I went to Cancun for Spring Break and—never mind that."

Hunter mentioned something about Camden not being affected by the HPA's memory-altering serum. The HPA uses the serum on any human who gets involved in the supernatural world who isn't on the HPA's payroll. It's how they keep humans from helping creatures without having to hurt the human. The only time the HPA would not immediately erase a human's memories is because they want to use them, or they think they have valuable information.

"Well, their goal is to save humanity. I bet they do everything in their power to save a human before they destroy them," Alyssa says.

"And to think I thought I was special," Mr. Augustine says with a smile.

Alyssa laughs. "That too."

Silence drifts over us, and we sit at the table and stare at the stacks of books. None of us have any idea what we're supposed to do, just that we're supposed to do something. I study my chipped nail polish and then crack my knuckles.

"Let's go to the city after school. I'll call Cian to see if he can track down any family members of Camden's or Ella's," Alyssa finally says.

"I'll drive you two," Mr. Augustine says.

"Will telling you it's too dangerous stop you from wanting to help?" He's already more involved than I want him to be. I can't live with myself if another innocent person gets hurt because of my life.

He shakes his head. "Not a chance."

"Then I guess you can come. But I have to warn you. In a fight, I tend to run."

His eyes shine in the light. "Don't worry, so do I."

## HUNTER

"The board wants you to focus on Creature 1252," Dr. Sullivan says.

I don't pay attention to the numbers assigned to the people in the cells, so I glance at my log sheet to verify she's talking about Dmitri, which she is, like I expected she would when Dmitri informed me he doesn't eat.

I shift my eyes to the monitor instead of meeting Dr. Sullivan's gaze. "Sure, no problem. What do you want me to do exactly? It's weird to go into his cell without reason."

In my peripheral vision, I watch her pull a manila folder from her bag. She sets it on my keyboard. I flip it open, reading over what appears to be a hundred page questionnaire. *You have to be kidding me.*

"You want him to fill this out?" I lift my glare to hers and raise an eyebrow. There's no chance I'd get anyone to fill this out, not even some random person on the street.

She crosses her arms. "Don't be ridiculous. Those are the topics I want you to bring up. Find out as much information as you can. Do whatever it takes, Hunter."

"Can I bribe him?"

"What do you mean?"

"Can I give the dude things in exchange for his answers?" She's making me spell things out. I know she knows what I mean. She just likes to make things complicated—and annoying.

"Do whatever it takes," she says again.

She swiftly turns around and heads toward the elevator. Smiling over her shoulder, she steps on and waves.

I scan over the contents in the folder.

*What year were you born? What was your childhood like? Did you have parents? Did you have siblings? Were you born in the United States? Did you attend school?*

All of the questions are pretty basic, except for a few that ask about special abilities and how they discovered they had them. I toss the folder on the desk and lean back in my chair. I don't need help with coming up with things to say to Dmitri, but now I know what I need to avoid. It's the only way I know how to keep everyone here alive. I hope it works.

# 12

# DESTINY

**NADIA**

ALYSSA GRABS MY hand and tugs me faster. "Come on, we're almost there."

Mr. Augustine sits in his Land Rover, watching us walk toward a row of newly built condominiums. After speaking with Cian, he gave us the address of an enchantress who might help us find Camden's family.

"Sounds like a party." I shove my hands in my pocket. Music trickles through the air, causing goosebumps to crawl over my skin.

Alyssa stops in her tracks. "Looks like one, too. Ready?"

Twisting my mouth to the side, I shift my weight from one foot to the other. "I don't want to stay long. This place makes me nervous."

Alyssa smiles and links her arm with mine. "We won't. Just long enough to find out any useful information about Camden."

The music increases in volume as a woman with wavy purple hair saunters onto the porch of a ground floor level unit. I relax when I see a broad shouldered incubus leaning against the wall, guarding the door. His size alone is intimidating, and it makes me feel safer knowing someone's on watch.

I follow Alyssa up the short steps, and she smiles at the incubus. "Great place," she says.

The incubus opens the door and allows us in without a word.

I peer around the cramped living room. A leather sectional couch rests in the corner and two recliners face it with a table in between. People stand around in small clusters, but it's impossible to hear their conversations over the pulsing music.

"Can I help you?" a woman with short midnight black hair and light blue eyes asks.

I lean closer to her. "Actually yes. I'm looking for anyone who might know an enchantress's son named Camden."

The woman presses her lips together and peers over her shoulder at another woman with long jet-black hair that reaches her waist. Her radiant blue eyes shine in the soft lighting from the chandelier. All enchantresses have the same identifying features of black hair and blue eyes. They're always confident and in control, fearless, and good. It's rare to find an ill-intentioned enchantress. Their powers are innately benign and used only for what they feel is right.

"Hey, Liv," the woman calls. "These girls know your brother."

## HUNTER

I pull into the driveway of my old house. Jacqueline called me when I was ten minutes from my house and told me Dr. Sullivan invited her to dinner. Jacqueline was uneasy about it, so she asked me to join her. It's like my mom to use someone to get me to agree to what she wants. I guess I couldn't avoid her invitation forever.

Sitting in my car, I contemplate reversing. A shadow hovers in the bay window, drawing my attention to the house. Without even seeing her face, I know Dr. Sullivan watches me, waiting for me to come to the door. Her wispy hair falls over her shoulders and light reflects off her gold-rimmed glasses perched on her head.

I'm not sure if she was expecting me or not. I wouldn't be here if it weren't for Jacqueline. I turn off the engine and groan, rubbing my hands over my face. It takes all my willpower to unbuckle my seatbelt. After another minute of watching my mom in the window, I slide out and slam the door shut.

Gazing around the empty street, I shuffle up the stone path to the porch. The stairs creak as I climb them. I tap the screen door and lean my back on the wood siding.

The door whines as it opens, and Dr. Sullivan beams a smile. "Oh, Hunter, I had no idea you'd be visiting. Where's your key?" She wears a pink, button-up blouse with a gray cardigan over it. It's been a while since I've seen her without a lab coat, and she looks years younger.

I offer an amiable smile. "Forgot it. Agent Camille mentioned she was having dinner with you. My plans fell through, so I thought I'd crash the party."

She wraps her arms around me, and I stiffen. "Well, I'm glad you did."

Kicking the snow off my boots, I leave them in the mudroom and shrug out of my jacket. I follow Dr. Sullivan into the living room. The room looks different from what I remember—it's been remodeled. The dark wood paneled walls have been painted light blue and all the family pictures have been replaced with watercolor paintings of flowers. In place of the rickety TV stand, a white bookshelf with a new flat screen TV mounted on the wall above it gives the room a modern feel. The green, lumpy couches that belonged to my grandmother have been replaced with a light gray sectional, and instead of the black coffee table, a white, faux-leather ottoman with hidden storage takes up most of the living room.

This house doesn't resemble the home I used to love. It changed after Dr. Sullivan proved the board was more important than I was. I'm a stranger now.

I cross my arms over my chest. "You've redecorated."

Dr. Sullivan smiles as she takes in the room like it's the first time she's seen it. "It's beautiful, isn't it?"

"The way it looked before was fine."

She scrunches her nose. "You just don't like change, Hunter. Never have."

I bark a laugh. I can't help it. She thinks she knows me, but she has no idea what I like and dislike anymore. I open my mouth to set her straight, but instead I ask, "Where's Mason?"

She frowns for a split second. "He's in his room. Want me to call for him?"

I shake my head. "It's all right. I'll get him."

Blinking her watery eyes, she nods. She doesn't want me to leave, but I'm afraid I'll say something I'll regret if we do anymore bonding. Outside of the HPA, Dr. Sullivan feels more motherly and less controlled. Now's not the time to share our true feelings. Hers are pretty obvious at this point. She's hurt, but I'm far worse off. She nearly destroyed me.

"Tell him dinner will be ready soon," she says, turning away to head toward the kitchen, trying to hide a tear rolling down her cheek.

I sigh and shuffle down the hallway, stopping at the first door on the right to peek in to see that my former room is empty besides a few boxes of crap I left behind because I didn't have any room for them. I close the door without a second glance and knock on Mason's door.

"Give me a minute, Mom," he yells.

I crack the door and say, "It's me."

The door swings open, and Mason shrugs into a black

thermal shirt. His brown hair, a shade lighter than mine, is cut short and styled with hair wax, and he's had the studs in his earlobes stretched a gauge and plugged with skull earring plugs. He hasn't shaved in weeks and looks older even though he's a year and a half younger than me.

"Damn, Hunter, I never thought I'd see you in this house again." Mason moves out of the way so I can enter and shut the door.

"Me either, but Agent Camille asked me to," I say.

"So, you'll visit for Camille, huh?" He grins and wags his eyebrows. "I didn't think she was capable of focusing on anything but her job."

I roll my eyes. "It's not like that."

"That's too bad. She's hot."

"She can also kick your ass," I say.

My brother laughs. "I'm cool with that."

For a moment, it feels like nothing has changed at all between us even though we're no longer housemates. If only I could forget that Mason is on the HPA's side, it'd be a lot easier to be around him. I was almost certain I could change him after I woke up in my body with him at my bedside when Jacqueline put me back. It's a shame my mom has him brainwashed.

Mason sits in his computer chair, resting his elbow on his desk. He wiggles the mouse and glances at the screen before turning back to me. Something's on his mind, but he doesn't say it. Silence falls between us, and I lean back on his bed and look at the ceiling.

I clear my throat. "So, how's everything going, bro? Dr. Sull—Mom driving you insane yet?"

His lips press into a line and then he shrugs. "She's never here anymore. I spend most of my time counting down the days until I can leave."

I frown. "Leave?"

He nods. "Mom didn't tell you?"

"Tell me what?"

"I was recruited to join the SATF in Virginia. I leave this summer."

A knot tightens in my stomach. Joining the Special Abilities Task Force is practically a death sentence. I'm afraid he won't survive the virus they'll inject him with that'll alter his DNA and give him abilities he now only dreams of.

"You serious? Are you crazy? You know most people don't survive the alteration." My resolve cracks and anger rushes over me—not at my brother, but at my mom and the HPA. They've convinced him to risk his life for this organization built on the blood of innocent people and lies. Mason's in too deep, and I don't think I'll ever be able to save him.

Mason raises his brows. "I'd be crazy not to take this opportunity. They're letting me in earlier than usual because the board believes I can handle it. Apparently, they're creating an elite team. I'm pumped."

I stand up. If I talk to my brother any longer about the HPA's plans for him, I might confess what I know—the problem is he won't believe me. Not now—not after he knows what our mom did and he still takes her side.

I open the door. "And if you can't handle it?"

Mason narrows his eyes. "I can. I know it. Why can't you be happy for me? You jealous or something?"

I turn away. "Yeah, that's it." Clenching my jaw, I walk away. Mason's making a huge mistake, and my mom is letting him. I just hope he really does make it out in the end.

## NADIA

"You know Camden?" Liv asks. "Where is he? He's been missing for a few days. I've been so worried."

Alyssa reaches out and touches Liv's arm. "We've never actually met him. But we thought you'd want to know he was captured by an HPA agent. He's alive, but we don't know for how long."

Liv gasps and covers her eyes. "I knew I shouldn't have agreed to let him stay here. I should've made him leave with our parents. If I could leave the city, I would, but the sisterhood wants me to stay."

Covering her face, Liv cries into her hands. I slide my arms around her and hug her, patting her back. She's in the same position my father was. The council making him stay in a city too dangerous for anyone who stands out. But at least with enchantresses, they have their power to protect them. Not a single enchantress has ever been caught by the HPA.

"It's not over. They have my dad, too. That's why we're here. We're looking for people to help."

"Doing what?" Liv asks.

"I want to invade their termination facility and break them out," I say.

Liv stares at me with wide eyes. "You're insane."

I sigh. "I'm not. I know how the HPA works and with the right help, I know we can be successful. This isn't my first time dealing with them."

Liv crosses her arms. "I don't know."

Alyssa touches my shoulder. "Come on, Nadia. Maybe Cian can think of someone else."

"Your name's Nadia?" Liv asks.

I nod. "Yeah, why?"

"I've heard about you. You're the girl the council kicked out."

I sigh. It shouldn't surprise me that Liv knows. The council made an example of me. I see a million questions line Liv's eyes. I peer around the room to break her gaze. I'm not in the mood to relive the events of Hunter's release or my punishment.

I rub the scar on my shoulder through my sweater. It's where the real Agent Camille stabbed me. "It's a long story. Where's the bathroom?" I need to change the subject.

Liv points to the dark hallway next to a small open kitchen. "First door on the right."

"Thanks." I turn to Alyssa. "Try to convince her. Maybe she knows someone else willing to help."

I move past her and cross the room to the short, three door hallway. Stepping into the bathroom, I turn on the light and shut the door. I stare at my reflection in the mirror for a moment before splashing cold water on my face.

A knock sounds on the door, and I turn to open it. Alyssa stares at me with wide eyes with Liv standing behind her.

"What's wrong?" I ask.

"The guard spotted a white van coming around the corner," Liv says.

Fear grips my chest. "We're okay, right?"

Alyssa rubs her hand over her green eyes. "It's better if we don't stay and find out. Mr. Augustine is waiting for us in the complex."

Stepping from the bathroom, I turn toward the living room. Silence falls over the condo, the music now off and the lights dim. Tension hangs thick in the air. Liv leads us toward the back bedroom and away from the front of the condo. As she opens the door, a scream pierces the silence.

Chaos breaks out. The sound of a window shattering cuts deep into my soul. I race behind Alyssa and Liv and slam and lock the door behind us.

Someone bangs on the door. "Let me in, please!"

I take a deep breath and turn the lock before opening the door. A girl my age dashes into the room, and I slam the door behind her and lock it. She grips her knees, panting. I glance at Alyssa, and she motions for me to follow Liv who's already outside.

"We have to hurry," I say, following Alyssa to the window.

The girl doesn't move. I step through the window, and as I turn to call to the girl, the door smashes open. A tall, blond agent kicks it in. "In the back, Rosaline!" he calls.

Without stopping to see the second agent, I race next to Alyssa and behind Liv, leaving the girl behind to face her fate.

"You tried to save her," Alyssa says, breathing hard next to me.

I nod. "I know." I just wish I had tried harder.

## HUNTER

My fork clinks my plate as I scrape up the last bit of my piece of turkey pot pie casserole. I hate to admit it, but Dr. Sullivan is a great cook, and I actually miss that about living here.

Jacqueline lifts an eyebrow and pats her lips with a napkin. She kicks me under the table. Narrowing my eyes, I lift my foot to nudge her back. She grabs my foot with one hand and pinches hard enough to make me flinch.

Jacqueline smiles at Dr. Sullivan. "This was delicious, Dr. Sullivan, thank you for inviting me."

"You're welcome, Camille. And please, call me Andrea when I'm not wearing my lab coat."

I roll my eyes. "Why did you, anyway?" The dinner table conversation revolves around superfluous and platonic topics like the upcoming forecast, how good dinner was, and how boring today has been without divulging into specifics.

Dr. Sullivan sips a glass of wine and sets it back on the table. "Is it hard to believe I only wanted to treat one of my most talented agents to dinner?"

I scowl. "You always have an agenda, Dr. Sullivan."

Jacqueline shakes her head, and my brother's eyes shift between me and our mom. He looks ready to throw his plate at me but grips the edge of the table instead.

Dr. Sullivan cracks a fake smile. "You know me so well, Hunter." She turns to Jacqueline. "I'm not sure Hunter told you, but Mason was invited to join a special division of the SATF. Unlike you, Mason will train with other new recruits as a team, and they'll specialize in taking on greater supernatural threats such as the council."

Jacqueline bares her teeth as she forces her mouth to smile. "Congrats, Mason. What an honor."

I cough as I choke on my water. Congratulations isn't what I was hoping Jacqueline would say. She shouldn't be encouraging Mason to sign up for his possible death.

"Is it really an honor?" My voice comes out low, and it takes all my strength not to get up and leave.

"I can't believe you're seriously still mad."

"I'm not mad. I think you're crazy. You know you're most likely going to die, right?"

"Hunter!" Dr. Sullivan says. "What has gotten into you?"

I take a deep breath to control my emotions. While I do think my brother's decision to undergo a near fatal procedure is a terrible idea, what really bothers me is that he's risking his life for a cause he could never understand while being brainwashed by our mom. Even if he does survive the alteration, it'll be the death of our brotherly relationship because he'd be programmed to kill my girlfriend. I'd be forced to pick a side. If it came down to Nadia or Mason, I'd choose Nadia. I just wish we were all on the same side of things.

"Is it wrong that I don't want my brother to die?" I ask.

Dr. Sullivan reaches across the table and touches my hand. "Have faith, Hunter. He's a great match. I believe Mason is strong enough to survive—just like I knew you were strong enough to survive the sin-eater." She shifts her gaze to Jacqueline. "And look at your partner and what a success she is. I bet she doesn't think she made a terrible choice."

Jacqueline blinks a few times like she's unsure of how to respond. "Of course not," Jacqueline says after a second. "This was my destiny."

I don't know whether to glower at Dr. Sullivan or laugh at Jacqueline. Dr. Sullivan refers to when she traded my soul—disguising the fact she risked my life for her ridiculous idea of the greater good by saying she knew I wouldn't die. *Whatever lets her sleep at night...*

I take the high road and ignore Dr. Sullivan's comment and look at Jacqueline. "Sure was."

"It's my destiny, too, Hunter," Mason says, speaking up.

Furrowing my brows, I push my chair back. "I'll leave you to discuss your destinies. If you'll excuse me, I have to get going. I have an early shift tomorrow." I don't look at anyone as I leave the dining room.

Shoving my feet into my boots, I grab my jacket without putting it on. I open the front door, freezing air hitting me, stinging my face. I can't sit around and pretend I'm okay with all this. Not now. Not when Nadia's dad is locked in a cell. And especially not when I'm questioning my own destiny. I thought my destiny was to change the world—but it's not so clear to me anymore.

I have no idea what to do.

# 13



## NO CHANGING THE PAST

### NADIA

CIAN'S EYES LIGHT up when we step into the hallway leading to The Haven. My heart still races from almost getting captured by the two agents who raided the condo. I hope people made it out safely.

It's been months since I've seen Cian in person, and I forgot how short the troll was. Blue-rimmed glasses perch on his wide nose above his reddish-brown mustache and beard. His black slacks drag on the floor as he hops from his chair in front of the computer built into the wall.

Liv slips past me. "Cian, Drea's was raided. I don't know

who got out."

"How terrible. It's getting out of control," Cian says.

Liv nods. "I'm meeting with a few of my sisters here, but I wanted to let you know I'm in to help those who were taken." Liv glances over her shoulder at me. "Nadia thinks we can break into the termination facility. I don't have time to hear her plan, so can you call me later and fill me in when you decide something? I want my brother back. Also, call Blake for me, will you? I heard his niece went missing." The words spill from Liv's mouth. It's so much to take in. Drea must be the first enchantress Alyssa and I met. I'm afraid to mention it, but if the man, Blake, she mentioned is missing his niece, I bet it's the girl Ella Hunter told me about.

"Will do," Cian says. "I didn't know your brother stayed."

She sighs. "He wouldn't leave me."

I hate other people are going through what I am, but I'm relieved I'm not alone. Everything doesn't feel so hopeless when strangers don't mock me and think I'm crazy for wanting to do what's never been done—unlike the council.

Liv touches my shoulder and looks between me and Alyssa, and then to Mr. Augustine behind us. "I don't know if it was fate or luck, but I'm so happy you found me when you did. If you need anything from me, let Cian know and he can find me."

I nod and hug the enchantress. Liv waltzes through the door to The Haven and leaves us in the hall.

Cian rolls up the sleeves on his blue and white striped button-up shirt and offers me his hand. "Nadia, doll, I'm so sorry about Dmitri. He's a tough man. He'll be okay," he says. I was hoping to avoid this conversation because it's hard enough as it is to keep myself together without the reminder.

I try to smile but fail. "I'm glad someone thinks so. The council thinks he's dead."

His grin twists into a scowl. "Screw the council. They're good for nothing."

"You don't have to tell me that." I glance behind me at Alyssa and Mr. Augustine. "Cian, this is—"

"Been years since you've been around here, Sandy." Cian offers out his hand to Mr. Augustine.

Mr. Augustine steps closer to greet the troll. Of course Cian would know him. He knows everyone it seems. I wonder why he doesn't start his own council and kick Mr. Soto to the curb. At least then things would get done.

"Things have been difficult since Abraham died," Mr. Augustine says. "I've stepped back from your community and stick to the library at Northern Bell." He looks at me with his sad, glassy eyes. "Until just recently. I've taken it upon myself to watch over Nadia and Alyssa."

I grimace. I didn't know Mr. Augustine lost what sounds like the love of his life. I wonder if that's why he remained friends with my father after my mother died. They were connected through their grief.

"It's a tough life, ain't it?" Cian says.

My bottom lip pouts. "Like I'm living my own nightmare."

A few people enter the hall behind us, cutting off our conversation. Opening the door, Cian ushers us toward the club. I grab Alyssa's hand. She's been awfully quiet this entire time, and I wonder what she's thinking. And then I see it—her glassy eyes staring off at nothing. From her expression, a vision consumes her thoughts. And it doesn't look like a good one. I tug her forward with Mr. Augustine following us.

Cian motions for the people in the hall to wait and follows us into the club, shutting the door. "Follow me to the back. I'll get someone to cover my post."

## HUNTER

I sit in my car in Dr. Sullivan's driveway, anger consuming me so much so that I know if I took off now, I'd probably get pulled over for speeding or something. Shadows edge my vision, clearing with each deep breath I inhale. I should suck it up and go back inside and apologize, but I'm not in control of my emotions. The last thing I need is to start a fight over something like this, especially since it's not what really ticks me off.

A knock on my window startles me, and I jerk to look at Dr. Sullivan.

Dr. Sullivan waits for me to roll down my window and says, "You should come back inside. I have dessert."

Gripping the steering wheel, I train my eyes at my dashboard. "I was just leaving."

She reaches in and touches my shoulder. "It's okay to be worried about your brother, but he needs you to be strong for him, too."

I grind my teeth. "You're right." I want to drop the subject and leave already. "Thanks for dinner. It's not often I get a home cooked meal."

"Your dad's sister was never into cooking. She used to buy store made things for holiday dinners." She gazes at the garage door, reliving her memories from a time where my dad didn't abandon us for the shy, blond librarian he met while teaching at the university. Tosha. It takes me a minute to remember her name. I only met her once before they moved across the country. I wish it could be so easy for me. I guess I'm like my dad in a way. I'd drop my mom and Mason for Nadia. I will drop them as soon as I can.

Leaning forward, I hang my head and slouch against the steering wheel. "Nothing wrong with that."

She purses her lips. "You're right. I'm being petty."

I'm surprised by her realization. If only she could see all the other wrongs in her life. She used to be a good person—a great person. I miss the mom who would've never traded her son's soul for business. I won't ever forgive her for that. I don't care if that's how I met Nadia. I could've died.

"It must be hard." What I really want to say is that it must be hard living with herself. Maybe this is why my dad left her. He knew she was crazy. If only he'd taken me and my brother with him. I doubt Dr. Sullivan or the HPA would've let him, though. It's better this way. My dad is safe far, far away from here.

"Sometimes I think about what I did wrong." Dr. Sullivan

stands straight, pushing her gold-framed glasses on top her head. "What I could've changed."

I can ramble a whole list of things—one being putting everything in front of us. I don't say anything, though. Instead, I pull my phone from my pocket and look at the screen. "It's getting late. Tell Mason I'm sorry."

I doubt he'll forgive me so easily even though he was so quick to forgive our mom. I don't understand how he can be so brainwashed when he knows the truth about what happened to me. I was hoping he'd be one of the first people on my side, but in this moment it's hard seeing anyone from the HPA on my side. I have to be ready to fight when I do choose to tell someone the truth about it all, just in case they don't believe me.

Opening my door, she leans in and slings her arms around me. I keep my hands on the steering wheel for a long moment and then pat her back once, caving to prevent the awkwardness. It's hard pretending I don't detest her, but I have to do it so she doesn't question my motives for why I do what I do. The moment I can put this all behind me, she'll be the first one to know.

"I'll see you around."

She smiles despite the sadness in her eyes. "Please, try to be there for Mason. He needs you."

Without responding, I roll up the window, and Dr. Sullivan turns away. She's wrong about Mason. My brother doesn't need me, but I do need him. He knows what really happened to me. He was there when I woke up after being brain dead. If only he could realize how manipulative our mom is. Once he does, he could help me.

## NADIA

The door creaks open and in walks a man with a chiseled jawline and well-defined arms. His shaved head glistens with sweat as he sweeps his midnight blue gaze around the room before stopping on me.

He shuts the door behind him, and Cian gets to his feet and holds out his hand. "Blake, my friend. I'm glad you're willing to join us."

"I couldn't stand around and do nothing while my niece is in the hands of the HPA. I'm willing to do anything," Blake says.

"Even break into one of their facilities?" I ask.

His brows pinch together for a minute. Crossing the room, he strides to my table and sits across from me next to Mr. Augustine. Cian pulls up a chair and leans his elbows on the table.

"If there's a plan, then yeah," Blake says.

I suck in my bottom lip. The plan was to have my father come up with a plan with the help of Jacqueline. All I know is we need to get in and save them but not much else. I'm not a great fighter like my father, and I barely survived the last encounter with an agent. I'm afraid we won't be successful. Not with me leading anyway.

"You have to tell them what you know, Nadia," Alyssa says. "If you don't, Jacqueline will die. I saw it."

My heart hammers against my ribcage. I'm nervous to give

away the secret I've been keeping for months. My father should've heard it first. I wish I were honest with him from the very beginning.

"Who're you talking about?" Cian asks. "That name sounds familiar."

I sink down in the booth. We're in a private room away from the noise and excitement of the club. I don't meet anyone's eyes but instead focus on the hum of the soft music buzzing through the walls.

Finally, I take a deep breath. "You've met Jacqueline Matthews, Cian. My father brought us here once before I was cast out from the compound and the council's protection. Everyone thought she was a necromancer."

His eyes light up. "She had curly hair? Pretty lavender eyes?" He throws a sidelong glance at Alyssa. "I thought she died. That's why you were thrown out of the compound."

I twist my lips to the side. "That's what I told them."

Mr. Augustine watches us quietly. He pulls his handkerchief from his pocket and wipes his forehead. Alyssa picks at her chipped, fiery orange nail polish and waits for me to continue.

"Why would you lie about that, Nadia? You could've saved yourself and your dad a whole lot of trouble."

I fidget. He's right, but I know the council would've figured out a way to cast me out regardless. "How else was I going to explain her dead body?"

Cian rubs his hand over his eyes. "You're not making any sense."

Alyssa taps her fingers on the table. "Just tell them, Nadia or I will."

Closing my eyes for a second, I gather my thoughts. I should call Hunter and have him send Jacqueline here, so I can make sure she's okay with this, but I don't have a lot of time. Too many people are counting on me.

"Jacqueline was a sin-eater, hosting the soul of a boy in her mind, and I discovered him while inflicting a nightmare on her. I talked her into releasing him. His body happened to be held at an HPA affiliated hospital, which made things complicated." I take a deep breath. I'm not going to tell them about Hunter. Not yet. Jacqueline is enough. "We got into some trouble, and Jacqueline took a knife for me. It killed her body but she was able to transfer herself into the body of the agent who stabbed her."

Cian, Blake, and Mr. Augustine all lose color in their faces as shock and disbelief smack them on the head. It sounds ridiculous coming from my mouth, and I'm not sure they're going to believe me.

Blake holds up his hands. "Let me get this straight. Your friend is not only alive, but she possesses the body of an HPA agent?"

"Yeah, Camille's dead now."

"Who's that?"

"The agent."

Mr. Augustine twines his fingers together and stares at me. "Why on earth didn't you tell Dmitri?"

My heart aches when he says his name. I wonder if I had told my father the truth the moment I came home all bloody and beat up, dragging behind me the corpse of the girl I told him was my friend, if things would've played out differently. If he wouldn't have been caught in the first place. I push all the what-ifs out of my mind. There's no changing the past.

"She asked us not to," Alyssa says, chiming in. "You have to understand. Jacqueline was tired of running from the HPA and thought if she stayed there among them, she could make a difference. Change the world even. But she didn't want to give up her identity. It would've been too risky."

I blink away my tears. "And I was going to tell my father after Jacqueline came to me and told me the HPA was holding Camden prisoner. We were going to ask for help."

Alyssa grabs my hand. "We were just a little late. I picked up visions of Nadia's future, not Dmitri's."

Mr. Augustine, Blake, and Cian look at us and then to each other. The drawn out silence makes me shift in the booth, uncomfortably, and I tuck my hair behind my ears.

"Will she meet us?" Blake asks, breaking the silence.

I roll my shoulders, tension knotting my muscles. "I can ask. I'm not sure when I'll get to see her though. It's pretty tricky to get together without putting each other at risk."

Blake runs his hand over his shaved head before crossing his arms. His dark blue eyes gleam like two sapphires as he searches my face, trying to determine if I'm lying. He clenches his fists, the veins in his muscular arms bulging, tightening his screen-printed T-shirt a size too small as he bulks up by thought alone. The shifter might try to use his ability to intimidate the truth from me, but I've already given him enough.

He tugs on his long beard. "Walking outside is a risk these days. She can manage."

I frown. I don't like the way he says it, like he's forgotten Jacqueline is a creature like us and not really a member of the HPA. He doesn't care if she risks her life as long as it benefits him. He reminds me of how Mr. Soto treated my father.

"I think you're the one who can manage," I snap. "They'll kill her if they discover her."

"You don't think the HPA will think twice about killing my niece?" Blake asks. "My sister is freaking out. Ella was supposed to be safe at the compound."

"My dad's in there, too, you know." I glare daggers at him and shift to look at Alyssa. She presses her lips together and shrugs.

Blake stands up and paces. "Your father was supposed to protect her!"

My heart hurts thinking about my father and that poor girl and her parents. I even feel bad for Blake. "Ella's okay for now. Jacqueline is taking care of her."

His eyes shadow. "Just do whatever it takes to get Jacqueline here."

I nod, clenching my jaw. "I will."

# 14

## CHANGE THE WORLD

### NADIA

HUNTER'S PHONE RINGS and goes to voicemail. It's past midnight, and I'm sure he's sleeping, but I need to talk to him. Peering over my shoulder, I smile at Alyssa and Mr. Augustine sitting in the front seats of Mr. Augustine's Land Rover.

I shift my eyes up to the cloudless night sky. The stars look like a million shimmering pearls on a blanket stitched of black satin. I feed change into the payphone, huffing a few breaths to watch it fog the air. Mr. Augustine thinks I'm calling Jacqueline. As far as he knows, Hunter doesn't exist. It's better this way.

"Hello?" Hunter's voice comes out raspy, deeper, reminding me of his dreams.

Pressing the phone harder to my ear, wishing I could be with him right now, I listen to him clear his throat. "I miss you," I say.

"You okay?"

I lick my cold lips. "It's been a long night. Was almost captured by an agent when I was in the city, but things are getting better. I found Camden's sister and Ella's uncle, and they're willing to do anything to get their loved ones back."

He groans into the phone. "You sure you're okay? It kills me that I can't be there to protect you."

"It just kills me that you're not here," I say, smiling into the phone. Hunter doesn't think this, but I'm a predator by nature. Even if the HPA scares me, I don't think I could just hide and let him protect me. We'd fight together. I'd protect him. "There are others who need your protection first. Like my dad."

He breathes into the phone. "So, what do you need?"

"You. Can you meet me in a few? I don't have a lot of time to talk now." I gaze at Alyssa again, narrowing her eyes.

Something rustles through the line before Hunter answers with, "Where?"

I tap my fingers on the metal phone housing. I wish I could ask him to come to my house, but I don't know when Mr. Augustine plans on leaving. The large, black duffle bag on the backseat means it could be a while.

"I can't go far. The street over from mine?"

"Sure," he says. "I'll see you soon."

Hanging up the phone, I turn and smile. Not because I'm happy, but because I know that I will be happy soon enough—when I see Hunter. I glide to the car and hop in the backseat. Mr. Augustine reverses before looking at me in his rearview mirror.

"Jacqueline will try to stop by tomorrow morning." It's possibly a lie, because I haven't talked to Jacqueline yet, but it's something to hold Mr. Augustine over for a while.

Alyssa shifts in her seat and stares at me. She can see straight through me but doesn't call me out on it. She'll understand. She has to. She knows how important Hunter is to me—to us. He's going to help get my father back so our family can be complete again.

Mr. Augustine parks in the driveway and turns on the overhead lights. We sit in the car in silence for what feels like forever. "I can stay here tonight, if you want," he finally says.

He looks like he really doesn't want to leave us, his eyes lining with fear and worry. I don't have the heart to tell him we're used to being alone. My father was never home two days in a row.

"You can sleep in my father's room," I say after a long moment.

"I'll make you girls a giant breakfast in the morning," he says, a smile outshining the dark emotions on his face.

Alyssa grins from the front seat. "Nadia doesn't eat, but that means there's more for us."

A few minutes later, I glance out the back window and see the flash of headlights illuminate the night. Hunter's BMW drives past, and I want to drop everything and run to him. Instead, I run into the house, open the garage, and then help Mr. Augustine get settled in.

I wait a few minutes for Mr. Augustine to turn the shower on and then go to Alyssa's door. "Tell Mr. Augustine I went to inflict a nightmare." I don't wait for her to answer but instead wave and sneak off into the night.

## HUNTER

Like a beautiful apparition gliding down the dark street, Nadia comes into view in my rearview mirror. She wears only a tank top and jeans, and I unlock my doors so she can hop in.

Her pale blond hair cascades in a mess around her shoulders, and she runs her fingers through it before leaning over to kiss me. Her lips send a shiver through me, and I shrug out of my jacket and lay it across her lap before adjusting the vents to blow hot air on her.

I glance at her bare feet. "You look like you're in a hurry."

She sighs. "Mr. Augustine is spending the night. I had to wait until he got in the shower."

I raise my eyebrows. "What for?"

"He wants to help break my father out."

"When?"

She sighs and leans her elbows on her knees. "Soon. That's why I'm here. I know our plan to get Camden out was ruined when my father was taken, but I still need Jacqueline to give me what she knows. We'll need it for those who are going to break into the termination facility to save who they can."

"You're not helping, are you?" The thought of Nadia breaking into the termination facility scares me more than the idea of me getting caught as a traitor.

"I want to, but we've agreed the fewer the people the better. An army would only attract attention. We need to go unnoticed."

I release a relieved breath. "How can I help?" I can do as much as Jacqueline, and it'll be more in my control. It could be my opportunity to leave. I don't want to sit around and do nothing.

She shakes her head. "No, don't even ask. No one knows about you, and I need to keep it that way. They wouldn't trust you, either. I need Jacqueline."

"I don't like this at all."

She shrugs and gazes out the window. "You don't have to."

## NADIA

Hunter stares at me like I told him his dog died. His hazel eyes beg me to rethink the situation. He wants to help, but I can't see it ending well. The HPA will kill him or he'll die trying to be a hero. I need my hero alive.

I touch his chin, leaning in to kiss him. He sinks into me, kissing me back, running his hands over my shoulders, trying to gather me in his arms despite the armrest between us. If I didn't have to hurry back, I'd stay right here with Hunter until the sun rises.

He pulls away, a hardened look steeling his usual soft features he always gives me compared to anyone else. "I don't want you to get hurt, Nadia."

I blink my vision clear of tears. "I won't get hurt. I'm not leading an army to battle or anything. I'm more worried about you. You're working with the HPA and my father's friends don't know you're actually on their side. A lot can go wrong. I don't want you anywhere near that facility. I don't know how things are going to happen, just that they are going to happen."

"That's why I need to be involved."

"The less you know the better if things don't pan out."

"What about Jacqueline?"

"She already agreed to do what she could."

Glancing out the back window, I watch as a figure appears on the corner. Alyssa crosses her arms, wearing a heavy coat over her pajamas. The street lamp light shadows her face, and she just waits and watches the car without coming any closer, giving me and Hunter space while reminding me the world still spins even if I try to pretend it doesn't.

I meet Hunter's gaze. "I have to go. Please, ask Jacqueline to meet me here tomorrow morning. Tell her not to wear her uniform. It'll freak people out."

He blows out a long breath. "This kills me you know."

"I know."

With a pout, I kiss his cheek and climb from the car. Cold air fills my lungs, and I shiver despite not being cold. Hunter pulls away from the curb and leaves me standing on the snowy sidewalk.

Alyssa saunters closer and holds out a pair of boots. "Just because the cold doesn't bother you, doesn't mean you should go running through the snow without the proper gear."

I smile. "Thanks, Mom."

She glares. "That's not why I'm out here. I had a vision."

I swallow the lump in my throat. "My father?"

She shakes her head. "No, but I saw Hunter decide he's not going to be a bystander."

Of course he won't sit back and not get involved. "What does that mean?" I ask, rubbing my eyes.

"I honestly don't know."

I sigh. "I'll call him in the morning."

Hooking her arm with mine, she tugs me to stroll with her back home. "You better. I think if he gets involved, it'll complicate our plans."

"When have things ever been simple between Hunter and me?" I ask.

She smirks. "Exactly."

## HUNTER

I wait for Jacqueline outside her apartment. I don't want to risk telling her over the phone, plus I need to see her reaction. Maybe I can convince her to let me help since Nadia's dead-set against it.

Headlights illuminate the inside of my car, and I don't move to get out until Jacqueline parks her old 1986 Mercedes Benz in the carport. Jumping from the car, I meet her at her front door.

While opening her front door, she asks, "Are you checking to see if I survived the longest dinner of my life? It almost felt like an interrogation. Then of course, I had to return to work and nearly kill myself from boredom."

I shut the door behind us. "Maybe it was an interrogation."

She punches my arm. "Don't say that."

"Sorry. I'm sure it wasn't, but that's not why I'm here. Nadia wants you to go to her house in the morning. She told a few people about you, and they want your help to plan a break-in at the termination facility."

She glances around like she's being watched. "What about you?"

I drop my shoulders. "I'm still figuring out my place in all this. She doesn't think it's a good idea for me to help, because people might not trust me."

Instead of looking at me, she stares at her reflection in the wall mirror next to me. "They probably won't. Not when it comes to putting their lives in someone else's hands. Even though I'm in this body, I'm still a sin-eater, and they'll recognize that if I let them."

Pulling her black hair from its disheveled ponytail, she combs her fingers through the tangles. She doesn't say anything, sinking deeper into her thoughts. She plops down on her leather couch and kicks off her boots, tucking her socked feet under her, leaning her elbow on the couch's arm.

I shuffle around the couch and sit on the heavy wooden

coffee table. "You can tell them I'm on their side."

She doesn't answer and doesn't attempt to look at me, finding the blank TV more entertaining. It's like she's pretending I'm not here, like she used to do when I was trapped in her head. Hoping she feels the weight of my stare, I glare at her for a few minutes until I can't take the silence.

I reach out and guide her chin up to look at me. "Jacqueline, I can help."

Swinging her arm out, she smacks my hand away. "I'll talk to Nadia about it."

"You have to let me help," I say, clenching my teeth.

"You can help by keeping Nadia safe. You both should stay far away from this mess. You've been through enough, don't you think?"

"Haven't you?"

She stands up and crosses her arms. "I think you need to go home and think things through."

I get to my feet and put distance between us. "You didn't answer my question."

Jacqueline stiffens, raising her fist like she'll punch me and throw me out. I take another step back and shove my hands in my pockets, holding my ground. She doesn't scare me like she used to, but she could take me down in that new body of hers, and pain isn't my thing.

Jacqueline sighs, dropping her hand to her side. She shuffles toward her bedroom and hovers in the doorway. We glare at each other, both unwilling to back down. I'll stay here all night if that's what it takes to convince her I should be a part of this. That I can help.

After a few minutes pass, Jacqueline says, "I have a lot to make up for, Hunter. You've changed me, and I can't sit around and look out for only myself anymore."

"You don't think I've changed?"

Her lips curl in the corner. "I'm well aware of how different you are."

"Then you should know why I want to help. We're a team. We should be doing this together."

"Nadia needs you alive."

"You don't think she needs you?"

Shaking her head, she says, "If something happens to me, you're the one who has to keep fighting. You're supposed to change the world, remember?"

I glare because she makes sense. "I don't think I can."

"I'm not going to sit here and give you a pep-talk, Hunter. I'm tired." She closes her door, leaving me standing in the middle of her living room.

It's hard to let other people handle things. I feel as if I'm trapped in Jacqueline's mind again with no control over anything, like I'm just watching the world through a glass window. And I want to shatter it. I want to knock the whole wall down and take control.

But I know in the end, Jacqueline may be right. I just wish doing nothing would stop feeling so wrong.

# 15

## SELFISH TO SELFLESS

**NADIA**

VOICES HUM THROUGH my door. I heard Mr. Augustine let in Cian, Blake, and Liv twenty minutes ago, but I can't find the will to leave my room. Alyssa's vision haunts me, and all I can think about is Hunter getting hurt if he doesn't do what I ask and not get involved. I'm afraid of what it'll do to our relationship if his attempt to help prevents my father from getting his freedom. Good intention doesn't always have a good outcome. We both know this better than anyone.

The scent of bacon and coffee sneaks in under my door, making my rattled nerves queasy. Forcing myself to stand up, I change into something that isn't damp and stained with mud. I pull a brush through my tangled, pale blond hair, and apply lip balm to my cracked lips.

A tap sounds on my door, tugging my attention away from my thoughts of Hunter. Alyssa opens it and peeks in, her green eyes glinting in the warm sunlight beaming through my open curtains. She looks well-rested and happier than she did last night. At least one of us is ready to face the day.

She slips into my room and plops on my bed. "Jacqueline will be here soon."

My shoulders relax. "I wasn't sure if Hunter was going to pass on my message."

"He'll come around. Next time you meet him, let me know, and I'll talk to him myself and tell him to stop being an idiot." She sits up straighter, puffing her lips. "Why are boys so insistent on saving the day?"

I giggle. "He just wants to be helpful."

"Or something."

"Nadia? Alyssa?" Mr. Augustine knocks on the door. "Breakfast is ready."

I glide to the door and swing it open. Mr. Augustine stands in the hall, wearing Alyssa's flower-printed apron over his dark denim jeans and green sweater. The dark circles under his eyes make him look older. He probably hasn't slept at all. Not that I can remember. I was too wound up in my own thoughts to concentrate on anything except for the moon sinking into the horizon to allow the sun to start a new day.

"Did I make you too nervous to sleep?" I ask, looking at the carpet, the new thought sneaking into my mind. I wouldn't blame him if thinking about my ability kept him up all night. He saw me nearly lose control in the library.

He forces his mouth to smile. "I'm not afraid of night-mares, Nadia, and no, I just have a lot on my mind."

I compel my own mouth to smile. "Maybe you should forget about us. It really isn't your problem."

He touches my shoulder, drawing my focus to him. "Nonsense. Your father would do the same if I had children of my own. Also, Emily would haunt me if I let something happen to you."

"My mother would understand."

Waving his hands, he bats something imaginary in the air. "Stop trying to get rid of me. I'm not afraid of the HPA. You need my help." He looks past me at Alyssa, who's watching us silently from my bed. "Now, come join us in the kitchen. Breakfast is ready."

Alyssa stands up. "She doesn't like to eat food, Mr. Augustine. You'll have to tempt her with something else."

I grin at my best friend.

Mr. Augustine sucks in a breath. "Then just come and enjoy the scents."

Before we can tease him anymore, the doorbell rings. I eye Alyssa and push past Mr. Augustine to glide into the living room to answer the door. Jacqueline stands on the porch, wearing her HPA uniform under a baggy hoodie. The blue of it matches her eyes, and my gaze drops to the weapons around her tiny waist. Hunter didn't tell her to come in street clothes, and I wonder if he did it on purpose.

I step back to let her in. "You might want to lose the weapons."

She looks past me into the empty living room. "I'm not going to hurt anyone."

"I know that, but these guys are pretty unpredictable. You're terrifying dressed like an agent," I say, waving my hand at her. And she really does look terrifying in the skin of the agent who tried to kill me and did kill her.

She lifts a delicate eyebrow, shifting on her boots while straightening her shoulders. Her loose black hair falls in her face like a veil. "They'll get over it."

I sigh, drooping my shoulders. That's what I told Hunter last night when he told me he didn't like I wasn't including him in any of our plans to get my father away from the HPA. I wonder if both Jacqueline and I will be right about it.

Glaring, I say, "You're stubborn."

"I like my belt. Makes me feel powerful."

"You are powerful."

She smirks.

I roll my eyes. She's not going to lose the belt. I just hope she knows what she's doing. "Fine, whatever. Just let me go in first."

She looks at the kitchen door nervously. "They are expecting me, right?"

I grab her hand. "Yeah, they asked to meet you. They're hoping you'd be willing to help us."

She follows me to the kitchen door. "I'll do everything I can."

## HUNTER

"Want today's newspaper?" I ask.

Dmitri lies on his cot with his fingers laced together on the back of his head. He's still wearing the plain black clothes he arrived in despite the pile of clean, white scrubs neatly folded on his pillow.

He doesn't move to get up and waves his hand at the discarded day-old paper on the desk. "You can leave it over there."

Pressing my lips into a line, I shut the door behind me. I cross the room with my eyes trained on Nadia's father and toss the newspaper from two feet away. I spin on my feet to face him, and we stare at each other for an uncomfortable minute.

I clear my throat. "Need anything else while I'm here?"

"No, I'm fine. Thank you," he says.

Shifting my weight between my feet, I say, "I don't get it. Most people ask for a million things—or at least to go home. But you—" I point my finger at him and then drop my hand. "You just sit there. You have to want something."

I have no idea what I'm doing, but I have to try to make an effort so the board doesn't get suspicious. I want him to talk to me, to get to know me so when this is all over, he'll trust me with Nadia, but I also don't want him to give away anything.

"I really am fine. If I think of something, I will ask." He

grins and glides to the desk and swipes the newspaper. Just as fast, he returns to the cot and flops back on it.

Because of his inhumanly speed and skills in combat, Dmitri could've taken me out right then, but he didn't. And I know he wouldn't. I don't know why I have to convince myself he's not a monster. I know he's not.

I peer at him once more and stride to the door to open it. "I'll be back in a while to check on you."

"Why bother?"

I turn to meet his dark gaze. "Because it's my job."

"You can see me from there." He points at the camera in the corner.

"It's my job," I repeat.

Shutting the door, I lock it and gaze at him through the window. He meets my eyes again, but I don't turn away. After a few minutes, Dmitri finally turns his eyes toward his newspaper, and I step out of view.

I need to get him to trust me.

And soon.

## NADIA

"Jacqueline's here," I say as I waltz through the door. "Nobody freak out. She's in her uniform."

Jacqueline's shoulder grazes my arm, and she steps up next to me. Everyone freezes, like I triggered a real life pause button. Blake holds his fork halfway to his mouth. Mr. Augustine extends his arm, offering sugar to Liv. Alyssa smiles and slams her mug on the table, jumpstarting everyone into action.

"Nadia told me you wanted to talk," Jacqueline says, shuffling forward to the table. She touches Alyssa's shoulder and smiles without sitting down. She hides her nervousness well, though she's obviously on guard with her stiff movements.

She reminds me of myself.

"You're standing right in front of me, and I still don't believe it," Blake says. "What are you? How can you stay hidden among them? They always know."

Alyssa slides out the chair next to her, motioning for Jacqueline to sit. I hover behind her, resting my hands on the chair back. All eyes study Jacqueline, every detail about her, from her hair to the way she positions herself with her hands under the table.

Jacqueline shifts, the chair squeaking on the tile. "The HPA altered this body's DNA. I've been gifted with the ability to conceal my aura. I can read other's auras, too. In a year or so, they'll assign me to a team with people like me."

Liv leans across the table and grabs Jacqueline's hands. "How? How did they accomplish this? This could be the beginning of the end. How many altered ones are there?"

"I don't know the details. When I took Camille's memories, there was a void. They put her under to do the procedure. And there are only a few of us. Not many humans survive the alteration. Like less than one percent."

I knew the body Jacqueline has inhabited was different, but I didn't know all this. I never asked, either. It's amazing. If the council finds out about her, they'll want her back. I'm sure of it.

But then, where would that leave me?

Cian laces his fingers behind his head. "What made you decide to stay? You could've run and found protection."

Jacqueline lifts her head. "I'm over running. The HPA took everything from me, including my body, and I'm tired of being scared. This way, I always know where they are and I can help people. I want to make a difference."

"So, you'll help me get my niece back?" Blake asks.

"And my brother?" Liv adds.

We're all tied together by the people the HPA took. I know I can trust Blake and Liv, because we all want the same thing. I just hope it all works out. I hope Jacqueline agrees.

Jacqueline tilts her head to look at me. I offer a small smile. Alyssa touches her arm, and I think about how this is what it was supposed to be like when I first met Jacqueline. It's how it should always be.

"Yes, I'll do anything I can. Do you have a plan?"

Blake grins, a hint of madness in his eyes. "We're going to invade the facility. We just need you to get us in. We'll get ourselves out."

I grip the back of Jacqueline's chair, my heart sputtering. The more I hear the plan, the more real it gets—and it scares me. We're going to need a miracle.

Jacqueline swivels again in her seat. She doesn't respond but just stares at the backs of her hands. It's a lot to ask of her, and if the HPA discovers she was the one to let us in, they'll kill her without question.

Finally, after what feels like eternity, Jacqueline whispers, "It'll be tricky, but I think we can do it."

My gaze falls to Alyssa, staring into space. It takes her a minute to compose herself, and she doesn't tell anyone she had a vision. Her forehead creases in worry, and I want to drag her from the room and ask her to tell me what she saw.

Reading my expression, she pushes from her chair and excuses herself from the table. I wait a minute before I race after her into the living room. She takes my hands, eyes lined with tears, and then she hugs me.

"Hunter's going to mess everything up. You have to call him and tell him to stay away from the facility. You have to beg him to listen."

I comb my fingers through my hair and rub my head. "Cover for me. I'm going to call him now."

She nods, and without a second look back, I rush out the door.

## HUNTER

My prepaid cell buzzes on my desk, and I glance from it to the monitor. Nadia knows I'm at the facility and that it's hard for me to talk to her here. Grabbing my phone, I shove it in my pocket.

The only place without a camera is the bathroom, and I'm not sure if it's bugged with a microphone. The HPA might be paranoid enough to do something so crazy. I'd hate to be the one with the job of listening to the recording from the hypothetical microphone.

When I reach the single stall bathroom, I lock the door and pull my phone from my pocket, waiting for it to ring again. I stare at the dark screen for what feels like forever, and then finally, an unknown number displays on the screen.

"Agent Hunter," I say, pressing my cell hard into my ear.

Static cuts through the line, and I glance at the screen. Cell service is pretty bad. I'm teetering on losing connection.

"Hello?" I ask.

"Hunter, it's—" The line cuts to static, and I switch ears to see if it makes a difference.

"What?" I wave the phone around, looking for a stronger signal. I find one in the corner of the room, next to the toilet. "I couldn't hear you."

"Can—meet—after—" Nadia's voice fades in and out. "Important."

"You want to meet me?" I ask.

"Yes."

Just when I'm about to respond, the line cuts off, and I'm left with silence. I tuck my phone in my pocket and open the bathroom door. I can't spend much longer in here or else security will be suspicious. I plop back down at my desk to look at the monitor and watch as Ella and Dmitri have a conversation through the wall.

Seeing Dmitri comfort her gives me an idea. I know exactly what he wants and I think I can give it to him.

## NADIA

The line cuts off, and I throw the grimy receiver at the metal box. It clatters down the side and dangles from its cord. I yank my long hair in my hands and take a breath. I hope he heard enough to come to me as soon as he's off. I pray I can talk some sense into him.

A horn honks, and I startle, spinning on the frozen sidewalk to meet Jacqueline's gaze through the windshield of her old, green Mercedes. She cranks her window down and sticks her head out. I stroll from the payphone and cross my arms.

"Alyssa said you'd be here," she says.

I shift on the balls of my feet. "I was telling Hunter to meet me when he gets off."

"Oh, good," she says. "I agree it'll be bad if he's around when things go down."

"When is it happening?" I ask, pressing my lips into a line, anticipation making me nervous though I won't even be there.

She taps her door frame. "Blake didn't want to wait, so I'm sneaking them in tonight."

"Tonight?" Fear and hope course through my veins. That means I'll get to see my father again before morning.

She sucks in her bottom lip. "As long as things go according to plan."

"Are you scared?"

She shrugs. "My part is simple. I'm more afraid for everyone else." I step back from the car when Jacqueline's phone rings. "I have to take this. I'll see you later, Nadia."

My heart clenches at her words. I hope they're true. What she's doing is dangerous, and I can't support her like I did when we returned Hunter to his body. I hope the others treat her as one of us despite her uniform. I don't know how I'll live with the guilt of getting her hurt all over again.

Jacqueline's come a long way since the first time I met her after I discovered Hunter in her head. She went from being the most selfish person I know to the most selfless.

I hope it helps her in the end.

# 16

## NOTHING WILL EVER BE FINE

### HUNTER

I LEAN AGAINST the door and watch Dmitri read the newspaper to Ella. After waiting my entire shift for permission from the board, I was reluctantly allowed to let Ella visit Dmitri as long as I remained in the room.

My feet prickle with numbness, and I eye the empty chair at the desk. Dmitri tucks Ella into the crook of his arm and flips to the next page. They talk so quietly that I have to strain to hear them. I'm tempted to move closer, but my legs stiffen, refusing to budge.

"Do you think Agent Hunter will bring my mommy here to visit?" Ella brings her green eyes to mine.

I drop my gaze to the floor without answering.

"Let's hope not," Dmitri says.

"But I miss her."

I can feel the weight of Dmitri's gaze on me, but I make a point to find the tiles much more interesting, though I watch them in the edge of my vision. "I'm sure she misses you, too. But you don't really want her to come here. Remember what I told you?"

I expect her to repeat what he told her, but she doesn't. She swings her thin arms around his chest and buries her face into his side. He's very fatherly, and I wonder if Nadia has fond memories of spending time with her dad. I hope so. I hope they're better than the ones I have with mine.

"Good, girl."

A beep rings in my ear, and the door swings in and hits me in the back. I stumble forward, yanking my dagger from its sheath. Turning, I raise my hand to Jacqueline hovering in the door. Her eyes widen, shadows clouding her expression.

"You're still here?" Her high-pitched voice rises with surprise. She glances from Dmitri to Ella, and then back to me. "Your shift ended an hour ago. I thought the charge had escaped. I didn't see you on the monitor. Why didn't you log this?"

"I was going to on my way out," I say.

She nods toward the hallway. "Fill me in."

"I can't leave them alone."

Jacqueline frowns and turns to Ella. "Come on. Back to

your room."

Tears spring from Ella's eyes, but Jacqueline swoops in on her and grabs her hand, yanking her from the bed. Ella has to run to keep up with Jacqueline.

I shrug at Dmitri, leaving him in the room, and lock the door behind me.

Jacqueline pounces the second I turn away from the door. Grabbing my hand, she drags me back to the monitors where I see Camden sleeping on his cot, Ella in the fetal position on the floor, crying, and Dmitri still sitting on the cot with the newspaper.

Jacqueline leans into me. "You need to leave."

My brows knit together. "What's up?"

She gathers my things and hands them to me. "Your shift is up. I know you have things to do."

"I'm fine. I was really getting somewhere with Creature 1252."

"I can take over," Jacqueline says.

I open my mouth to argue. Jacqueline's acting stranger than usual, and I want to know what she's not telling me, but she won't because of the camera. "Agent Cam—"

"Go pick me up some dinner, Hunter. Please, just do it."

## NADIA

I sit on the snowy curb on the corner of my street. Hunter should've been here hours ago, and he hasn't been answering his cell phone. What if he forgot? What if something happened? All the what-ifs slice through me, opening up fear inside me to spill out onto the cold ground.

I hate that I have no other way to reach him. All I can think about is something came up. That Alyssa's vision couldn't be avoided. That maybe it wasn't our fate to rise up against the HPA without starting a full blown war, one I'm not sure we could ever win, not when Hunter is trapped on the opposite side.

Pushing to my feet, I dust the snow off my wet jeans. I glide in the direction of the convenience store where I usually call Hunter. Mr. Augustine felt obligated to help Blake and Liv, seeing that the HPA would most likely let him go if he were caught so Alyssa waits at home alone for any sort of word from the others.

It'd be easier if I pushed past my fear and just called Hunter from home or the emergency cell phone I share with Alyssa. But it's too risky. Who knows what kind of technology the HPA has. They can create their own versions of creatures, like the body Jacqueline inhabits. They could probably trace a phone back to me. Calling Hunter's burner phone is hard enough.

I reach the payphone and sigh. This is the fifth time I've walked here, the second time in the dark. Every time I try to call, I get Hunter's voicemail. My hand trembles as I dial his number again. Each ring sends cold dread down my back and then I hang up. "He's just busy," I say out loud. "Call him back."

A car horn blares, surprising me, sending my heart nearly

falling out of me. I swing around to meet Alyssa's bone-chilling, hard expression. She waves through the window, motioning me to close the distance.

Rushing to her side, I wait for her to roll down the window. Warm air hits my face. "Come on, Nadia. My vision about Hunter hasn't changed. We need to find him," she says. "They should be breaking into the facility soon, and he can't be there. Jacqueline said everyone is gone by nine."

I feel sick to my stomach. "Let me call Hunter one more time. I'm sure it's nothing."

"Hurry."

I race back to the payphone and shove my coins into the slot. My breath fogs the cold air, and my pale hands turn red from being exposed to the elements for so long. My heart drums in my ears as each ring passes and tears well in my eyes. *Hunter's okay. He has to be okay...*

"Agent Hunter."

A cry of relief rips from my mouth. I lean my back on the metal box and motion to Alyssa that Hunter picked up. "Where are you? You were supposed to meet me hours ago. I was so worried."

Hunter breathes into the phone. "I'm sorry, Nadia. I got hung up with your dad and kept missing your calls."

"Will you be here soon?"

"Yeah, I'm just pulling back into the facility to take Jacqueline some dinner and then I'll head over. I need to check on her real quick. She was acting weird, and I'm afraid something happened with the board." A car door slams, and I hear his footsteps.

I dig my fingers into the palms of my hands. "Hunter, leave now. Jacqueline was acting strangely because the break-in is happening tonight. Maybe even now." My voice echoes through the silent air. "Please, you can't be there."

I hear a door close. "Why didn't you tell me?"

"I was going to, but you didn't answer your phone."

Hunter curses under his breath. "I have to go."

"Don't hang up on me!"

"I think this is all a misunderstanding." Hunter's voice sends a chill down my spine. "Stay back. I'm not going to do any—"

The line goes dead.

I thrust the phone at the wall, tears burning my eyes as I stumble back to Alyssa's car. "We have to get to the facility."

Alyssa reverses without waiting for me to buckle my seatbelt, and I clutch onto the dashboard. My head fogs with worry, with despair and anxiety. It's hard to see because the world is spinning. My heart aches, making it hard to breathe. I should've told the others about Hunter and included him in the plan. I just thought that it was better if he didn't know. I didn't want him to be at the facility—he wasn't supposed to be at the facility—but he's there anyway. And now, I know he's in trouble.

I hope we aren't too late.

## HUNTER

My head throbs, black stars peppering my vision.

Slumping over, my knees hit the hard floor, and I cover my head to protect myself from the creature. A man, wearing all black, stomps closer to me. His shaved head glistens with sweat, and his long beard twitches as his skin ripples like a thousand spiders crawl beneath the surface. I wince at his closeness, trying to roll away, but he swings his leg back and kicks me in the chest.

I gasp as the air escapes from my lungs. It takes everything in me to scramble back before he kicks me again. My head spins, and I grip the wall, trying to pull myself to my feet. I can't fight from the floor, not with him stopping me from getting to my feet.

My stomach heaves, bile rising in my throat, and I spit and cough to clear my airway. I need to get out of here before he comes closer. I have to do something to protect myself.

"What are you doing? Come on."

I rub my hand over my eyes and see a black-haired woman talking to the creature. Her hair is the same color as Jacqueline's, but she's shorter and less muscular.

"He saw us, Liv," the guy says. "I have to take care of him."

"I know you're mad, Blake, but you're not a monster. Don't be cruel. I'll meet you downstairs." The woman, Liv, struts off. I almost beg her to stay. She'd be the one who would show some pity on me, not this guy.

The offsite security team only checks in on the zones periodically when the caretakers are still on shift, and the front gate guards don't know what's happening because I saw them watching TV a few minutes ago. If I don't think of something fast, he'll kill me. I know it.

Hands shove me in the back. Falling forward, I hit my stomach on the edge of the desk. It cuts into me like a blunt knife, but I manage to swivel sideways and swing my arm. My fist connects with the guy, Blake's, arm and he rolls his shoulder, a sadistic smile on his face. He jabs his hand forward, and my nose screams in pain from his sucker punch. Sticky blood pours from my nostrils. He's going to beat me to death with his bare hands.

"Please man, stop. I'm not your enemy," I say, covering my nose. "I'm here to—" Blake's fist flies at me again. I jerk to the right and throw myself back. He's not going to let me talk. Nadia hasn't told anyone about me, and Jacqueline is somewhere else, so she can't see what's happening. Blake's so concerned with trying to kill me that I can't explain I won't hurt him and I want the same thing he does.

I manage to get to my feet and hobble to the back of Phillip's desk. If I can reach the alarm, I could bring in an army of agents to stop this dude from killing me. I don't want to, because I know Nadia would be disgusted by it, but I'm not going to let this guy murder me, either. She'll have to understand. Being a traitor in this uniform puts me at risk with the HPA, but it also puts me at risk with creatures. No one is my friend in this moment.

The edge of the desk scratches my back through my shirt, and I land hard on my hip. I crab walk backward to put some distance between us and then slide my knife from its sheath.

I grip the knife in my shaking hand, and the guy kicks his leg again. I catch his black pants with the blade, and he yells out as I slide it across his shin. Before I have a chance to bring the knife up again, he knocks me back with another fist to my face. My ears ring, and I lose focus, dropping the knife. It clatters on the tiled floor.

The guy swipes it up and aims it at me. "You really do want to die, don't ya?"

I roll to my hands and knees and crawl back toward the desk. "Please, Blake. Let me talk. I thought you weren't a monster."

"You took my niece. I'm not here to talk things out." He kicks me in the side, and I drop to the floor. He laughs, his deep voice echoing through the air. Rage rushes over me. If I were strong enough, I'd tackle him and smash the smile off his face. It's supers like this that give them a bad reputation. Just when I thought the HPA was really horrible for their beliefs, I now think they're a little right. I want nothing more than to kill this guy. He's evil. It's him against me.

Stepping on my chest, he presses his weight into my ribcage. I claw at his pants, trying to knock him off me, but he doesn't budge. It's hard to breathe through the pain. Black shadows rim the edges of my vision. If he stays on me much longer, I'll lose consciousness. I'll be a dead man.

With my free hand, I reach for my weaponry belt again. The man moves his boot from my chest and crushes my hand to the floor. I yell and cuss and spit as the bones in my fingers snap under his weight. Swinging my free hand out, I punch the back of his knee, and it gives out on him. He drops on top of me with his knee on my stomach.

My gut heaves, and I hit my head on the tile from the sudden shift in pressure. I flail my legs, thrusting my knee into his back, and knock him off me. Tears blur my eyes, and blood drips from my nose and onto the floor. I grit my teeth and pull my taser from my belt and jam it into the back of his neck before igniting him with a jolt of hot electricity.

He yells out, thrashing, but he doesn't go down like I expect him to. He's back on his feet in seconds, blind with rage and smelling like burnt flesh. I roll out of the way as he swings his leg to kick me again. He hits air, throwing him off balance, and he falls to his knees next to me. Grabbing the collar of my shirt, he jerks my head up, his sweat and saliva hitting my face, and before he has a chance to slam my head into the tile, I taser him in his side this time, causing him to jerk away.

He yells, knocking the taser across the room.

"If you kill me, you won't make it out of here alive. I can help you," I say, blinking hard to keep consciousness.

"Liar."

Getting to his feet, he grabs the discarded knife from the floor. The elevator dings, stopping him in his tracks. He glances from me to the elevator and then back to me. I take the moment to slide the rest of the way to Phillip's desk. Reaching under it, I slam my palm on the alarm.

I'm not going to die today.

## NADIA

"We're ten minutes away," Alyssa says. "Call Mr. Augustine again."

My fingers fumble on the buttons of the cell phone. I'm agitated no one is picking up their phones for me. I could've warned them if they'd answered. Then, we wouldn't be in this mess. I just hope Hunter is okay. *Please, let him be okay.*

It rings and rings and then Mr. Augustine's voicemail clicks on. "Still nothing."

Alyssa blows out a breath and crosses two lanes, stomping on the accelerator. "Try again."

"It's pointless." I hit redial anyway.

It rings twice. The line finally clicks, and a murmur of voices rush in my ears before a heart-stopping alarm rings through the phone. "Nadia? Nadia, can you hear me?" Mr. Augustine yells.

"What's going on?" I ask, my voice high pitched and breathless.

"An unexpected agent hit an alarm. I have to go," Mr. Augustine says.

"Is my father with you?" I ask. I want to ask about the agent, but I'm too afraid of what he'll tell me.

"Blake! What have you done?" Liv screams in the background. "You should've just tied the agent up."

Fear tugs at my chest. "Mr. Augustine? What happened?"

"I have to go," Mr. Augustine repeats. "Don't worry. We'll

be fine."

The phone clicks off, and I throw it on the floor. My stomach heaves as I cry into my hands. It's like I'm losing everything, and there's nothing I can do to stop it. Nothing will ever be fine. I should've just accepted it a long time ago. I can feel deep in my soul that Hunter is hurt or worse. And with the memory of the alarm still ringing in my ear, I'm not sure if anyone is getting out of this alive.

# 17

## PERSONAL NIGHTMARE

### HUNTER

THE DEAFENING ALARM nearly steals my consciousness. Voices scream through each quick pause in the blaring sound, and I sit on the ground, leaning my back on the desk. I peek around the edge and watch as the black-haired woman, Liv, grabs the hand of Ella and runs to the door with a bald man on her heels.

The alarms cut off, my heartbeat now resonating in my ears. I can't hear what the people say, but as they reach the door, Agent Rosaline kicks it open and holds up her tranquilizer gun.

Liv holds her hand up and yells, "Don't move!"

Agent Rosaline frowns, keeping her gun trained on them, but remains frozen like she's under some sort of spell.

Liv turns to Dmitri, Camden, and Blake. "I can't protect all of us, and more agents are coming."

"Just get Ella out," Dmitri says. "We can take care of ourselves."

"I'll carry her. It'll be faster." The bald man kneels, and Ella hops on his back.

"Go first, Sandy," Liv says to the bald man with Ella.

Liv nods and they rush through the door past Agent Rosaline. The moment they disappear, Agent Rosaline shoots and sends a dart into Camden's shoulder. Dmitri catches him as he falls and yanks him a few feet back.

Agent Rosaline shoots another dart. Dmitri ducks, the dart hitting the wall, smashing to pieces. Blake charges her way, wielding my knife, but Agent Rosaline twists out of his way and elbows him in the back. He loses his footing and smacks against the window with the palms of his hands. Before he has a chance to turn around, she stabs a tranquilizer into his back.

He reaches around, contorting his body in an unnatural position and yanks the dart out. Spinning, swinging his arm, he launches the knife at Agent Rosaline. It jams in her shoulder, and she stumbles back, catching herself on the desk. She uses it to launch herself at him, and before he has a chance to move, she tackles him to the ground.

In one fluid motion, Agent Rosaline draws her own knife

and rams the blade into the guy's back and hits his heart. He slumps under her, and she huffs, catching her breath.

I shift to stand up and meet Dmitri's obsidian eyes. They line with fear and worry, and I stagger back to my feet, heading in his direction. If he were going to kill me, he would've already. I know how fast he is, ten times faster than Nadia, and he could take me out in my condition in seconds.

I cradle my hand and nod to the elevator. "You have two choices. Take Camden and go back to your cell or try to fight your way out."

Dmitri lifts Camden over his shoulder, and I limp behind him and follow him into the elevator. I hold up my taser, as if it'll somehow protect me, but I know I won't have to use it. Dmitri is a smart man.

My cell phone rings at my side, my stomach clenching because I know it's Nadia. She'll hate me for sounding the alarm. She won't forgive me for ruining the one chance to get her father out.

We enter the green zone, and Jacqueline's eyes widen as she sees me escorting Dmitri with a knocked out Camden back to the cells. Once I lock them in, I slump to the ground as pain and grief washes through me. I'm broken mentally and physically, and I don't know how I'll manage to pick myself up off the floor. I don't know if I want to.

Voices echo into the corridor, but I close my eyes. I can't focus.

Darkness takes me.

## NADIA

"I can't drive any closer," Alyssa says. "We'll get caught."

I feel sick. My stomach rolls, and I breathe through my nose. Yanking my hair back, I tie it in a ponytail and glance at Alyssa. "Let's walk the rest of the way."

Her eyes glass over, and she grips my knee. "We'll get caught that way, too."

"Then what do we do!" I have to get to the facility. I have to see my father—I have to see if Hunter is okay. The thought of living without either of them makes me want to curl up and die.

Alyssa wraps her arms around me. "I don't know. I wish I knew, but I don't."

Her cell phone rings, and my heart stops beating for a few seconds before kicking into overdrive. I don't have to look at the number to know who it is, but I'm terrified to talk to Mr. Augustine.

Alyssa reaches for the phone on the floor and hits the speaker-phone button. Static buzzes from it, and I wince. After a second, we hear Mr. Augustine gasp a few times, like he's out of breath, and then he says, "Nadia? Nadia? You there?"

I dig my fingers into my palms. "What's going on?"

"We need you to pick us up. We had to abandon the vehicle."

"Where?" Alyssa asks, already pulling away from the curb.

"South Mesa and Riverdale Drive."

I puff a long breath through my lips. "We'll be there in a

few minutes."

A smile tugs at the corner of my mouth. They made it out alive. I'll get to see my father again and hug him and ask him to leave the council. I know he'll do it this time, especially after how they reacted to his kidnapping. They would never have to even know.

I'll even tell him about Hunter.

*Hunter...*

My insides tighten, and I push his hazel eyes from my mind. I can't worry about him right now. It'll only make the pain worse. Instead, I imagine the smile on my father's face and how proud he'll be of me for not giving up on him. He'll be proud of how I figured out how to save him with the help of his friends. He'll know I can survive in this world.

I will keep on surviving.

## HUNTER

"Is he alive?"

Jacqueline's voice swirls around me. It feels almost like I'm trapped in her head again. I try to open my eyes, but I can't feel my face. It's numb with pain, and the pain is the only reason I know I'm still in my own body. Without the pain, I'm afraid I'll lose myself. I need to get up. I need to find Nadia and beg for her forgiveness.

But, I can't move.

I can't see.

I'm nothing.

## NADIA

Alyssa pulls to the curb, and I glance around for signs of my father. There aren't enough seats in the car for everyone, but I'm not leaving anyone behind. It's unsafe to make several trips. The HPA will search the area for their lost prisoners.

Alyssa points out the window. "Over there."

Three figures emerge from the thick brush on the side of the road, none of them tall enough to be my father. My heart sinks into my stomach, panic sweeping over me. Mr. Augustine flings open the back door, and I blink a few times to clear my tears. He, Liv, and a young girl, who I suspect to be Ella, slide onto the backseat. Mr. Augustine grimaces when he meets my eyes and shuts the door.

Alyssa drives away from the curb without saying a word. There's no need for it. It's obvious the others aren't joining us.

On the mournfully silent ride home, I let my tears stream freely down my face. It's hard to hold it together when my life is crumbling to dust. My heart aches as I imagine the pieces drifting away from me forever.

The empty neighborhood greets us with a light dusting of snow on the street. No one is out this time of night. I'm thankful for the shadows that obscure the pain in my eyes. The night air wraps me in its black depths and hides the tears that won't stop. I wish I could float to the sky and fade away into its never-ending darkness.

Gliding to my room, I sink into my bed without turning on the light. I'd give anything to close my eyes and sleep. To experience what it's like to dream again. I'm afraid if I'm allowed to think about everything that happened tonight, I'll live my own personal nightmare. I want to think of the best case scenario, that both Hunter and my father are fine, but I can't get my hopes up. I must prepare for the worse thing imaginable—that they're both dead.

My bedroom door creaks open, and a small figure slips into my room. A veil of low light peeks through my curtain and reflects off Ella's fiery red hair. She reminds me of Alyssa, and I wonder if that's why my father fought so fiercely to protect her—if that's why he gave up his freedom, and possibly his life, for this girl.

Ella sits on the edge of my bed and touches my leg. Shadows cover her face in the darkness, but her green eyes reflect what little light comes into my room. She wears a pair of Alyssa's pajamas and the too-long sleeves scrunch up to her elbows.

She stares at the floor. "Alyssa said Dmitri was your daddy."

I force myself to sit up and lean against the wall. "Yeah." I don't know what else to say. Hearing my father's name is like taking a red-hot iron to my chest.

"He's going to be okay." She sounds so certain that I almost believe her. I want to believe her so badly.

"I hope so." The words burn in my throat, making my voice come out low.

Ella shifts and scoots closer to me. Tucking her feet under her, she slides her arm around me. She rests her head on my shoulder, and I lean my head on hers. My sadness eases as she comforts me, and it reminds me of my father. It makes my heart hurt a little less when I imagine she learned it from him.

"He will. Hunter likes him and won't let anyone hurt him."

My mouth falls open at Hunter's name. Of course she knows who he is. He's the one who has been watching over them.

"Did you see Hunter before you left?" It's a risk asking Ella about him, but I can't stop myself. I need some sort of clue about what to expect. If she saw him, he could still be okay. *Unless the HPA found out...*

She shakes her head. "I was too scared to look. There was this loud alarm that hurt my ears and then a lady blocked the door. It's why Dmitri had to stay behind with Uncle Blake. Liv couldn't help everyone."

I imagine the alarm went off to notify the facility there were intruders, but how did they find out? Jacqueline swore up and down that everyone would be fine, that it would be easy enough. I should've gone with them—things could've been different. *Things could've been worse, too.*

I push the thought away. I guess it's a good thing she didn't see Hunter. Maybe he left when our phone conversation got cut off.

"So, my father's still alive," I say.

She squeezes me. "I think so. They like him there."

A small smile plays on my lips. I know Ella is wrong about the HPA liking my father, but I'm not going to say anything.

She needs to hold onto her naivety as long as she can. The world is a much better place when you believe everything is going to be okay in the end. I wish I could think the same way she does. I haven't thought that way since my mother's death, and if something happens to my father, I don't think I'll ever think that way again.

Ella's breathing changes as she starts to drift off to sleep. My stomach burns, and I slide out from under her and glide from my room. Mr. Augustine and Liv murmur to each other on the couch. When their eyes meet mine, grief washes through me all over again.

Alyssa struts in from the kitchen with a few mugs of coffee on a tray, and she sets them on the coffee table. She flops onto the armchair, and I perch on the arm of the couch.

I finally find my voice to talk to Liv and Mr. Augustine. "So, what happened? What went wrong?"

Liv stares into her steaming mug. "Blake let his anger get the best of him when we ran into an unexpected agent."

My heart pounds, and Alyssa eyes me. This is all my fault. Hunter wasn't supposed to be at the facility. He was supposed to be meeting me. I consider telling Liv and Mr. Augustine about Hunter now, but what good will it do? Telling someone the secret I fought so hard to protect after the fact won't change anything. I made a mistake that caused things to fall apart.

Alyssa takes a sip of coffee and rests the mug on her knee. "I saw Blake's death," she says.

And now a man's dead because I wanted to protect

Hunter—I still do.

Mr. Augustine releases a long sigh and rubs his handkerchief over his head. "I was hoping they'd just put him in a cell like the others."

Liv frowns. "Blake would've never let that happen."

I tap my fingers on my knee. "What happened to the agent?" I look at Alyssa again. "I mean the one who pulled the alarm?"

Liv's electric blue eyes meet mine. "Blake did a number on him. I'm sure he regrets ever stepping through that door."

My stomach lurches, my vision darkening around the edges as her words cut deep into my soul. I need to get out of here. I'm sick with worry and grief to think Hunter was hurt by someone I asked help from. It's my fault he was in that situation. I should've involved him. Things would've been different if I had.

Guilt consumes me. It squeezes my chest and snakes its way into my mind. It's all I can feel. I can't escape it. What if this turns Hunter back to the HPA? What if he thinks I've clouded his judgment all along and that creatures are as awful as the HPA says we are? What if he hates me and can never forgive me?

I need to get out of here.

My eyes sweep around the room. I jump to my feet and glide to the door, ignoring the voices calling my name. I rush off into the night. It's all I can think to do. I just want to forget everything.

# 18

❧

# STAR-CROSSED

❧

## HUNTER

A RHYTHMIC BEEP lulls me in and out of sleep. Machines click and swoosh, and every so often, it feels like ice water pours into my veins. My eyelids flutter and glaring light sends shooting pain through my head, so I concentrate on keeping my eyes shut.

"Hunter? Can you hear me? It's Mom."

I press my lips together and cringe at the pain of putting pressure on my split lip. Dr. Sullivan is the last person I want to see. By the sound of crinkling paper, I know she has a dozen papers with a thousand questions on them for me to answer.

"I feel like crap," I mutter.

"It's the drugs wearing off. I can administer some more painkillers if you need them."

My stomach flops, and I force my eyes to open. "I'll live. I just need to go home." I hit the button to raise the back of my bed and swing my bare legs over, touching my feet to the cool tile. It takes a minute for everything to register, but I notice my hand is in a cast and I'm covered in bruises.

Dr. Sullivan's heels click as she crosses the room. She touches my shoulder, and I wince in pain. "Lie back down. You need to rest."

"I can rest at home."

She digs her nails into my shoulder. "Just stay a few more hours until you're cleared."

I sigh and slump back. Pain bursts in my head, my eyes blurring. I swear under my breath and rub my good hand over my eyes. It takes a few minutes to find my concentration. Dr. Sullivan stares at me in pity.

I almost don't hear the knock on the door through the pounding in my ears, but a few seconds later, the door swings open and Jacqueline struts in. She looks me up and down and then meets the gaze of Dr. Sullivan. They hold each other in a stare for a minute and turn to look at me.

Jacqueline sits on the edge of my bed next to me and gently touches my chin with her fingers as she studies my face. "That monster got you good," she says.

I blink a few times. "I put up a good fight, though."

The last thing I want to talk about with Jacqueline is getting my ass kicked, but with Dr. Sullivan listening to us, there's not much else to say. I wish she'd leave already, so I can find out about Nadia. I hope she's okay.

"What were you doing there anyway, Hunter?" Dr. Sullivan asks, interrupting us.

I rub my face with my good hand again. "I stop by when I can't sleep. I was making progress with Creature 1252. He was starting to trust me."

Dr. Sullivan tugs a pen from her lab coat pocket and makes a note on the top sheet of paper on the clipboard she had tucked under her arm. "I think he still does. I watched the video and how he listened to you after the supers took the girl. Are you comfortable with returning to the green zone?"

I nod. "It's my job."

Dr. Sullivan turns to Jacqueline. "And you, Agent Camille? Are you comfortable returning to the green zone?"

"If you allow me to."

"Mistakes happen. None of this was in your control, Camille," Dr. Sullivan says with a sad smile. At least she believes Jacqueline and doesn't suspect she was behind everything. She looks between the two of us and taps her pen on the clipboard. She raises her eyes to mine. "One more question. Do you think the intruders were sent by the Creature Council?"

I shrug. "I was too busy trying not to get killed to ask."

Jacqueline stares at her hands. "No, the little monster they took called the terminated one Uncle Blake. This was personal."

Dr. Sullivan writes something down and looks over at me and smiles. "Rest up, Hunter." She turns to Jacqueline. "Will you see him home if he's cleared?"

Jacqueline nods. "Yes, ma'am."

Dr. Sullivan saunters from the room, and Jacqueline rests her hand on my good one. Her red eyes glass over with what looks like the weight of the world on her shoulders. She wipes her eyes and clears her throat but doesn't say anything.

After a minute of somber silence, I say, "See if you can get me cleared now. We can stop at my house, and then I have somewhere I need to be."

## NADIA

I sit on the snowy steps of Northern Bell High. It's been three days with no word from Hunter. His phone goes straight to voicemail, and I couldn't leave a message even if I wanted to. Mr. Augustine won't allow me to stay at home and mope, because he says my father would want me to keep living.

But this isn't about my father.

It's about Hunter.

I don't even know how to contact Jacqueline.

"Hey, girl. I missed you in Econ." Evie sets her folder on the cold steps and sits next to me.

I look at her in my peripheral vision. "Wasn't feeling it today."

"I don't feel it every day," she says with a laugh. "Want to get out of here?"

I open my mouth to tell her no, but then the word, "Yes,"

slips out instead.

"I think I saw Alyssa at her locker. Should I invite her?"

Staring at the frozen lawn, I nod. "Yeah, she'll be pissed if I ditch without her."

Evie stands and rushes inside. The door swings open a minute later, and Evie and Alyssa barrel out toward me. I get to my feet and run behind them as we race to Evie's old SUV.

She knocks trash off the seat so I can slide into the front next to her. Alyssa hops in back, sitting in the middle to lean forward. Evie starts the engine and reverses, grinning at me. I shift in my seat to smile at Alyssa, who meets me with a smirk.

"I haven't seen you smile in days," Alyssa says.

Evie looks at me in her peripheral vision. "Something happen?"

I shrug. "I can't reach Hunter."

She frowns. "Did you stop by his house?"

I regret even saying anything. "His aunt hates me." I've never met Hunter's aunt, and he never talks about her. They're only roommates who cross paths every few weeks because if Hunter isn't with the HPA, he's with me.

Evie taps her fingers on the steering wheel. "I'll do it for you. What's his address?"

*No! No way. This will get us all killed.*

"Not going to happen." I lean on the door. "It's really okay."

Alyssa leans between the seats. "Take I-35 to Lakeview."

I grimace and shift in my seat. "Are you crazy?"

Alyssa shrugs. "You want answers, don't you? Nothing bad will happen. Promise."

I don't argue. Evie accelerates onto the freeway, and I press my head into the headrest. My need to see Hunter outweighs my fear of getting caught, and I put my fate in Alyssa's ability.

Evie turns and smiles again before looking back at the road. "Don't look so worried. I bet it's all a misunderstanding. I saw the way Hunter looked at you. You're meant for each other."

But what if we aren't? What if we're star-crossed and only bad will come from our love? It's possible that we're not good for each other or for other people for that matter. I hate even to think it, but what if the only real way to have a normal life is if I'm alone?

*You don't want a normal life.*

But maybe I do.

## HUNTER

"I need help," I say. My jeans hang halfway down, my casted hand making it difficult to do anything without assistance.

Jacqueline turns from the wall to look at me. She laughs. "Seriously?"

Heat rushes over my face. "Never mind. I'll just walk like a penguin to keep them up."

She laughs again, pushes from my bed, and meanders over to me with a smirk plastered on her face. She tugs up the waist of my jeans and slides the zipper.

"Watch it," I say.

She grins as she buttons. "Next time ask Nadia."

I roll my eyes. "Come on. She gets out of school soon."

"Think she's there after everything?"

"I won't know until we get there."

The doorbell rings, and I hear my aunt pad to the living room. I shuffle into the hallway and lean against the wall. Jacqueline comes up next to me, and I hold my index finger to my mouth.

"Evie? What're you doing here?" my aunt says.

"Hi, Christine! I didn't know you were Hunter's aunt. I was just coming here to visit."

I peek around the corner and see the friend Nadia introduced me to the other day. I'm shocked seeing the girl on my porch, but more surprised she knows my aunt.

"That's sweet of you." My aunt turns away from the door and calls, "Hunter! You have a visitor."

I turn my gaze to Jacqueline, whose brows knit in confusion. She's never met Nadia's classmate so she doesn't understand how complicated this situation is.

*It's nothing. It's just a coincident.*

I inhale a deep breath, my chest aching because of my two broken ribs, and hobble into the small living room. My aunt smiles at me, her brown eyes crinkling in the corners, and she tucks her dark blond hair behind her ear.

I swallow and clutch the back of the couch. "Evie? What're you doing here?"

Jacqueline comes up behind me and stands next to me. Evie's eyes glance to her and back to me. She frowns before forcing a smile. Heat crawls up my neck. I probably look guilty even though there's nothing going on between Jacqueline and me, and I don't have to worry if Evie tells Nadia.

Evie crosses her arms. "I came because Na—"

"I'm glad you're here," I say, cutting her off. "Do you two know each other? I thought I heard you say something."

My aunt offers me a small smile, one of pity because of my condition. "Evie is Dovina Thompson's daughter."

My head spins, and I stumble into Jacqueline. I blink a few times as cold fear drains the color from my face. Dovina Thompson is a doctor from Northern Trinity Hope Hospital. She's an HPA member, which means that Evie's friendship to Nadia is toxic and could possibly get her killed. How she managed to end up at the same high school as Nadia is alarming.

"You look like you've seen a ghost, Hunter. You need to sit down," my aunt says, coming around the couch to me.

I pull out of her grasp. "I'm fine. I just need to eat something. I have some leftover Chinese food in the fridge. Mind heating it up?"

My aunt nods and struts to the kitchen.

I bring my eyes to Evie's. "Dr. Thompson has a long commute."

Evie shakes her head. "I live with my dad."

Things start to make more sense. "I'm sorry. I didn't even know Dr. Thompson had a daughter."

Evie shrugs. "It's nothing. We don't see each other often. My parents split when I was young. My mom's a workaholic and my dad thought family should come first."

It's possible that Evie doesn't know anything about the HPA or the supernatural world. While it's a lot safer now for Nadia, Evie is still dangerous by association. Any attention Evie gets from her mom is attention from the HPA. It could be a disaster.

Evie fidgets and glances at the open door behind her. "So, are you two...?" Her voice trails off.

My stomach churns as nausea sweeps over me. I lower my voice so my aunt doesn't overhear. "Camille is my coworker. I can't drive in my condition, and she was about to take me to Nadia's."

"Oh, awesome, okay. Well, I just saved you a trip." Stepping closer, she whispers, "Nadia told me how Christine hates her, so she's waiting in the car with her sister."

I'm guessing she's talking about Alyssa, and that explains how Evie found out where I live. I hobble to the coat rack and use my good hand to toss half my coat on. Jacqueline laughs, and I glare at her, but I don't ask her for help. I'd rather freeze than have her hold this over my head.

I glance over my shoulder as the microwave beeps. "Hey, Aunt Christine, I'm going to grab a bite to eat with Evie instead. I'll see you later."

I don't wait for her to respond but instead let Evie help me walk out to her car with Jacqueline meandering behind us. She parked a lot farther than I'd have liked, but I'm glad. I wouldn't want to risk Nadia getting caught.

We reach the corner of my street, and I spot pale blond hair blowing out the window of an SUV. When I see Nadia's beautiful face, all my pain magnifies, and I stumble a few feet before Jacqueline and Evie steady me. How am I going to tell her that her father is still in a cell because of me?

How I'm the reason a man died?

How I wouldn't forgive me either?

## NADIA

Hunter's so bruised and broken that my heart shatters into a million pieces seeing the pain he's in. His eyes shine with unshed tears, and his lips pull down in the corners as he grimaces when he should be smiling.

I jump from the car and rush to him, my feet pounding on the salted street. I don't touch him when I reach him, and just stand a foot away, studying his face. His right eye shadows with a blue bruise, and an angry cut splits his bottom lip. The bruises on his neck match a handprint, and he walks with a limp. His hazel eyes convey more than pain—they're shrouded in a mix of fear and uncertainty.

He reaches out his hand, his eyes squinting in pain, and he touches my cheek. His scabbed fingers feel rough as he runs his hand along my skin. I touch his shoulder, making him wince, but I want so badly to hug him. That's when I see the white cast on his other hand, the tips of his deeply bruised fingers peeking out. I can't believe this happened to him—that I let this happen to him.

"Oh, Hunter," I whisper.

He swipes a tear from my cheek. "I'm okay, really."

"How could I let this happen?"

He presses his finger to my lips, leans down, and whispers, "I have something important to tell you."

# 19



# WHAT WE NEED FOR CHANGE

## NADIA

ALYSSA, JACQUELINE, AND Evie take a walk while I get some alone time with Hunter. Hunter and I sit in the third row of the SUV, hidden behind tinted windows. I run my finger over his swollen jaw and lean in and graze my cool lips across the bruise.

He shudders, tilting his head to meet my lips. He kisses me hard despite his split lip and I taste coppery blood rolling over my tongue. He sinks into me, and I slide my arms around him, holding him as gently as possible.

He leans his forehead on my shoulder, releasing a shallow breath. "It feels like it's been forever."

I suck in my top lip and nod. "I thought you were dead."

"I almost was."

Tears leak from my eyes. I blink to clear them, but they keep pouring, blurring my vision. It's like my body tries to save me from seeing the look on Hunter's face, the pain in his expression as he remembers what happened.

I sniffle. "This is my fault."

He tucks my hair behind my ear. "It's not. You were protecting me."

I shake my head. "I was protecting my father. I knew if you were there, they'd fail."

"You mean they failed because of me, not just because I was there. You should be blaming me, not yourself. I ruined the only opportunity Dmitri had to escape. A man died, too."

I twine my fingers through his. "I'd never blame you. And Blake, it was his choice. He knew the risks and he would've never let the HPA take him alive."

He nods, holding my gaze. "So, what now?"

"We move past this. It's all we can do. You need to heal and watch over my father until I come up with another plan."

I kiss his cheek and breathe in his scent—a mixture of musk, antiseptic, and a hint of citrus. It's comforting, being in his arms, and my fears hide in the shadows of my mind. I can't think about the terrible things happening in the world or what horrifying things may come. I need to think about Hunter and how he's alive and with me, and how much I love him.

Shifting in my arms, he gazes out the window. A million

thoughts swirl behind his hazel eyes. I wish I could hear his thoughts, just for a second, so I can tell him not to worry—that in this moment it's me and him, and the world is all outside the car. In this small space, we are each other's world, and we're okay.

He rests his cast on the armrest of the door. "There's something else I need to tell you."

My heart stops at the tone of his voice. I'm not sure it's going to start back up again. I inhale a long breath through my nose to settle my nerves. My head pounds as my heart's frantic beating now drums in my ears.

He squeezes my hand. "You need to keep your distance from Evie."

I frown, surprise and confusion washing through me. "What? She's my only friend at school besides Alyssa."

"Nadia, listen."

I hold my hand up as anger rushes through me. "No, you listen, Hunter. You can't tell me who I can and can't be friends with. Did you really think this conversation would go in a positive direction? Evie drove me here to see you. She's a good person. You don't even know her."

He cringes at the high-pitch sound of my voice. "I'm not telling you to stop being her friend. Just be careful. How much do you know about her?" His brows furrow as he sits up straighter.

"Where is this coming from?" I don't understand how our conversation could shift from the failed attempt to save my father to who I can hang out with at school.

He glares at me for a second before sighing and pressing his lips together. "I went about this all the wrong way. I'm sorry."

My shoulders relax. "The last thing I want is to be angry at you. Now, please, tell me why you suddenly hate Evie."

He closes his eyes. "I don't. It's just that she knows my aunt."

I twist my lips to the side. "What are you saying?"

Lacing his fingers through mine, he meets my eyes. "Evie's mom is an HPA doctor."

## HUNTER

Nadia's angry, indigo eyes shift to ones filled with disbelief. Her pale lips part as she blinks away her never-ending tears. Her hand trembles in mine, and I bring it up and kiss her knuckles. I shouldn't have told her now. It wasn't the right time, not when she has so many other things to stress about, but I had to do it before something happened. It would've never been the right time anyway.

She runs her free hand into her hair and sits with her head bowed. "I can't believe this." Pushing to her feet, she hunches over as she swings the back door open. "Stay here. I need to find Alyssa."

My body screams in pain as I snatch the back of her jacket. "Wait, Nadia, I don't think Evie's an immediate threat. She lives with her dad. I don't think she knows about any of this. I wanted to warn you just in case."

She eyes me over her shoulder before slumping onto the

seat. "I thought the HPA grooms everyone to serve them."

I shake my head. "Some people don't involve their kids until they think they're ready. You'd be surprised how many people want to give their children a normal childhood."

Her gaze drops to her hands. Without having to say it, I know she's thinking about my mom and how she puts the HPA before me and Mason. I don't think any less of my childhood because of her selfishness. I always had Mason. It's only been the last few years I despise her for—how she destroyed my relationship with my brother, and how she wouldn't think twice about doing it again.

On the other hand, I couldn't imagine how terrible it must be to be thrown into this world without a clue. Unless I tell Evie first and show her the truth, the HPA will taint her view on things.

"I hope Evie never finds out," Nadia says.

I shift my legs. "At least not from the HPA."

Her eyes light up. She's thinking the same thing I did. "You think if she found out from me, we could get her on our side first? I could show her she can trust me."

I shrug. "I don't know if I want you to tell her. It could go horribly wrong."

"Or this could be what we need to make a change."

Nadia sounds so convincing, but I have a hard time believing it'll be as easy as she thinks it'll be. The HPA is very persuasive. Evie doesn't stand a chance against them. They'll brainwash her the moment they suspect she's a creature sympathizer, even if she's not a part of the organization.

I rub my finger across the top of her hand. "Let's think about how to save your father first."

She glances at me from under her long, white lashes. "This can't wait. I'm going to tell her today."

I sigh. "Nadia, please, just think about it."

"I have. She needs to know before it's too late."

Her mind is set and there's nothing I can say to convince her otherwise. "Then we'll tell her together."

## NADIA

My hands tremble as I watch Alyssa, Jacqueline, and Evie stroll down the street in our direction. I've never dreamed of telling a normal human about me, and I don't know exactly what to say to make me not sound like a monster. Maybe I'll tell her about Alyssa first, because her ability is more acceptable to humans.

Hunter sits on the side of the backseat with the door open, and I stand outside the car and lean between his legs with his arms wrapped around my neck. His cast rests heavy on my collarbone, and I hold his free hand.

Alyssa meets my gaze and presses her thin lips together. She's already seen me make the decision to tell Evie about our world, but I can't tell if she knows the outcome. I stroll up to Alyssa and pull her away without looking at anyone.

"Evie's mother is an HPA doctor. I'm going to tell Evie about our world before the HPA can feed her lies," I whisper.

Alyssa nods. "She'll believe us and take our side. Unless something happens to change her mind about our world, I see her as an ally."

I shift my eyes to Evie, who offers an ear-to-ear grin. Her red and brown hair blows behind her, and she pulls her jacket tighter.

Jacqueline raises her eyebrows, stopping a few feet back. "I should get you home, Hunter. You look like you're going to pass out."

Hunter puts his feet on the ground. "Blame Nadia. She's about to do something stupid."

I glare at him. "Not doing it would be stupid."

Three pairs of eyes glance between us, and Alyssa tugs on her red braid. She nods, barely moving her head, encouraging me. I can't believe this is really happening.

"I don't—"

I raise my hand and cut Jacqueline off before turning my eyes to Evie's. "I have something I need to tell Evie," I say.

Evie points to herself like she misunderstood me.

I nod. "I need you to listen carefully with an open mind." Pushing away from Hunter, I close the distance between us.

"You're freaking me out," Evie says.

I puff air through my lips. "Please, don't be scared. That's the last thing I want. But, you're going to think I'm crazy."

"Okay." Her voice sounds barely above a whisper.

A million thoughts swirl through my mind. How am I supposed to tell her about the creatures in the world and how they integrate themselves among humans? Or how there are humans who hate us because they don't understand, and how her mother is one of them? What if she doesn't believe me? What if she does but is afraid? What if she tells someone? A lot can go wrong. *You want her to trust you, so you need to trust her, too.*

I clear my throat. "Do you believe in the supernatural?"

She frowns. "Like ghosts?"

I shrug. "And other things."

"I don't know, maybe. Why?"

At least she thinks there's a possibility. "Because Alyssa and I—" I glance at Jacqueline. "And Camille are different."

She narrows her eyes, shifting on her feet. "Are you witches or something?"

The fact that she's not screaming is a good sign. I shake my head. "Not exactly, but we have special abilities."

She looks at Hunter behind me. "What about him?"

The SUV squeaks, and Hunter limps to me. "If I did, I probably wouldn't have been beaten up."

Evie laughs nervously. "You're joking with me."

"I wish they were. It'd make my life a lot easier," Hunter says.

I'm surprised he's speaking up. He was dead-set against telling Evie and now he's directing the conversation.

"You see, Evie," Hunter continues. "My Aunt Christine doesn't hate Nadia. She actually doesn't know about her because she's special." He smiles at me. "But people like my mom and your mom, they don't see it. They think Nadia is a monster out to destroy humanity. They'd like nothing more than to lock

Alyssa up in a cage, and Camille, well, they'd murder her again if they knew."

Evie blinks a few times. "Again? What? You're right, Nadia, this does sound crazy. And my mom? My mom is a doctor. She wouldn't hurt anyone. She took an oath."

"Anyone who was human," Jacqueline says. She looks Evie up and down. "She's never told you any of this? Do you know what the Human Preservation Agency is?"

Evie's eyes light up. "I do know that name. My dad said my mom was brainwashed into thinking that company was her new family. It's why she left us." She pinches the bridge of her nose. "So, why are you telling me all this?"

I wait for her to look at me. "Because I needed to tell you before the HPA brainwashes you and convinces you we are bad. When Hunter realized who you were, he wanted me to distance myself from you. But I felt you'd be on my side, though. You're one of my only friends. I didn't want to ruin our friendship."

Her eyes soften, and she smiles. But then, just as quick, she furrows her brows and glares at Hunter. "You know you can't tell Nadia who to be friends with. And you said your mom works for that company, too. But, you don't hate Nadia. Why?"

Hunter blows a breath through his lips. "It's a really complicated story, but I'm a reformed guy. I also work for the HPA, but it's because I want to protect Nadia."

"You're working for the enemy?"

I laugh. I can't help it. I'm so relieved Evie believes me and that she already thinks the HPA is our enemy. I touch her shoulder. "Camille does, too. They're a team. They want to change the ideals of the HPA. We can trust them—but only them. You can't tell anyone about us. It could get us all killed, including you. If anyone asks, play stupid. I'm serious."

Her mouth opens and closes and then she shakes her head. "This is a lot to take in."

I fidget. "I know it's hard, but I didn't want to keep lying to you, and I know you'll keep our secret."

Evie blinks a few times. "Well, thanks for trusting me."

Jacqueline clears her throat. "Not all of us do."

I glare at Jacqueline. "This is what we need for change."

Evie purses her lips. "I don't understand."

Alyssa slings her arm around Evie's shoulder. "You will soon enough. I saw it."

Hunter chuckles from behind me. I tilt my head to his chest and smile from Alyssa to Jacqueline, and then to Evie. She crosses her arms and looks from the ground back to me and then shrugs.

"Alyssa is a seer. She sees what the future is like when a decision is made," I say.

Alyssa grins. "And you decided to trust us."

Jacqueline grimaces. "For now." She turns to Hunter. "I need to get you back home. My shift starts soon."

My heart aches having to leave Hunter. Turning to him, I gently wrap my arms around his neck. He leans down and kisses me. Tears trickle from my eyes. I can't help it. It hurts so much to leave him.

He brushes my hair behind my ear. "Call Camille if you need anything." He turns to Jacqueline. "Get Alyssa's phone number. We need to stay connected. Things might be different now."

Alyssa and Jacqueline trade numbers, and Jacqueline memorizes the nine digits without taking the small slip of paper. I hug Hunter once more and bury my face into his shoulder. I already miss him when Jacqueline helps him walk home. I turn away before he disappears around the corner.

Evie shifts her weight from foot to foot. "Now what?"

Alyssa smiles as we all get into the car. When she shuts her door, she leans between the seats and says, "Head to the city. It's better to show you."

# 20

# THE BEST INTENTIONS

### HUNTER

I COULDN'T STAY at home any longer. I hate feeling like a prisoner. It took a lot of nerve calling my brother, but I needed him for a ride. I convinced Mason to drop me off at the termination facility, despite him still being angry. He didn't speak the entire ride, even after I apologized, and I know our relationship as brothers is doomed. He didn't stick around after dropping me off, and I waited in the parking lot for thirty minutes before I mustered up the courage to walk through the door.

"Agent Hunter, I'm surprised to see you. Agent Camille said you'd be out for a few weeks," Phillip says.

I hobble past his desk toward the elevator. "Only death could keep me away from here," I mutter and hit the down button.

Phillip laughs. "I see a seat on the board in your future."

I don't respond, and the elevator dings open, cutting our conversation short. I don't think I could fake it another minute. Jacqueline turns to look over her shoulder and frowns when she meets my gaze.

She stands up and crosses her arms. "You're supposed to be at home."

I shrug. "I have a job to do."

"I'm pulling a double shift to cover you."

I roll my eyes. "I don't care. You can make sure I don't pass out or something. I can't stay home. I need to keep busy."

She sighs. "Fine, but I don't have to like it."

Smirking, I hobble down the corridor to Dmitri's room. It's been a few days since I've been here, and I need to see for myself that he's okay and that the HPA didn't punish him for the invasion. I punch in my pass code and swing the door open.

He sits up on his cot and frowns. "You look awful."

I chuckle. "I feel awful."

"You should be at home healing."

"Why does everyone keep saying that? I have a job to do, so I'm going to do it." I grip the wall to steady myself. "Now, if you don't mind, I have a few questions for you."

Dmitri's eyes shadow. Leaning back, he laces his fingers behind his head. "Go on."

"Why didn't you try to escape?"

He tilts his head toward the ceiling. "I've become quite comfortable here."

## NADIA

When we enter the hallway to The Haven, Cian raises his eyebrows and scoots off his stool to stand. He sets his magazine on his chair and smiles, but it's not like the normal, flirtatious smile he usually gives. This one's forced, almost bitter, and his eyes don't crinkle in the corners.

"Does Sandy know you girls are here?" he asks.

I shrug. "We ditched." I turn toward Evie. "This is Evie. She's cool, I promise."

He looks her up and down and then crosses his arms. "You girls should just head home. You know the city is a bad place right now."

I lift my hand and touch his scruffy cheek. "Come on, Cian. My father would be disappointed you sent us away from what he considers the safest place around."

His gaze drops to the floor. I know it was a low blow, but I want Evie to see how normal everyone is. This might be my only chance to convince her we're not all monsters and that she can trust me.

Alyssa steps up next to me. "We won't be any trouble. You can trust us. Evie is special. I saw a vision about her, and she's on our side."

Cian puffs air through his lips. "Fine, but don't stay long. The patrons are suspicious of new people, especially nonmembers."

I beam my brightest smile and kiss his cheek. He opens the door, and I hook my arm through Evie's. Alyssa follows behind us as we make our way into the noisy club. We dance our way through the pulsating crowd on the dance floor until we reach the black leather booth in the far corner, near the kitchen. It's the best spot to sit, with our backs to the wall, and closest to the back exit. We should be safe. *Well, Evie should be safe.*

Evie sits between Alyssa and me, and we watch the other patrons. I peer over the crowd to see what kind of creatures hang out today and lean on my elbows, knowing that most of the creatures are harmless.

"This place is amazing," Evie says. "I would've never guessed anyone here was different."

Alyssa nods toward a booth with four attractive men, most likely in their early twenties, clinking their glasses together. "Don't let their pretty faces fool you. That's a clan of ogres."

Evie frowns. "Really?"

I nod. "Most creatures have human-like qualities, but once you know what sets a creature apart from a human, they're easy to identify." I lean closer. "Watch when one of them talks. You'll notice their bottom teeth have a pretty bad overbite and their lower canines are sharper than normal."

"I see it," Evie whispers.

"Also see how their ears curl at the tops?"

An ogre with shaggy, black hair glances up. I scoot closer to Evie, like my closeness alone will keep her safe. The man's jaw shifts, and he smiles, revealing rotting teeth. He obviously over-heard us, and it takes everything in me not to glide up to the booth and snap at him for trying to scare my friend.

"Oh, crap," Evie whispers.

Alyssa raises her hand to her mouth and blows the man a kiss. His jaw falls back into place. Human-like teeth slide in front of his rotten ones as he makes himself appear more human than ogre. He winks, and I release a breath, laughing nervously. It's always hard to determine how a creature will react.

"They're hot-tempered, strong, and violent, but easily charmed," Alyssa says. "As long as you don't badger them, they'll leave you alone."

Evie nods. "Good to know."

I touch her knee under the table. "Don't be scared."

Evie glances at me. "I'm not. Everything is just so strange. Unbelievable, really. Now, tell me about someone else."

I nod toward Maddie, the bartender. "She's a pixie. They're known for their incredible resourcefulness, food and drink talent, and well, pixie dust. When you look at her closely, you'll see her pointy ears and notice she leaves a glitter-like dust on everything she touches."

Evie's eyes widen. "That's so cliché."

"Don't tell them that. Being dusted is not fun."

"Seriously?"

Alyssa slides to the edge of the round booth. "Want to see for yourself?"

**HUNTER**

"Does that mean you're willing to cooperate?" I ask, wobbling on my shaking legs to the chair at the bare desk. I sink into it and rest my elbows on my knees, holding my head up.

Dmitri stares at the ceiling. "To an extent. I'm not oblivious to what the HPA does."

I gaze at the blinking camera, wondering how many eyes watch besides Jacqueline. "Why?"

"You're questioning why I'm cooperating?"

"Suppose I am."

Dmitri rubs his chin. It's not until now that I notice he doesn't grow a beard. Not because he chooses not to, but because he can't. The HPA doesn't provide razors so I know he's not shaving it.

He stares at the ceiling for another minute before saying, "I guess it's to show you I'm not the human-terrorizing, man-eating, child-snatching creature the HPA swears all non-humans are."

I rub my hand over my head. I'm not going to ask him what he is because I already know the answer to that. I'm afraid he'll be willing to tell me, which means the HPA would know, too. I can't risk them knowing about Nadia's species.

"So, you don't eat food or people, you're not a baby stealer, and you don't live to traumatize humans."

"Correct. My job in life is to protect people."

I blink the surprise from my face. I think he expected me to ask what he does, and he was smart enough to offer an explanation. Sure, it's what he does for the council, but it could pass off as a special ability.

"Do you have a name?"

"You're well aware my name is Dmitri."

I chuckle. I can't help it. The HPA is probably glaring at me behind their monitors, too. "I meant your kind."

"It's not really a kind. The council calls me an escort, and I don't know any others like myself in the States."

My heart slows, feeling a lot better knowing he isn't going to mention Nadia. "That's a terrible name."

He lifts an eyebrow, not understanding what I'm implying, which is probably for the best considering he's my girlfriend's dad. "Would you prefer a protector?"

"That works," I say, sitting up straighter. "You mentioned there is no one like you in the U.S. Does that mean you're not from here?" It's strange sitting here, talking to Nadia's dad like we're good friends. I hope we have the chance to be friends one day. I hope when all of this is said and done and I meet him as Nadia's boyfriend and not an HPA agent, he'll remember my kindness.

"That's right. I'm nomadic by nature. I lived all over Europe as a child."

I'm surprised because of his lack of accent. I'd have never guessed. I wonder if Nadia knows. *He's her father. Of course she knows.*

I open my mouth to ask another question, but a knock on the door interrupts me. Staring at the small window, I wait for the door to swing open, but it doesn't. Instead, the person knocks again. My gaze shifts from Dmitri to the door, and then I struggle to get to my feet. I meander to the door and hit my code to unlock it and exit into the corridor.

Dr. Sullivan stands three feet away with the biggest smile I've ever seen her offer, taking up most of her face. Her dark hair twists off her shoulders in a clip, and her gold-framed glasses hang from her lab coat pocket. She tucks her clipboard under her arm and steps closer. She slides one arm over my shoulder in a half hug before pulling back to smile again.

I stiffen, a knot forming in my stomach. "What?"

"The board is impressed by your sudden breakthrough with Creature 1252." She squeezes my good arm.

I wince as her fingers dig into me. "Why?"

"Because he agreed to cooperate. We'd like to study him more in a laboratory setting."

*Oh, crap.* "I just got him talking."

"I know, and it's great, but the board would like to have someone more qualified take over. You can assist them with interrogation if they feel they need it."

This isn't good news. The board is no longer going to sit back and just watch Dmitri. If he's being transferred to the lab, it means the study will be invasive and possibly deadly. He'll be a lab rat until they decide there's nothing more they need from him or until they accidentally kill him. It also means I won't be his caretaker anymore and no one is nicer than me.

I clench my jaw. "What if he trusts only me? Wants to cooperate with only me? I think you should give me more time.

Just tell me exactly what you want."

Dr. Sullivan shakes her head. "I know you want to prove what an excellent agent you are, but this isn't the way. I don't have time to train you and give you the resources you need to do something we have trained professionals for. You know this is just a holding area until decisions are made."

There's nothing I can say to change the board's decision. I just hope they give me time to prepare for it. I'll break Dmitri out on my own as soon as the last shift leaves for the night. I'll have to trust that Dmitri can help me get out with him, too. I'm not in the best shape to run—let alone fight. "When is that happening?"

"Ten minutes. No one knows other than you, Agent Camille, Agent Rob, and Agent Rosaline."

I clench my jaw. It'll be impossible to get Dmitri out in less than ten minutes. I stare through the window at Dmitri. The HPA moves fast and unexpectedly for security reasons. I need to call Nadia now and tell her what's going on. I won't have complete access to her dad much longer and then there is nothing Jacqueline and I can do to help him.

"Okay, mind if I sit down until then?" I lean against the wall, feigning a look of extreme pain.

"Oh, yes, relax. I don't want you to hurt yourself anymore than you already are. If it weren't important, I'd have you stay here," Dr. Sullivan says. She turns toward the entrance of the corridor. "Agent Camille? Please come help Agent Hunter."

Within a few seconds, Jacqueline arrives at my side and

hooks her arm around my back. We leave Dr. Sullivan in the corridor outside Dmitri's room, and Jacqueline guides me back to the monitors.

I lean into her, getting as close to her ear without looking suspicious, and whisper, "Give me your cell phone."

As she's helping me onto the seat, she slides it from her pocket to mine. She scribbles a number on a piece of paper, and I memorize it and tear it up to shove in my pocket. Jacqueline doesn't say anything. We stare blankly at our two charges on the monitor. At least Camden still has a chance.

I hear the click of Dr. Sullivan's heels before I see her. She smiles as she emerges from the corridor.

She taps her watch. "Seven minutes, Agent Hunter." Glancing at Jacqueline, she says, "Join me, Agent Camille. I need you to get the van ready."

Waiting a few seconds after they leave, I shuffle to the bathroom and lock the door behind me. I dial Alyssa's number and it rings and goes to voicemail. I swear under my breath. If someone doesn't pick up, I don't know what I'll do.

I redial and wait again. This time, a cacophony of noise bursts through the line, and I pull the phone from my ear. After listening to the music and laughter for a minute, the line finally goes silent, but my ears continue to ring.

"What's the matter?" It's Alyssa.

"It's me," I say. "Is Nadia around? It's important."

"Sure, Hunter, let me go get her. It'll be a minute."

The music and noise blasts through the line again, and

sweat beads on my forehead. A sudden knock on the door startles me. I swing my gaze from the phone to the door, and then back to the phone.

"Give me a second," I yell. "Can't a guy go to the bathroom around here?"

No one answers, but the knocking stops.

"Hunter?"

I was too distracted by the knock that I didn't hear the line go silent. I press the phone to my ear and whisper, "I only have a second, but they're transferring your dad to the lab. I'm going to try to intervene in the transfer, but I don't know how successful I'll be. I love you."

She gasps. "No!"

I cringe at the fear in her voice.

Another knock bangs on the door. "I have to go, Nadia. I'll call you back as soon as I can. I'm part of the transporting team."

"Hunter, wait. Don't hang up. Tell me where the lab is. I want to help you."

My chest tightens. "Let me do this, Nadia."

"You could barely walk the last time I saw you. I'm not letting you attempt to be a hero."

The knocking becomes incessant.

"I'm coming!" I yell. Pressing the phone to my ear one last time, I say, "I'm sorry, Nadia. I'm not letting you get involved. Your father wouldn't want you to either. I'll call you soon. I love you, okay? I promised I'd fix things. Now let me."

I hang up the phone and flush the toilet before running the faucet. Nadia's never going to forgive me for not letting her get involved, but I don't see how to protect her any other way. I just hope in the end she realizes I have the best intentions and that we can somehow get through this.

Opening the door, I meet Agent Rob's snarky smirk. He steps back to get out of my way, and when I pass him, he turns and swings his arm around my shoulders. Pain screams through my chest, and I groan. He watches me in his peripheral vision, smirking at me for an uncomfortably long time, gauging me.

"Tough doing things one handed," I quip, shoving him a few inches away.

His cocky presence alone aggravates me. He thinks he's better than everyone. It probably bothers him I was the one who got Dmitri to talk, since he's always in the field, making Agent Rosaline do all the dirty work.

"Need to work on your combat. I could kick your ass into shape. You look like hell, Sullivan."

"So do you."

He shoulders me, and it takes everything in me not to rip the taser from my belt and shove it into his neck. He's one of the few agents I disliked from the first time we met.

Jacqueline and Agent Rosaline lean against the counter, watching the monitors when we make it back to the viewing area. The elevator dings open, and out walks Dr. Sullivan again, this time holding a black duffle bag. She hands it to Agent Rob, and he looks through it without letting any of us see it.

He reaches in, pulls out a cloth bag, and tosses it to me. "Here, Sullivan, Creature 1252 is your responsibility. You'll also be riding in the back with me."

# 21

## NOT MADE OF TRAGEDY

### NADIA

THE ROOM SPINS, and I can't catch my breath. I'm terrified, hurt, disappointed, and furious. Hunter has lost his mind if he thinks I'm going to sit back and do nothing. He's even crazier if he thinks I won't hunt him down myself. I'm a fighter. I can't just hope for the best.

Fingers lock onto my shoulder, and I twist to meet Alyssa and Evie. Without even having to look in the mirror, I know my eyes are wild and I'm probably pretty scary to normal humans. My nightmare inflictor side crawls to the surface, begging to take hold of my humanity. It's been a while since I've felt like

I was losing control. This might throw me over the edge.

"We have to go. My father's in trouble," I say.

"Can you drive us back to school?" Alyssa asks Evie.

Evie glances between us. "That's at least an hour with traffic. I can drop you off where you need to be."

I wring my hands together. "It's not that simple. The HPA has my father."

"So, let me help. I'm not afraid of my mom's company."

I squeeze my eyes shut. "You should be."

Alyssa grabs my hand. "She's made up her mind. Don't worry. The HPA won't kill her if they know her mom is an HPA doctor."

Evie pleads with her eyes, and even though every ounce of my being screams this is a horrible idea, I can't tell her no. I need her. I lead Alyssa and Evie out the back exit. We reach Evie's SUV without another word. Evie idles in the quiet parking garage, waiting for me to give some sort of direction, but the problem is, I have no idea what to do.

Without a plan, I'll fail.

"I don't know where to go. Hunter wouldn't tell me where the lab was." My stomach twists in knots.

Alyssa leans between the seats. "Get on the highway and head north."

"To the termination facility?" I ask.

Evie looks in the rearview mirror. "Then what?"

I knock on the dashboard. "I don't know. Just drive."

If we can make it to the termination facility before they

transfer my father, there might be a chance we can stop them. As long as they're outside of their heavily guarded facility, we can free my father. If Hunter is with him, he'll help us. Now is a better time than ever to leave.

Traffic on the highway slows us down some, but Evie weaves from lane to lane, managing to get us down the highway faster than I expected. As soon as we're out of the city limits, the roads clear and we speed north well over the speed limit.

Alyssa hands me her phone. "Call Hunter again."

I nod and redial Jacqueline's cell. It rings and goes to voicemail. I hit redial again. I'll keep calling until he picks up if I have to. He'll have to shut the phone off if he's going to ignore me.

After the sixth time of no answer, my heart sinks. I hit redial again.

I have a terrible feeling about this.

## HUNTER

I sit in the back of the van with Agent Rob. Dmitri is bound to the seat with a breathable cloth bag over his head despite there being no windows besides the one that separates the front cabin area from cargo. Even then, it's curtained as a safety precaution.

Jacqueline's cell phone rings in my pocket, and I pull it out and silence it. I don't even have to look at the number to know who's calling. It's the sixth time in the last few minutes, but I can't answer it. I wouldn't even if I could right now.

In just a few miles, we'll be far enough away from the termination facility that agents won't immediately arrive if either

Agent Rosaline or Agent Rob were to call for help. If the van stops any sooner, my plan won't work.

I wish I had a minute alone with Jacqueline to discuss things with her. She's great at handling sudden obstacles, but I wish I could've made sure she was ready to leave the HPA with me. I know she was tired of running from them, and it's why she stole Agent Camille's body, but what choice do I have now?

"What do you need a personal cell phone for? Something to hide, Sullivan?" Agent Rob's voice pulls me from my thoughts of how to subdue both him and Agent Rosaline without crashing the van. We'll need it to get away.

I lean back and glare at him, adjusting Jacqueline's phone without telling him it belongs to her. "None of your business, Rob."

Agent Rob narrows his eyes, and I know where this is going. We're allowed to use our HPA issued cell phones for personal use, and most people do, but he's right about why someone would get a separate phone and it is to hide things. It's not unheard of though. He's questioning me to piss me off. "Well, maybe it's the board's business." His lips twist into a crooked smile.

The phone vibrates in my pocket, the humming resonating off the metal walls. I tug it out again and hit ignore. The second it goes to voicemail, it rings again. Nadia's not giving up. I sigh and go to turn the power off, but Agent Rob jerks forward and snatches the cell from my hands. I lunge at him. Swiveling on the bench, he kicks me in the side, sending explosive pain through my ribs.

He lifts the phone to his ear and says, "Agent Rob speaking."

A blood red color sweeps over my vision as rage rushes through me. I've never wanted to hurt someone so much in my life than I do right now. I take a few breaths to ease the pain in my chest and swing my good arm to try to knock the phone from his hand. He leans back, and I miss.

He holds his finger up. "The wrong number, you say? If you are trying to reach Hunter Sullivan, then this is the correct number."

I grind my teeth. "Give me the phone, Rob."

He shakes his head. "What's your name? I can pass on the message for a beautiful girl like you." He grins, licking his lips. "How do I know you're beautiful? Your voice and the fact that Hunter is trying to kill me as we speak."

*Hang up, Nadia. Come on, hang up. Stop talking to him. Stop it. Hang up the phone!* I can't keep the thoughts from coming. If it weren't for my need to keep her safe, I'd scream them out so she could hear them.

Agent Rob laughs. "You want me to tell you where we are?"

I lean back in the seat across from him. I didn't want to have to hurt him, but I will if he continues this conversation. I know what Nadia's doing, and I can't let her use Alyssa to find us. All it would take is for Agent Rob to make one decision that could set things into motion.

Agent Rob wags his eyebrows. "Let me see. I have to open the curtain and take a peek. What will you do for me in return?" He chuckles and peers at me before shifting in the seat again. Moving the curtain over an inch, he peeks out. "I'll give you a hint. The street name starts with an S."

I reach for my tranquilizer gun. I can't stop myself. I need to get Agent Rob to hang up the phone, and the only way I see him doing so is if we either fight for it, which I don't think I could win in my condition, or if I use the tranquilizer. This will risk everything, but I don't see another option.

I yank the gun free, hold it up, and pull the trigger.

## NADIA

"I got it," Alyssa says. "They're heading down Shadow Ridge."

"How do you know?" Evie asks.

"The moment he decided to open the curtain, I knew what he would see."

A whizzing sound and a thump rings out, and I drop the phone in my lap, startled. My hand shakes as I bring it back to my ear. Low voices come in and out through the receiver. Something's happened, but I have no idea what.

I find my voice. "Agent Rob? You there?"

A breath of static buzzes through the line. "I told you I'd call you when I could, Nadia." It's Hunter. He's breathless and his voice sounds hoarse, but it's really him.

"That would be hard to do if you're dead."

"Did you say Nadia?" Another voice cuts over mine, and my heart races. It's my father's voice. It's unmistakable.

I dig my fingers into my palms. "Let me talk to him."

Hunter sighs. "It's dangerous. I'm not alone, and Rob can wake up any minute."

Tears rim my eyes. "Don't do this to me, Hunter. Don't do this. You have to let me talk to him!"

The line falls silent, my heart breaking the longer it draws out. I check the phone to see if Hunter hung up on me, but we're still connected.

"Nadi? Nadi? Is it really you?" My father's voice wraps around me like a comforting hug, and I lean into the seat.

I hit the speakerphone so Alyssa can hear him, too. "Yeah, Dad. Alyssa's here, too."

"I don't understand. You know Agent Hunter?"

"It's a long story, and we don't have time. We're coming to get you."

My father doesn't respond, and I can hear murmured voices in the background. "She's going to get herself killed." Hunter's voice cuts through my heart like a blade. "You have to convince her not to, Dmitri. I'll get you out myself."

Alyssa's fingers grip my shoulders. "If Hunter tries to stop the van, all the possible outcomes leave someone dead, Nadia."

I inhale a deep breath. "You can't stop us, Hunter."

"Nadi, please, just stay away." It's my father. My heart cracks and crumbles into a million pieces at his plea. "I don't want you to get hurt."

"I don't want to lose you. They'll kill you."

"It's okay. I'll be okay. I love you so much. Never forget

that."

The line cuts off, and a scream burns in my throat, threatening to rip me apart. Tears drip down my cheeks, my shoulders shaking in silent sobs. My father has already given up on life and hope...on everything.

On me.

He doesn't think I'm strong enough or capable enough. He still sees me as the fragile girl who hid under a table and watched her mother die. That's not me. I'm not made of tragedy. I'm made of the best parts of my life—love, faith, and survival.

Alyssa touches my shoulder, and I shift to look at her. Evie doesn't say anything but just gazes out the windshield, slowing down only a little. Alyssa's green eyes shine with tears, her bottom lip quivering, and the only thing keeping us from falling apart, together, is that both of us want to be strong for each other.

I blink the tears from my eyes and rub my tear-stained cheeks. I can't believe I'll never see my father again. I won't believe it. I'm not going to let things end like this. I'll see him again if it's the last thing I do. I have to try. I can't live with myself if I give up without knowing if I could've saved him, saved Hunter and Jacqueline, too. I'm not afraid of failing. In this very moment, I'm only afraid of doing nothing.

I breathe deep to slow my heart rate. "I can't let him give up."

"It's going to be messy, but the odds of us all surviving are better because we outnumber the agents. Just remember, things can change at any second," Alyssa says. "Right now, we can catch up to them, but I don't think we can stop them."

Evie switches lanes. "I'll go faster." She slams the throttle, and I jolt back with the sudden acceleration. "Where do I exit?"

Alyssa leans between the seats. "Five miles at Mariposa Street. Then turn left."

I grip my knees. I hope we can get there fast enough before it's too late.

## HUNTER

Dmitri hands me the phone, and I stare at it in the palm of my hand. Things feel so final. I don't know what else to do. I'm guilty and frustrated, and can't look Nadia's father in the eyes. How do I tell him about everything? Should I even? *He deserves to know.*

"You love my daughter." It's not a question. Dmitri isn't stupid. I'm sure he's confused, but my love for Nadia is obvious. I feel it not only within me, but in everything I see, hear, and touch. But, sitting with her father while he heads to the end of his freedom and possibly his life, it's hard to feel anything but grief and self-loathing. I did this to him. I didn't fight hard enough.

I lift my eyes from the phone. "This isn't how it's supposed to be. I should've run away when I had the chance. I stayed because I thought I could make things better, but things are worse."

He studies my face, and it's hard to keep my eyes focused

on his. "This isn't your fault, Hunter."

"It is, but I never wanted this. I did it because I didn't see any other way. I love Nadia and she loves me, but it's like we're not meant to be together no matter how much I want it."

Dmitri doesn't say anything for a minute. He frowns. "Why didn't she tell me?"

I shrug. "Would you have welcomed me with open arms?"

He presses his lips together. "Fair point."

I run my hand through my hair. "Don't be too mad at her. She only wanted to protect me and—" I glance at the curtained window. I lean in and whisper, "Jacqueline Matthews."

Dmitri's eyes widen. Out of everything, he seems the most surprised to discover Jacqueline isn't dead. He leans his head on his hands and stares at the floor where Agent Rob lies face down between the seats. He'll be out for another few minutes and then I have no idea what I'll do about him. If murder wouldn't sit so heavy on my conscience, I'd open the door and roll him onto the street.

Dmitri sits straight. "I'm trying to wrap my head around this, but I just don't understand. I saw Jacqueline's body with my own eyes."

I swallow. "Well, her body's dead. She body jumped into Agent Camille. It was sort of the same way I got my body back."

His lips form an O-shape. "You're the boy."

"Funny, isn't it? I used to despise Jackie. We've grown on each other, though. She's the one who convinced me we could make a difference."

"I think she's right. This is exactly what my kind needs."

I furrow my brows. "We haven't exactly changed anything for the better."

Dmitri grabs my shoulder the way a dad would reassure his son. "Don't you see? You are making a difference because you're on our side. The only other person able to think outside of the HPA when she was one of them was Veronica Sanders. But now, there's you. And I bet more will come around."

I sigh and rub my good hand over my hair. "Not fast enough. I can't exactly save you on my own."

Dmitri leans back. "But you can save Nadia. You can save everyone I know and care about. I'm okay with my fate, Hunter. I'm not afraid to die."

I frown. "I see where Nadia gets her bravery from."

He smiles. "She didn't know how brave she really was until the day she set you free."

# 22

## AS MY WORLD FALLS APART

**NADIA**

MY HEART RACES when Evie exits the highway. The world whizzes by, and I concentrate on the cars in front of us. We merge onto a narrow street. Evie side swipes a plastic garbage can and sends trash flying into a few yards.

"Turn right at the stop sign. We're going to go through the neighborhood and hopefully cut them off at an intersection," Alyssa says.

I turn in my seat. "We're going to catch them, right?"

"I don't know."

Evie follows Alyssa's directions, and we wait at a stop light.

As each second passes, my stomach twists into another knot. I don't think I'll ever feel fine again. If it weren't for my father, I'd curl up in a ball and try to fade away into nothing. Life has never felt so tough to deal with. Not even after my mother was murdered. At least then, I had my father to pick up the pieces.

"We're coming up to Shadow Ridge," Evie says.

"Make another right but slow down. I don't think they're here yet. They're taking surface streets as a precaution." Alyssa sits back in her seat and latches her seatbelt. I eye her in my visor mirror, and she offers a small smile. It's enough to give me hope.

"What am I looking for?" Evie says, lifting off the accelerator.

"A white van," I say.

"Like the one coming up?"

I jerk to look out the back window. The white, unmarked HPA van is unmistakable. It's a few blocks down and driving at a slow pace, a few miles per hour under the already slow speed limit.

"That's them," Alyssa says. "I see Jacqueline in the front."

"Jacqueline?" Evie asks. We only referred to her as Camille in front of her so she wouldn't know.

"Camille," I say. "Camille's real name is Jacqueline."

"Oh..."

Evie slows down even more. I peer out the back window and watch as the HPA van closes the distance between us. My palms sweat and my legs shake. I haven't thought this through.

Now that they're so close, what am I going to do? Nicely ask the driver to pull over? Expect Hunter and Jacqueline to protect us from the other agents?

I grip the dashboard, the white van nearing two car lengths behind us in the left lane. Evie clutches the wheel, her hands turning white. She's waiting on me or Alyssa to say something, but I can't make a decision yet. I'm afraid it'll be the wrong one.

"If they pass us, they'll get away," Alyssa says.

I grab the wheel and jerk it.

Evie screams. "What are you doing?"

The SUV swerves and the van honks its horn. Time slows and it's like I'm watching everything from outside the SUV. My white hair blows in the breeze, hot tears branding my cool cheeks. Snow sprinkles around me, hugging me in its icy embrace. I'm watching my own worst nightmare kick into motion. Except this isn't a dream. It's my life and at any second it might be over.

I blink a few times, the van's horn echoing in my ears. "Slam the brakes!"

## HUNTER

I tap on the window to get Jacqueline's attention. Agent Rosaline screams and slams the breaks.

"No," I whisper, recognizing the SUV in front of us.

Tires squeal, the smell of burning rubber fills my nose, and the ear-shattering sound of metal grinding against metal rips through the air. The world spins, and I slam into the divider between the front seat and the cargo area. I hit my casted hand on the window, my shoulder screaming in pain. Tumbling back, I land hard on top of Rob, who's now under my legs. Black stars pepper my vision, the sound of the crash deafening, and my chest burns as the air forces its way from my lungs.

And then all falls silent and the world stops.

I slump against the wall in an unmoving world, staring at the roof of the van, shifting my weight to my good hand. Fingers lock around my ankle, and I turn my eyes to Agent Rob. He leers at me while pulling his knife from his weaponry belt. Dmitri doesn't move but sits how we had him when we first put him in the van.

Agent Rosaline yells out from the front seat. "We need back up!"

"Be there in five, Agent Rosaline," a male voice says, blaring from the speaker.

I shake my head to clear my thoughts. I need to get Dmitri out of here. I need to protect Nadia. I need to get away from the HPA now or else none of us will survive this.

Rob scowls at me. "You tranquilized me, you son-of-a—"

"Now's not the time, Rob." I swallow and clear my throat. He can't know I'm not on his side. It's the only way to get out of here.

"Agent Hunter, Agent Rob!" Agent Rosaline screams.

Agent Rob jumps to his feet and pushes past me, throwing the back door open. He leaps out, and I follow on his heels, leaving Dmitri behind.

The freezing air hits my face, my eyes watering as a gust of wind blows around me. My boots crunch on the gritty street and when I reach the back corner of the van, my chest tightens. Nadia stands ten feet away with a crowbar gripped in her hands.

Agent Rob closes in on her.

## NADIA

I swing the metal crowbar I found in the SUV at the windshield, cracking the glass. Jacqueline sits in the front seat with another agent. She's a twenty-something-year-old brunette with a pixie cut and high, sharp cheekbones. Her chestnut eyes widen, and she cringes as I swing the crowbar at the windshield again.

"Well, aren't you a pretty little thing," a deep voice says. I turn to meet the eyes of a tall, broad shouldered agent. He points his knife in my direction and grins, mocking me with the way his eyes travel from my face to my boots. He wags his thick, blond eyebrows, the same color as his long hair tied back into a ponytail. "I don't think I could ever forget your face."

Stepping back, I hold up the crowbar. It takes me a second, but I recognize the agent from the raid at the condo. "Don't come any closer."

"Need some help?" My heart rises into my throat, meeting Hunter's gaze.

The agent turns to Hunter. "Stay with the prisoner, Sullivan."

Hunter doesn't move, and the agent doesn't notice. He steps closer, stalking me, making me feel like his prey.

I stumble back. "I don't want any trouble."

The agent's smile widens. "Funny way of showing it." He eyes the shattered windshield. "Just put it down, and I won't hurt you, pretty little monster."

"I have no idea what you're talking about." I glance at Hunter, and he touches the hilt on his knife. I don't doubt he would use it.

"You can't fool me, darlin'. I saw how you moved."

I grip the crowbar tighter to steady my shaking hands. "Please, just leave me alone."

"Now why would I do that? Backup's already on the way, and I'm not gonna let them ruin my fun."

I stiffen as he moves closer. He knows I'm not human, and no matter how much I deny his accusations, he'll never believe me. The only thing I can do is keep away the best I can.

The agent strides closer, raising his hand, and jabs his knife, taking me by surprise. I scramble away, slipping on the snowy street. I'm getting weaker by the second from the lack of nightmare inflicting and from the exhaustion of letting my fear and stress consume me. I don't glide because even if he doesn't think I'm human, I won't let him have the satisfaction of seeing my nightmare inflictor side. I'll only show him my humanity. It might keep me alive.

"What're you doing, Agent Rob?" Hunter steps closer. I release a breath. He'll never let the agent hurt me. "She's not actively threatening you. We have protocols."

"Screw you, Sullivan," Agent Rob says. "She got away from

me once in the city. I'm not letting it happen again." He lunges, and I trip over a piece of debris from the wreck. Falling hard on the ground, I roll to my knees. I crawl a foot back before using the side of the SUV to pull to my feet.

"Agent Rob!" Hunter yells again.

Brakes squeal on the other side of the center divider, and another white van pulls up, blocking the road. Two more agents jump out and run in my direction. I'm surrounded, and there's no way I can fight them all.

Turning from the agents, I watch Alyssa pull a bag off my father's head. His stare falls on me, and I nod my head for him to leave. His eyes shift to the approaching agents and the agent who gets out of the driver's side door.

My eyes flick to Hunter. He looks from my direction to the approaching agents. Shifting on his feet, he touches his weaponry belt. Before he can run toward me, Evie dashes from behind the van and charges Hunter. She jumps on him, and they collide to the ground.

It's like the world around me crumbles. Maybe Evie wasn't trustworthy after all. She's preventing Hunter from running to me—from saving me. I'll die here at the hands of these agents.

## HUNTER

My back hits the ground hard enough to expel all the oxygen from my lungs. I don't move. I don't know how to fix this. I can't fight off four agents. Glancing around, I spot Jacqueline's boots on the other side of the van from my perspective on the ground. She heads toward where Alyssa and Dmitri are.

"I'm going to get off you. I want you to capture me but don't hurt me. Alyssa said this was the only way to save you," Evie whispers in my ear. She shifts her weight, and I wrap my arms around her and pull her to her feet.

The sound of soft voices draws my focus behind me even though I don't turn my head to look. I can't take my eyes off the commotion going on in front of me. Agent Rob taunts Nadia with his knife. I'll kill him if he hurts her. I'll gladly take his blood on my hands.

"You need to hurry and leave." Jacqueline's voice reaches me, her unmistakable serious tone, speeding up my heartbeat. "I have a plan."

I turn to glance over my shoulder but only Dmitri remains. I hope Jacqueline's plan didn't include running away when things got tough. Anger and fear rush through me, and the edges of my vision shadow. How could I let this happen? How could I put Nadia in this danger? If it weren't for me, she wouldn't be in the middle of this.

And I'm a coward. I'm holding onto Evie when I should be wringing Rob's neck. But, Evie's warning rings in my ears, and I'm afraid she's right. I'm afraid I can't keep Nadia alive without my HPA identity. The HPA will kill me with her, and I refuse to let our love end like this. *Think Hunter. Think. Think!*

## NADIA

"Run!" I scream at my father.

He doesn't move.

The agents who were heading my way change direction and

head toward my father.

I'm too distracted as my world falls apart that I don't see Agent Rob close the space between us. Pain bursts in my shin as he kicks my leg. Falling to the ground, I crab walk a few feet from Agent Rob.

"They're getting away!" a voice yells out.

Agent Rob turns toward the voice, and it gives me a chance to crawl under the SUV. If I get to the other side, I can run. I need to get something between Agent Rob and me so I have time to pull myself together.

On my stomach, I shimmy out of view from Agent Rob.

"Hurry, Nadi," my father says. He kneels on the other side of the crushed SUV. "Just a few more feet."

"Think you can hide from me?" Agent Rob asks.

Agent Rob's voice strikes me in my heart. "Dad, run! They'll kill you," I scream. Ice pours through my veins as a hand locks around my ankles and pulls me out from under the SUV.

Agent Rob stands over me and grins. He aims the knife, and I close my eyes and wait for the sting of the dagger. I imagine hugging my father one last time and think about the memories I have of Hunter. I'll not let Agent Rob torment me with fear in my last moments of life. If I'm going to die, I'm going to die thinking of who I care about most.

## HUNTER

My world freezes as I watch Agent Rob stand over Nadia. His demented laugh echoes through the air, and I loosen my grip on

Evie and step forward. Touching the hilt of my knife, I get ready to yank it free.

"Oh, no," Evie whispers, the panic in her voice intensifying my own fear. "Oh, my God."

Nadia screams, the terror in her voice ripping my heart into a million shreds. Agent Rob drops to his knees, digging them into her stomach. Twisting his hand in her hair, he exposes her alabaster throat and holds the knife against her skin.

She screams again, her voice burning through my eardrums, turning the world dark. I'm afraid it's the last thing I'll ever hear from her.

# 23

BROKEN

NADIA

THE BLADE GLINTS in the pale, winter sunlight, sending a spark of light across my vision. I can't stop the screams ripping from my throat. I can't die like this. I *won't* die like this.

"Rob, no!" Jacqueline yells.

Tears burn my eyes, and I squeeze them shut. Two loud pops break through the sound of my screams and Agent Rob curses. I expect the dagger to cut through me at any second, but Agent Rob collapses on top of me, crushing me with his weight. The burning pain of not being able to breathe silences my screams.

Flailing, I kick and push at the fallen agent's heavy body. I blink a dozen times under a figure blocking the sun. Jacqueline stands over me in a halo of light, her black hair veiling her face, stuck to her forehead with sweat. She reaches out and grabs my hand.

"You saved me...again," I say. I grip the cold door of the SUV, steadying my weak knees. "Where's my dad?"

Jacqueline stiffens and surveys the area. "I forced him to leave with Alyssa, because the HPA would've killed him. Alyssa said they won't kill you. I didn't just blow my cover to let everyone die." I gaze down at Agent Rob's body. Jacqueline used her ability to kill him. She also tranquilized two other agents.

I meet Hunter's eyes. Hunter stands frozen with wide eyes twenty feet away. Evie gapes at me and Jacqueline, her fingers wrapped on Hunter's wrists. I'm not sure who holds who up, but they're both as surprised as I am.

The van honks its horn, turning my gaze from Hunter to another agent, who locked herself in the van. The agent saw everything Jacqueline did. She knows Jacqueline is a traitor to the HPA.

Jacqueline tugs my arm. "It isn't over. More agents will arrive any second."

I step over Rob, his body sprawled out on the snowy street. Because Jacqueline's given herself away, there's no way she'll make it out of here alive if she's caught.

"You have to body jump, Jacqueline," I whisper.

Jacqueline peers at two more white vans screeching to a

halt across the center divider.

Hunter lets go of Evie and turns to face me. "If you don't attempt to run or fight, we won't kill you." Hunter still pretends to be on the HPA's side.

Jacqueline ignores Hunter and turns to me. "There's no way to get close enough to those agents. I doubt I'll get physical contact to do it anyway. They'll tranquilize me and then kill me. I don't think I can kill all of them either. We're outnumbered."

I squeeze her hand. "Then we have to run."

She shakes her head. "Then they'll kill you, too."

Fear trickles down the back of my neck and wraps its icy fingers around my chest, squeezing me with an overwhelming feeling of dread, anger, and hopelessness. It can't end like this. Jacqueline and I are survivors. We always have been. It's what brought us together. We understand each other and respect each other. I can't let her give up.

"You don't know that. We could escape. Hunter won't let them hurt us." My gaze flicks from the ground to Hunter, and he looks so utterly devastated as if he's expecting me to die. It hurts to see him like this. He steps closer as the other agents draw near.

Jacqueline nudges me behind her. "He won't have a choice. He won't be able to protect you if they know he's on our side. Alyssa told me it's the only way."

"So, what do we do then?" I ask. My voice quivers, and I press my back to the SUV.

"You do nothing. Don't resist. Don't fight. Don't tell them you're anything other than human," Jacqueline says.

My heart hammers as her words sink in. She's already made up her mind. I know she's going to fight the best she can and then accept the fate that was given to her. I want to argue and beg for her to fight with me, but my tongue sticks to the roof of my mouth and exhaustion rolls over me. I don't have the energy to fight for my life or to try to save Jacqueline.

Tears spill from my eyes as the perfect idea swirls in my mind. This is my chance to make it up to Jacqueline. I can save her now. I never wanted this to be about me, and I'm not afraid of what will happen next. I was given a second chance when Jacqueline saved my life after I saved Hunter's, and even though she chose her new life with the HPA doesn't mean she deserves to die by their hands. She can live on still...through me. "You can take my body. I want you to. You're the one who can make a difference in the world, not me."

Jacqueline turns from the agents closing in on us. "I'm not killing you." She lets go of my hand and turns toward Hunter. "But you did give me an idea. Remember, don't fight and tell them you're human."

I open my mouth to argue, but Jacqueline rushes from me. She pulls her knife from her belt and bolts away from the agents coming toward me.

A pop echoes through the silent street. My shoulder stings as a tranquilizer sinks deep into my skin. I slide to the ground, hazy air washing over my vision. I peer over at Hunter as

Jacqueline charges at him, knife wielded, and then I fall into darkness.

## HUNTER

My gaze darts from Nadia to Jacqueline. Jacqueline's already given away her identity by helping Nadia, tranquilizing two agents, and killing Rob. If there weren't so many agents, I'd give myself away, too, but if I did right now, I won't be capable of protecting Nadia.

Jacqueline runs at me with her knife wielded, and it's like a heavy hand punches my chest. Her lavender-blue eyes widen with a wild desperation I've only seen in them once before. Frozen tears and clumps of black hair stick to her cheeks.

Jacqueline collides with me, her screams piercing through the air. She knocks me over, and we crash to the ground, her weight forcing the air from my lungs. I smack her shoulder with my cast to get her off me, but the position she holds me in gives me no room to fight or move.

She holds the knife against my throat, nearly snarling in my face. Everything I've tolerated about her now gone with the touch of icy metal to my neck.

I grip her shirt with my free hand. "You're crazy," I whisper, staring into her teary eyes.

"I don't know what else to do," she says. "I can't let them take me."

"So, you're going to kill me?" I ask.

Kneeing her in the stomach, I roll her off me. Her head hits the pavement, and she cringes. I press my cast against her shoulder to keep her down, but she doesn't struggle. She lies limply under me.

"Please, Hunter, kill me." Hot tears brand streaks on her temples as they trail into her hair before freezing. She looks as lost and afraid as the first time I saw her trapped in the termination facility before Dr. Sullivan struck a deal with her. This isn't the Jacqueline I know now.

She wiggles her hand, the knife she grips sparkling in the sunlight. Footsteps echo through the air, crunching on the mixture of slush and salt or pieces from the wreckage. Without having to look up, I know at least two agents cautiously move closer. Jacqueline drops the knife, and it clatters on the pavement. I pick it up with my good hand and look at my defeated expression in the gleaming blade.

"I can't do that to you," I whisper.

"Hunter, please. Do it. You have to do it." Her low voice, full of fear and venom, cuts through me. Her fingernails bite into my skin, her eyes begging me to go through with it.

I swallow my nausea at the thought of hurting her and shift to point the dagger at her heart. My stomach flips and twists, threatening to stop me, and it takes a few long, deep breaths to keep from getting sick. I steady my shaking hand, and the blade catches on the front of her black uniform. She doesn't take her eyes from mine. I can't look away, either.

I lean closer. "I won't forget you."

Glaring, she grabs my arm to push the blade harder, but I don't let her force me to stab her. She puffs air through her lips.

"Shut up, Hunter, and kill me."

A hand grabs my shoulder, and I swing my elbow back to knock the person away. Jacqueline squeezes her eyes shut. I do the same as I jam the knife into her chest. She cups my face, digging her nails into my cheeks. Her hands drop to the asphalt, and red-hot heat rushes through me.

The world spins, like everything bad that has happened in Jacqueline's life flows into my mind. I fall back to the pavement, covering my eyes with my good hand as Jacqueline's life flashes in my head. A projection flashes on the back of my eyelids. A little girl with curly, dark hair and bronze skin swings on a swing as a guy my age with dark hair shaved close to the scalp and golden brown eyes stands behind her, pushing her. The little girl has light purple eyes, and it's exactly how I imagine Jacqueline looked as a child. The guy, with skin a shade darker than Jacqueline's old body, grins and laughs as she squeals on the swing. His voice echoes through my mind. *I wish it could always be like this, Jackie. You know I'll do anything to keep you safe.*

The little girl kicks the ground to stop the swing and jumps off. She turns and wraps her arms around the guy's torso. It's like I'm invading a private moment between the two siblings, but it's out of my control.

Another image flashes through my mind. Jacqueline is more of who I remember in this vision. Her dark, curly hair hangs in a mess around her face. She kneels at a grave, alone and devastated—her emotions tangible as I watch her get up and dust dirt off her knees. *You were supposed to always take care of me. You promised you'd never leave me.* Jacqueline's voice echoes around me, and I sink deeper into my thoughts. It reminds me of when I was trapped in her mind. I try to push them away.

"Agent Hunter, can you hear me?" A different voice, separate for my mind, talks to me. I ignore it as another image forms in my head.

I'm staring at myself, just minutes ago, my hazel eyes wide, my lips hidden in a thin line. It's strange to see myself as Jacqueline saw me. The fear lining my eyes, how I clench my teeth, and how conflicted I looked. I shudder as I remember the feeling of how easily the knife went into Jacqueline and how she didn't even scream.

Dark fog nudges the red of my closed eyelids.

*"Open your eyes, Hunter. Act normal. You were doing your job. You saved the day."* Jacqueline's voice echoes through my head.

I do what she says and open my eyes.

My jaw tightens when my gaze falls on the body of Agent Camille. Blood seeps onto the snowy street from her body. I turn away as Agent Rosaline and another agent I've never met before rolls her body onto a black tarp.

I sit up on my elbows.

An HPA van blocks the street behind me, directing traffic down a side street, and another does the same on the other side of the center divider. I've been out longer than I expected, at least ten minutes, and the agents have almost completely cleaned up the accident and everything involved in it.

I stumble to my feet and peer around. Nadia isn't anywhere to be found, and my heart sinks into my stomach. I'll never forgive myself if something happens to her.

A hand touches my shoulder. "You should sit down, Hunter."

"I didn't want to kill Camille," I say. "But she attacked me." I turn to meet Agent Rosaline's puffy brown eyes. She blinks a few times to clear her tears away. I almost forgot about Agent Rob and how Jacqueline killed him. "I'm sorry about Rob," I add, even though I don't mean it.

"How did this happen?" Agent Rosaline's voice drips with grief as she mourns her partner. She runs her fingers through her short, brown hair, flattened with sweat, and nods toward the van. "I saw Agent Camille kill Rob with the touch of her hand. I know she wasn't a reaper. How did we not know she was a super?"

*"Tell her I was acting differently after the attack on the facility."* Jacqueline's voice echoes in my ears again. It's like she's haunting me.

I shake my head and climb in the van. "She was acting differently after the invasion. I think a super got to her."

Agent Rosaline closes the door, leaving me alone to walk to the driver's side.

I squeeze my eyes shut to push Jacqueline's voice away.

*"You're going to have to do a lot more than shake your head to get me out of here. Let's just say I need somewhere to stay for the*

*time being."*

"I'm glad you're not dead."

Jacqueline body jumped into me. I wasn't just seeing her life flash before my eyes. What I saw was what Jacqueline sees when she redeems a soul through her life visions. All the pain and suffering—the bad decisions, the cruel intentions, the wrong-doings. Jacqueline takes all that into herself and releases the souls pure so they find peace, but the remnants of the sins she absorbs linger in the shadows of her soul. I can feel them now.

*"If you keep talking out loud, they'll know. So shut up about it. We'll talk later. Just get through the day."*

The driver's side door opens, and Agent Rosaline hops in. She starts the engine, shifting in her seat to look through the curtained window. I follow her gaze and see two figures bound to the bench seat.

Nadia and Evie.

"I have orders to bring them to the termination facility for evaluation. They both seem human, but you never know. The board wants to investigate and run some tests. Figure out why they're working for supers."

I look out the windshield to hide any emotion I might be showing. "I'd like to know why, too."

"Don't worry, Hunter. We'll get our answers."

**NADIA**

"I'm scared."

If my hands were free, I'd reach out and hug Evie. "You

don't need to be. Your mother works for the HPA. She'll fight for you."

The leather bench seat squeaks as Evie shifts. "What about you?"

The black bag sticks to my mouth when I suck in a breath. I blow it away from my face the best I can. I lean closer and whisper, "As far as anyone knows, I'm human. I don't know how far that'll get me, though. I'm sure they'll see something during whatever tests they do." My saving grace is that I never told Evie what I am so they can't get that information from her.

"I'll tell my mom you're human. She'll help you."

"My ability is nothing really," I lie. "And my mom was human so I'm technically human, too." I'm relieved I didn't have the nerve to tell her what I do yet. The HPA can't use her against me.

Evie sounds so sincere about helping me, but I doubt her mother can do anything. Her mother doesn't know me, and I was a greater participant in the car wreck that allowed my father to escape.

While Evie was there, she's different because she was born into the HPA and whether or not she realizes it, she'll be forced to join their side. Because she didn't know about the creature world before she met me, they'll brainwash her one way or another.

I roll my shoulders. "It's better if you don't defend me. It's probably even better if you tell them we aren't really friends and you didn't know what you were getting into."

"But—"

"Really, Evie. I'm serious. I don't want you to be killed because of me. I should've never gotten you involved in the first place. It was stupid and unfair of me to do so." A tear drops from my eyelashes, soaking into the fabric of the bag. Evie could've been a really good friend in another life. I hate that our friendship is forced to end before we ever had a chance.

She sighs. "I'll go with things for now, but I won't stand back and watch them hurt you."

I don't want to break it to her, but she won't have a choice. The HPA steals that choice from everyone involved with them. They're about manipulation and control—about their community as a whole. They won't even think twice about the feelings of an individual.

"Thanks," I say. "You're a good friend."

The van jolts to a stop, and the engine cuts out. Fear swells in my chest, gripping my heart so hard it feels like it'll explode. My entire body trembles, causing my teeth to chatter. My insides ice over with terror and uncontrollable panic. I thought I was stronger than this. I thought I could get through this levelheaded. But, all I can think about are the horrors to come. I almost wish I'd died at the hand of Agent Rob because I'm afraid I'll survive whatever experiments and tests they want to perform on me. I'm terrified of the pain and anguish—of sadness, despair...of loneliness. I'm anxious of the unknown and of the thought of never seeing Alyssa and my father again. Of not seeing Hunter.

"Remember what I said about not knowing me," I say.

The seat shakes as Evie sobs.

"It's going to be okay. Everything's going to be okay. Be strong."

I'm not sure if I'm saying it to make Evie feel better or myself. I don't even believe the words coming out of my mouth.

The back door creaks open, and freezing air drifts in. My mind swirls with dizziness and fear. I gasp for the air that can't come through the fabric bag fast enough. A soft hand locks around my arm and gently squeezes it. My pulse slows, the touch feeling so familiar.

The hand lets go and then bright light blinds me as the black bag is removed from my head. The sunlight feels warmer than usual because of my hunger, but I refuse to let anyone in on my secret. *You have only a few days before you'll lose control...* I push the thought away. I'm stronger than my nightmare inflicting side. I have to be.

My vision clears, and I gaze at Evie. Mascara tears run down her cheeks, and she sobs when her eyes meet mine. I frown, my bottom lip quivering, but I use every ounce of energy I have left to control my emotions. I won't let them see me afraid.

"Get up and follow me."

My heart hammers against my ribcage. I shift my eyes from Evie's to Hunter's, and it's like the world crumbles around me. He sounds so cold and serious, nothing like the Hunter I love. I know he must fake it on the job, but it still feels like something inside of him died. Maybe this was all too much for him. I wish I could hug him.

Instead, I push to my feet.

"Take them to the blue zone for interrogation and testing," he says to a petite blond woman in a white lab coat. "They won't be any trouble."

Hunter's hazel stare drops to the ground. I blink my eyes a few times and study his defeated face, but he doesn't look at me again before I follow the blond woman in the lab coat.

The walls Hunter once broke down are being rebuilt, ten times thicker and so high, even the stars couldn't see over them. I'm lost and uncertain about what happens next.

My heart and spirit shatter into dust.

I'm broken.

# 24

## NEVER GIVE UP ON US

HUNTER

"What happened next?"

I lean my back on the hard chair. I'm aching all over and only want to crawl in bed and sleep away my pain and discomfort. I want to forget today ever happened. Maybe I'm living a nightmare. I can only hope to wake up from this mess.

*"Suck it up, Hunter. Nadia doesn't get to forget any of this."*

Jacqueline's voice echoes in my ears.

My heart hurts at the reality of her words. She's right. I breathe through my nose and think, "Stop listening to my thoughts."

*"Then conceal them."*

"I can't," I say. My voice echoes through the room, and I swear in my mind.

Lifting my glare from the tiled floor, I meet Dr. Amelia's eyes. She's president of the board and has the ultimate say in my fate with the HPA. I shift my gaze to Dr. Sullivan's and then across the other ten faces belonging to board members I've only met once before. I don't recall any of their names.

"You can't what?" Dr. Amelia asks, tucking a strand of orange-red hair behind her ear.

I shake my head. "I'm sorry. I need a minute." I rub my hand over my face, trying to conceal how troubled I am by today's events. They're judging my weaknesses, and I need to prove to them I'm strong. I need to be strong for Nadia. If they deem me to be unfit, I'll lose the little access I already have.

"You're upset," Dr. Sullivan says. It's not a question.

I don't look up. "Agent Camille was my partner. I didn't know some super killed her until I watched her kill Agent Rob. If I had known..." My voice trails off, and I grit my teeth, forcing anger into my voice. I hope I'm convincing. "I'd have destroyed the monster sooner."

*"Nice touch,"* Jacqueline says in my head.

I press my lips together to stop the smile from crossing my mouth. I hate that I'm playing host for Jacqueline, but I'm glad she's not dead.

"So you subdued Human 9208. What happened next?" Dr. Amelia asks again.

Shifting in the hard chair, I rest my elbows on my knees. "I released her. The super in Agent Camille's body attacked me. She almost slit my throat."

Dr. Amelia flips through a file in front of her. "Agent Rosaline said she saw you conversing with the possessor."

I lick my cracked lips. "I wasn't exactly having a conversation. I threw a few nice swear words at her and managed to knee her. I then took her knife and, well, you saw the body."

"How do you feel now?" The question comes from a blond woman who looks too young to be here. Her long hair is tied back in a bun and her red lipstick matches her nails.

I shrug. "Like I was hit by a bus."

She clicks her pen on the table. "I mean mentally. You've been through a lot."

I shrug again. "You know, I honestly feel fine. Nothing fazes me anymore. I could do without the injuries, but I still want to work. Maybe not in the field for a while."

I lift my gaze, and Dr. Sullivan smiles. She looks like a proud mother, causing agitation to sweep over me. She's a hard woman to please. It's taken me surviving death three times for her to realize how awesome I am. Unfortunately, she'll eventually be rudely awakened with the truth. I'm not her precious, overachieving son. I'm her enemy.

Dr. Amelia clears her throat. "As a precaution, I'd like you to meet with our mental health team for an evaluation. If all goes well, you may continue overseeing the green zone. You won't have any help for a while until we can assign another partner to you."

I sit up straight. "I'll be fine."

Dr. Amelia's eyes shine in the overhead lighting. "I know, Agent Hunter. You'll be better than fine."

## NADIA

*Beep.*

*Beep.*

*Beep.*

"Are you sure you read the results correctly?" A muffled female voice cuts through the darkness.

*Beep.*

*Beep.*

*Beep.*

"She's definitely human. Look at the results for yourself."

The dark world shakes, and I fall deeper into myself. I'm awake, but I can't move, talk, or open my eyes. I can feel the heat of whatever drugs the doctors have injected into me as they course through my veins.

I'm alone in my own personal void, afraid of what'll happen once they pull me out. Maybe they'll leave me like this forever. I can live through my memories and never have to experience pain and heartache again.

*Beep.*

*Beep.*

*Beep.*

"She's ready for transfer."

I'm not sure if I really am. I'm not ready for anything besides this comforting darkness. The muffled voices grow in volume, and the heat in my veins fades. The numbness gripping my hands and feet turns into a dull ache. I wiggle my fingers. The drugs wear off, and in a minute or two, I'll have to face the nightmare reality again—the HPA, the experiments, possibly what will be the end of my life.

I blink.

Blinding light halos my vision, and I study the shadow of a silhouette leaning over me. The light blinks out, and blue and black dots dance across my eyes. I blink again and watch as the blurry room comes into focus.

White walls and cabinetry, stainless steel instruments, white sheets, the sterile smell of a medical facility—it's all so overwhelming.

I shut my eyes.

"Don't be frightened."

A hot hand touches my cheek. I hold still, refusing to flinch and show how uncomfortable I am with my wrists and ankles bound to the rolling bed. The calloused fingers linger for what feels like minutes, and I force myself to open my eyes.

A young man with chestnut brown hair and dark coffee eyes studies me. He's dressed in a green button-up shirt with a white lab coat over it. Pinned to his front pocket, a gold name tag reads Dr. Harvey.

I turn my eyes toward the ceiling.

"You'll see your friend soon. What's her name?"

I press my lips together.

"I know it's a lot to take in," he says.

I blink.

Dr. Harvey shakes his head and pushes the rolling bed through double doors. I lift my head enough to peer at the tan painted walls, but there's nothing distinguishing for me to remember my way around if I ever get the chance to escape.

An elevator door dings open. Dr. Harvey wheels me into a cold cement corridor. Metal doors with small windows line the walls, but I can't see into them. Without having to ask, I know this is my prison. This is where I'll wait for them to kill me.

"Here we are," Dr. Harvey says.

He punches in a code into the door, and it swings open. Rolling my bed in, he unlatches my restraints and exits without another word. The room is much warmer, and I take a minute to gather my strength.

Hunger stabs me hard, and all the hair on my body stands on end. I sense Evie a few feet away. She's deep asleep and curled under a blanket on a small cot. I slip off the rolling bed and force my feet to the ground. Each step falls heavy, my hunger consuming me while my good senses scream at me not to mess up. But I can't resist the call of her dream.

I tug up part of the covers, slide on the cot next to Evie, and hug her. Within seconds, I'm in her dream.

## HUNTER

*"You should sleep."*

"I don't think I can," I think.

*"Just try."*

I shake my head and rub my eyes. "I need to see her."

*"Then go."*

## NADIA

I look around at the wreckage. Evie's SUV twists around a light pole with a white van idling behind it. Smoke and flames lick the metal, sparkling off the shattered windshield. A redhead rests limply on the steering wheel, and I'm caught off guard.

*Alyssa.*

Evie is trapped in a nightmare based on our reality. I touch my hand on the burning metal of the car, and it explodes under my touch. I inhale breath after breath of the delicious, cinnamon-tasting nightmare, and energy washes over me.

"Nadia, please, wake up. You have to wake up."

I glide around the totaled SUV and stop in my tracks when Evie comes into view. Her brown, red streaked hair veils her face as she kneels on the street next to a pale, ghostly figure.

My breath catches in my throat seeing my dream persona, created by Evie's mind. I'm doll-like with light blond hair and rosy cheeks, dressed in jeans and a tank top even though it's snowing. White snowflakes stick to Evie's hair and cover my own dream persona's face.

My stomach burns. I need to destroy her dream, yet I hate seeing what I'd look like dead. No one is ever supposed to see that.

The snow melts when my boots touch the pavement. "It's too late," I say. My voice comes out deep and smooth and eerily familiar. I turn and glance at my reflection in the cracked side mirror hanging from wires.

I'm Hunter.

In this moment, Evie's worst fear is not just the HPA but Hunter.

She opens her mouth to scream, and I crash into her. Wrapping my muscular arms around her, I suck in a deep breath of her disintegrating nightmare. I close my eyes so I don't see the look on Evie's terrified face as she explodes into a cloud of dream dust.

I pull out of the dream as it collapses and open my eyes. The urge to run away and hide overwhelms me, but I hug Evie and pet her tangled hair instead. She relaxes next to me and groans into her pillow.

I shake her and whisper, "Wake up, Evie. It's only a nightmare."

She jerks in my arms and pulls away, thrashing the sheet off us. I sit up and grip her shoulders so she can see my face. Her wide eyes shift from terror to relief, and she wraps her arms around me, crushing me to her.

She chokes back a sob. "I thought they killed you."

I press my index finger to my lips and nod my head toward the camera in the corner of the room. "Don't say anything about us. Remember what I told you? Did you tell them?"

Her brows furrow, and she presses her lips into a thin line. "I did, but my mom hasn't come. I think she disowned me."

I lean closer to her. "I doubt it. They're keeping you here to see if we'll talk."

"I really don't think that's true."

A knock on the door startles me, and I pull my legs up to my chest. A doctor in a white lab coat struts in. Her chocolate brown hair is styled around her shoulders, and she looks familiar. Shutting the door behind her, she turns and covers her mouth with her hand seeing us sitting together on the bed.

"I don't believe it. I thought the board was playing a joke on me." The woman steps closer, her eyes shifting from Evie's to mine and back to Evie's. "How in the world?" She takes a deep breath. "I don't understand. You have a lot of explaining to do."

Evie pushes from the bed and crosses her arms. "*You* have a lot of explaining to do, Mom. What is this place? Why are we here?"

Evie's mother pinches the bridge of her nose, closing her eyes. "You're here because you were involved in an accident that led to the death of one of our agents."

"It wasn't my fault."

Her mother's brows knit together. "One of our prisoners escaped."

Evie forces a laugh. "When did you quit the hospital to work at a prison?"

"So, you don't know?"

"Know what?"

I stare at my hands to keep myself from smiling. I didn't expect Evie to be so convincing. She might make it out of here with her memories after all. It's all I can ask for. I brought her into this mess, and I want to see her get out alive, unscathed, and unaffected by the lies and fears the HPA forces onto people.

I'll gladly accept my fate here if it means my father is free, Alyssa is safe, and Hunter doesn't give up on trying to change the world, even if it's my world he can't change.

"Never mind. Come on, I'm taking you home," Evie's mother says.

Evie's eyes shift to mine, and I tilt my head down just enough that she knows I'll be okay and this is what I want for her.

"What about my friend?" Evie asks as her mother guides her to the door.

Her mother peers over her shoulder and narrows her eyes at me. "I'm sure her own mom will come to pick her up shortly. Don't worry about her, just worry about yourself."

The door clicks closed, and the deadbolt slides into place.

My heart sinks into my stomach when I'm reminded of how my mother fell at the hands of an HPA agent, just like what will happen to me. I glance around the quiet room and lean back on the cot. Staring at the ceiling, I think about the life I gave up. I hope Alyssa is keeping my father together. He's done so much for me. I'd do everything exactly how I did all over again so he could be free. He makes the world safe, not me.

My mother once told me the most important thing in life was the people around you—not only family, but friends, acquaintances, strangers—they're the ones who create and inspire the world. They're good, bad, selfish, selfless, brave, scared, strong, weak, and different. But in the end, whether they're human or not, they're—we're—only people, and we have to share this life regardless.

Her words remind me of Hunter.

I've shared my world with him, and now, he's forced to share his with me. In the end, we'll both understand each other better than ever, and I know that neither of us will go down without a fight.

It's the fight that makes life worth it.

## HUNTER

Nadia sits on the edge of a cot in the same cell her father was in. Dread crawls over my skin and buries deep into my soul. I don't know how to face her, how to keep my emotions disguised, how to treat her as if she's not the most important person to me in the world.

*"You're going to do it because you have to, Hunter. Nadia will forgive you. She'll understand you're only doing it to save her."*

Ignoring Jacqueline's voice, I touch my finger to the monitor. Rainbow pixels cross the screen, my finger leaving a smudge print on Nadia's figure when I pull it away. I take a deep breath and force my legs to stand.

My instructions were clear. Find out as much information about her and find the connection between her and Creature 1252.

I wish I had time to prepare Nadia for this. Teach her how to answer my questions without giving away any telling information. I wish I could have two minutes alone with her so I can hug her and kiss her hair and see her smile.

*"We'll figure something out,"* Jacqueline says. *"We're all getting out of this alive."*

I wish I could believe her.

I shuffle down the cold corridor and pass Camden's room without stopping. It's hard to think about any other person here when I know Nadia is behind the last door on the right. I can feel her presence without seeing her. Her power and strength radiate through the walls and wrap me in her essence.

I knock.

"Leave me alone," Nadia says through the door.

My fingers shake as I punch in my code. I'm tempted to turn around and leave and just continue to watch her through the monitor. I crack my knuckles, easing the door open a bit to peek at her before she can see me.

She's moved from the cot to the corner of the room and stands guarded with her back to the wall, her arms crossed over her chest. I push the door open completely and hover in the doorway. My gaze shifts from the ground and up to hers. She stares at me with her intense, beautiful indigo eyes. She's so full of life and color that my tight nerves relax. She must've had the chance to inflict a nightmare, which will give her the strength to make it through this.

I swallow the lump in my throat. "I just wanted to introduce myself. I'm Hunter and I'll be your caretaker."

Her serious expression gives nothing away. She fakes her anger and hatred like I'm faking being an agent to protect her.

It doesn't hurt any less seeing her like this, though. She needs to keep her guard up at all times here, even with me. The HPA plays on weakness and works hard to break down walls to get the information they desire, the information I'll kill for to keep it out of their hands.

Sucking in her bottom lip, she narrows her eyes, burning my soul with unintentional hatred. Her nostrils flare as she takes a deep breath, and she drops her gaze to the ground. "And how long will that be?" Her low, razor sharp voice cuts into me.

I close my eyes for a second to hide my pain. "I don't know. I'm not in charge."

She shifts on her feet. "Then I have nothing to say." She turns and walks back to her cot and plops on it, curling her knees to her chest, staring at the wall.

I can't bring myself to leave her yet, so I lean against the doorframe and watch as she tries her best to ignore me. I know I need to leave her, that it's difficult for her to see me, but it's harder pulling myself away. I want her to know I'm here. I'll make things right. I'll figure things out. But, what if I can't?

I shake the thought away. If I can't figure things out, Nadia will. She's the bravest and strongest person I know. It's why I fell in love with her in the first place.

Rolling on her side, she meets my eyes again but doesn't say anything.

"I'm here if you need anything," I say.

The corner of her lips twists into a ghost of a smile, one only I'd be able to decipher. "I know."

And I really think she does. Life has always been hard on us. Nadia said it herself, maybe we're not meant to be together, but I'm not ready to give up.

I'll never give up on Nadia or myself.

I'll never give up on us.

# EPILOGUE

## STRONGER

### NADIA

I USE A purple crayon to mark off another day. Ten rainbow colored slashes decorate the paper calendar Hunter printed off for me. I'd go crazy without having a sense of time. There isn't a window to the outside world in my small cell and since I don't sleep, it's hard to track days. I'd forget if it weren't for my faking sleep every time my cellmate, Camden, slept.

The HPA separates prisoners by species instead of sex, and because both mine and Camden's DNA say we're human, I ended up with him. It's not as awkward as I expected because we've learned to give each other privacy—and it could be worse.

"You going to eat that?"

I drop my purple crayon on the small desk and turn toward Camden. His tousled, sandy blond hair stands in all different directions, and he desperately needs a haircut. He rubs his fingers through his unkempt beard and nods toward my cold plate of scrambled eggs.

"Go ahead. I don't like eggs," I say.

"You don't like anything."

I roll my eyes. "That's not true. I just don't like anything here...except you."

He smiles between bites. "I know. I hate that you're here, but glad I'm not alone. I thought I'd eventually go crazy."

I look away. I wish I could warn him that he might go crazy, not from the loneliness, but because of me. It's torture to resist his dreams, and I have given him nightmares out of necessity, but I really do try to keep them short.

The green zone is full to capacity since the HPA has gone psychotic and picks up basically anyone they even remotely suspect to be a creature or working with a creature. It's insane, but because of it, I'm able to get the nourishment I need. I'm still counting down the days until I get out of here. Hunter told me soon.

*Not soon enough.*

"We'll get out of here before that happens," I say with a wink.

"Doubt it."

Crossing the room, I touch Camden's shoulder. I lean

down and press my lips to his ears. "I promise we'll get out of here, and when we do, we're going to destroy this place."

His smile melts into a frown, and he turns to gaze into my eyes. "I almost believe you."

"I almost believe me, too."

## HUNTER

"How is she?" Alyssa stands a foot away with her arms crossed. Snow dusts her red hair, and she hugs her jacket tighter to her.

I rub my hand through my messy hair. "She's managing. I moved her into a room with Camden because the cells are filling up."

"That many? What gives?"

"The HPA is scared."

Alyssa glares past me. "They should be."

I shove my gloved hands in my pockets and shift on my feet. "You see something?"

She shakes her head. "I don't have to see something to know. I just feel it. Don't you?"

I shrug. "Depends on the day."

A horn beeps, and a black pickup pulls to the curb. Dmitri rolls down the window and nods at me. "Any changes?" he asks.

"Not since yesterday."

"Keep me informed."

"Will do."

Alyssa digs into her pocket and hands me a folded napkin. "Give this to Nadia with lunch. You won't get caught because she can flush it."

She hops in the truck, and Dmitri waves once before pulling away. I stand on the sidewalk of the empty street and let the freezing snow dust my face. It feels warmer than my heart does right now. It's hard to be strong when it feels like life is out of my control.

*"It's your job to get it under control."*

I hate to think it, but Jacqueline is right.

## NADIA

Hunter's eyes linger on mine for what feels like eternity. I'm afraid the moment I look away, he'll be gone for another few torturous hours. He sets the lunch tray on the desk in front of me, and I notice the corner of some paper sticking out from under the bowl of soup I'll stir a few times but won't eat.

"Do you guys need anything?" Hunter asks. He stares at me while he says it, his love for me radiating from him, giving me the strength and hope to survive another day.

"What do we have to do for it?" Camden asks.

"Answer a few questions." Hunter's eyes shift from mine, and he shuffles back to the door.

"I could use a sketchbook and a newspaper," I say. I don't need either, but I've formed the habit of asking for random things to give Hunter an excuse to always come back. It makes being locked in this facility more bearable.

Hunter smiles and crosses his arms. "The HPA would like to know your name," he says.

A thousand names swirl through my head. "Emily," I finally say. I don't know why I say it, but my mother's name comes out of my mouth. "They can call me Emily."

Hunter waggles his eyebrows, and I turn away. It's his way of saying he loves me without having to speak the words. I know he does regardless. His love is tangible. I raise one eyebrow, and he twists on his heels and exits, locking the door behind him.

I slip the paper napkin from my tray and up my sleeve and meander to the only place where I have privacy. I hide in the corner of the tiny bathroom and unfold the note. My heart bangs against my ribcage. I squeeze my eyes shut to stop the tears from coming.

It's not a note but a drawing.

Two people stand on the edge of a river with their arms around each other. Their backs face me, but I recognize my long hair and Hunter's dark curls. In the distance is a cityscape, shadowed in dark clouds, but the sun shines above us. There's nothing foreboding about the sketch, and we look happy. We look free.

In tiny print, disguised as the flowing river, a note reads, *You two will get through this. Things will be okay.*

"We'll survive this," I whisper.

Hunter and I have been through terrible times together, but it makes the good times even better. We'll make it through this and will be stronger in the end because of it.

Even though it feels like I lost everything right now, I still have hope for a better future with Hunter—with all the people I love.

Hope is the one thing that can never be taken from me.

To be continued...

Read on for a sneak peek at *Edge of Awake*, the final installment in the *Destined for Dreams* series.

# 1

## KEEP IT TOGETHER

### NADIA

WARM BREATH TICKLES my neck. I silently count as I breathe in—*one, two, three*—and then out—*one, two, three*—it's the only way to keep my breathing in rhythm with what it should be like for a sleeping person. My breathing is identical to my cellmate Camden Allister's, and it helps that his heavy arm drapes over my side and his chest presses into my back. I just wish he wouldn't breathe on me. It makes it hard to focus.

Because Camden's and my DNA reads human, the Human Preservation Agency determined it safe enough to house us together in their termination facility. Luckily for us, it also means the HPA won't be experimenting on us. They're only keeping us locked up because they believe we have information they can use to destroy the supernatural world. The information they think we have is what's also keeping us alive. Once we have nothing else to offer, we're dead.

I flop on my back and stare at the white sheet covering my face so they won't see I'm awake. The dull ache of hunger grips my stomach as my nightmare inflictor side begs to take control. Grinding my teeth, I try to think about other things. I can't invade Camden's dreams right now. It'd be too soon since the last time. If I inflict nightmares too often, I'll drive Camden insane. A person can only experience terror so much before they break. I couldn't live with myself if I hurt Camden—or anyone—with my ability. I'm not a monster despite what the HPA would think if they found out the truth about me. They want nothing more than to rid the world of creatures—and nightmare inflictors would be at the top of their kill list.

*One. Two. Three.* Breathe in. *One. Two. Three.* Breathe out.

I've never been so controlled in my life. It only took giving up my freedom to save my father, being thrown in a cell with a powerless enchantress's son, and the heavy weight of my immediate demise if I screw up to get to this point. I never thought I could be this strong and resist a dream, but here I am. It's not like I have a choice.

Despite the constant tears burning my eyes and the heartache clenching my chest, I manage to keep myself together. If it weren't for my boyfriend, Hunter Sullivan, visiting me every three hours during the day like clockwork, and staying for twenty minutes at a time, I don't know what I'd do.

When the HPA made the sudden decision to transfer my father from the termination facility to the HPA lab, I had to wing an unplanned rescue mission. Hunter and Jacqueline Matthews, the sin-eater posing as an agent, were part of the escort team, and because of this, I did something crazy. With the help of my best friend, Alyssa Callaghan, and my new friend, Evangeline Thompson, from my short enrollment at Northern Bell High School, we managed to run the HPA van transporting my father off the road.

After the car wreck, I tried to distract the agents, and it nearly got me killed. That single decision forced Alyssa and my father to flee without me. It was the only way to keep everyone alive—almost everyone—since the only possible outcomes were to fight to the death or to split up.

Evie and I stayed because Alyssa knew the board would think I was human since I'm only half nightmare inflictor, and she knew Evie would be okay because her mother is a doctor for the HPA. I'm not sure what's happened to Evie, but I know her life is forever changed—just like mine.

I don't despise Alyssa and my father for abandoning me, but I do regret Jacqueline had blown her cover by killing the agent who was trying to kill me. I was tranquilized before I could see her fate, but I know it wasn't a good one. Putting her in that situation will always haunt me.

As for Hunter—he kept his agent façade to protect me. He watches over me in the termination facility, and I'm sure he, my father, and Alyssa are devising a plan to get me out of here. I just hope it's soon. I'm at my breaking point.

Camden rolls closer, tugging me from my thoughts, and slings his leg over mine in his sleep. I squeeze my eyes shut and grimace. I don't know how people sleep next to each other with the constant shifting and moving, the tug-of-war for blankets, the fight over pillows, and the heavy weight of limbs threatening to crush me. But I don't have a choice. I have to deal with this until I get out of here.

I sigh and sit up. I'll either pretend to nap later or act sleep-deprived. I just can't take it anymore. If I have to pretend to sleep for another minute, I'll go crazy.

Pressing my feet to the cool tile, I pad my way across the room to the desk. I don't wear the slippers provided for me because I can't risk messing up and accidentally gliding. I need complete control to keep the HPA's board from discovering my nightmare inflictor half. If the HPA discovers I'm not completely human, they'll murder me without a second thought. It's hard being under a microscope all the time, but as each day passes, I find it easier to pretend to be human. If I ever make it out of here, I'll never have to worry about fitting in with the human population again.

I flip open the sketchpad and stare at yesterday's drawing. It's a stick figure with vertical lines drawn over it like prison bars. I'm not the least artistic, but boredom has opened up a new world I never thought of exploring. That's the answer I gave Dr. Harvey, the scientist who pesters me for information, when he asked me about my sketches. Every few days, he has Hunter retrieve the sketchbook for the board to analyze. They somehow think its contents will reveal all my dark secrets.

I pick a black crayon from the box and draw sixteen circles, adding four lines to each to make it look like a crowd of poorly drawn people. I give some hair while leaving others bald, and then I write names under each figure—Mike, Jamie, Christopher, Ted—each figure is given an imaginary identity I'm sure the board will go nuts over. The board thrives on information, so I make it up and lead them nowhere. I'll play this game as long as they're willing to go on wild goose chases that'll always leave them sore losers.

A beeping sound echoes through the quiet room, and I get up and walk to the wall, leaning my back against it. It's a habit I've grown used to after these eight extremely long weeks. Today is the last day of another month. I can't believe I've already wasted so many weeks of my life here.

The heavy door cracks open. Dr. Harvey covers for Hunter half the week so he doesn't have to take as many double shifts until they assign him a new partner.

*A new partner.* My heart sinks into my stomach thinking about Jacqueline.

I cross my arms. "You're here early."

Dr. Harvey rubs his hand over his day-old stubble. His chiseled jaw tightens as he clenches his teeth, and his dark coffee eyes shift from me to Camden sleeping on the cot. He tucks his hands into his lab coat pockets.

I stiffen. "Where's breakfast?"

"I'm not here for that, Emily," he says.

My heart hammers a million miles a minute. I gave them my mother's name as my own, and I'll never get used to people calling me by it, but hearing her name also helps me keep it together. If she were alive, she'd want me to fight and not give up. She believed in the goodness of my father, including his nightmare inflictor side, and she'd believe I could make it through this.

I press my hand to the wall for support. This could be it. They could deem me useless and send me to the black zone where I'd be murdered. Hunter isn't even here to save me. I thought he'd fight to the death with me if it came to it. *You don't want that. You want Hunter to live.*

I want to live, too.

It takes me a moment to find my voice. "Then why are you here, Dr. Harvey?"

"Please, follow me," he says.

I shake my head, cold dread seeping into my bones. "Not until I have some answers."

"It's only for some tests and questions, Emily. Don't make this difficult." Stepping closer, he leaves the door open behind him, strutting my way.

It takes everything in me not to scream for Camden. Even if we could take Dr. Harvey out, we'd never make it far even with the door open. There's nothing I can do. If I fight, they'll relocate me to another zone, but if I don't, they might kill me.

I swallow. "You could've just said that."

Dr. Harvey stops in his tracks and pulls out a pair of handcuffs from his pocket. "I have to restrain you."

"Why? I'm not going to run."

"Emily, hold your hands up." He sighs, waiting for me to raise my hands.

My fingers tremble as I hold them up. The cold metal cuffs cut into my wrists when Dr. Harvey tightens them. He jerks his head toward the door, forcing me to shuffle to it with him at my side, digging his boney fingers into my shoulder.

This is the first time I've left the cell since I was transferred from another one days after my arrival. But this time, I'm not walking thirty feet under Hunter's care. We walk in the opposite direction of the cell block, and I don't get a chance to look into the cells around me. I wonder how many others share my fate. I've only heard screams through the wall from the cell next to mine.

"Where are we going?" I ask, my voice echoing through the quiet corridor.

"Don't speak. Keep your eyes on the ground. If you disobey, I'll call for an agent to assist me, and they don't care about your wellbeing like I do." Dr. Harvey nudges me past a desk with a set of monitors toward an elevator.

I flick my attention up and back to the tiled floor. Dr. Harvey doesn't really care about my wellbeing. He only cares about what I have to offer—whether it's information or some new scientific breakthrough—and once I have nothing left, I'll only be a number on some scribbled notes buried in a file.

The elevator dings, and my eyes shift to a pair of black stilettos. A woman waits inside the elevator, but I'm too scared to look up to see her face. Dr. Harvey pushes me forward. Tension rolls through me, feeling the woman's gaze on me.

"It's nice to see you, Andrea," Dr. Harvey says.

"I thought I'd join you for the transfer and interrogation, Harvey," the woman says.

I crinkle my nose. Dr. Harvey is one of the few doctors that goes by his first name. I'm not sure what to think about it.

Dr. Harvey tugs my arm, forcing me to the wall and away from the woman. "While Human 9209 asks a lot of questions, she never gives anyone any trouble. Right, Emily?"

I don't open my mouth. He's trying to trick me. Instead, I just keep staring at the floor.

A hand reaches out and grabs my chin and pulls my head up. I slowly lift my gaze and stare into hazel eyes so familiar they almost shatter my blank expression. Andrea isn't just any doctor. She's Dr. Andrea Sullivan, Hunter's evil, heartless mother who was willing to give up Hunter's soul for information about creatures, and the woman I want to kill most in the world.

## HUNTER

I tie on the leather bracelet with a small engraved coin on it that Alyssa gave me three days after Nadia had given up her freedom for her father's. It's the only way to get past the spelled walls surrounding the non-human portion of her neighborhood. Without it, I'd constantly walk past and never find Dmitri's house again. He's tripled his security measures since losing Nadia, and I don't blame him.

Alyssa stands on her front porch, her red hair hiding under a fleece hat. She hugs herself, running her gloved hands up and down her puffy jacket. I raise my hand and wave. She motions for me to hurry, so I jog the rest of the way to her.

"You have ten minutes," she says.

My brows furrow. "What are you talking about? My shift doesn't start for another two hours."

*"Will you ever catch on that Alyssa is a seer?"* Jacqueline's voice rings in my ears.

I blink. "What did you see?" I add.

It's funny how our roles have been reversed. I never thought I'd ever host a soul, especially Jacqueline's. She didn't have a choice but to body jump into me to save herself after preventing Agent Rob from murdering Nadia. I'd let Jacqueline hitch a ride forever if I had to, because I could never repay her for her selfless actions.

*"We'll just call it even, Hunter,"* Jacqueline says, hearing my thoughts.

Unlike the time I spent in her head when my mother traded my soul to Jacqueline in a deal that would grant Jacqueline amnesty from the board, Jacqueline can now hear everything that goes on in my mind. I haven't learned to conceal my thoughts—haven't really tried either—but it's not as annoying as I thought it'd be.

Jacqueline is basically like my strongly opinionated conscience. She walks me through everything, like my own personal, annoying guardian angel, and helps me make good decisions about the board and Nadia. But, one thing she's made clear, is that if I even think about telling anyone, including Alyssa and Dmitri, about her, she'll make my life more hellish than it already is. I don't know what her plan is, but as long as it doesn't consist of fighting for control over my body, I'll do what she asks.

"They're going to ask you to go in early," Alyssa says, pulling me from my thoughts. "The board decided to interrogate Nadia. She'll make a very clear decision that'll leave people unhappy."

Alyssa opens the door, and I follow her in. Dmitri sits on the couch, leaning his elbow on his knee. He presses his cell phone to his ear and glances at me before dropping his gaze to the carpet. Alyssa shrugs out of her jacket, struts to the kitchen, and returns with a steaming cup of tea.

I bring the warm mug to my mouth, the heat defrosting my face, but a chill remains in my stomach as I think about Nadia. I wish Alyssa would tell me more, but I know she's already moved past the topic. If it were something serious, she wouldn't be so put together. Her confidence is the only thing preventing me from running out the door and back to Nadia.

*"Nadia's going to be fine,"* Jacqueline says.

I exhale through my nostrils. "Are you psychic, too, Jackie?" I think.

*"If you think anything other than that, then you don't know her at all."*

I clench my jaw. "I can still wo—"

"Hunter?"

I rub my hand over my eyes and meet Dmitri's stare. "Sorry, what?"

He sets his phone on the table. "I asked if there was any change in the situation?"

Shaking my head, I say, "The board is still interested in Nadia. I'm more concerned that they're a little too invested in her. The scientist assigned to her constantly watches the monitor over my shoulder."

"I don't like this," he says.

I cross my arms. "I won't let them hurt her, Dmitri. Trust me."

Alyssa comes up next to me, bumping my shoulder with hers. "He does."

*"Ask him about his plan."*

I force Jacqueline's voice away. "What about your plan? How's it coming along?"

Dmitri stands, towering a good six inches above me. He runs his chalky white hand through his inky black hair and puffs air through his lips. "I need another week at least. The council refuses to leave the compound."

"And then what?"

Alyssa flicks her eyes from Dmitri to me. "It's not the right time to tell you, Hunter."

I sigh. I hate being left in the dark, but I'm not going to argue. The last time I did, I ruined the plan to get Dmitri away from the termination facility. I refuse to ruin Nadia's chance, too. "Okay."

Dmitri reaches out and grabs my shoulder. "As soon as everything is set, I'll tell you. Just keep me posted about Nadia."

He turns away from me, ending the conversation. His phone rings, and he waves to me as he answers it, then walks to the kitchen, leaving me alone with Alyssa. She shifts her weight from one foot to the other and pulls a napkin from her pocket.

She holds it out to me. "Give this to Nadia after nine o'clock tonight but before breakfast."

I shove it in my pocket. "She misses you guys."

"I know." Alyssa flings her arms around me, and I keep my hands at my sides.

*"It's okay to pat her back, Hunter. She's not going to bite."*

"Shut up, Jackie," I think.

Alyssa pulls away and walks to the front door and holds it open. "You have three minutes, Hunter. I'll call you later if I can."

I leave without looking back. As soon as I'm out of the neighborhood, I untie the leather band from my wrist and tuck it in a hidden pocket of my jacket. Running the rest of the way to my car, I climb in and start the engine. I stretch my achy, still tender hand. I got the cast off only a few weeks ago, but the memory of nearly getting beaten to death during Dmitri's failed rescue mission still lingers in my mind. I regret getting involved. If I hadn't, everyone would be free, and I'd be away from the board now.

I pull away from the curb and drive. I want to be as far away as possible before the board contacts me. I wish I didn't have to answer to them. I wish Dmitri would hurry up with his plan. I don't know how much more I can take.

## NADIA

Dr. Harvey leads me into a small room with two couches and a coffee table. A folding table with a coffee pot, cups, and a plate of muffins rests against a wall with framed portraits. Along the opposite wall are floor-to-ceiling cabinets secured with combination locks.

Dr. Sullivan points to a spot on one of the couches, and Dr. Harvey pushes me toward it to sit down. I contemplate asking to stand but instead lower myself onto the worn, green cushion and rest my cuffed hands in my lap.

I listen to the clicks of Dr. Sullivan's heels as she crosses the room. "Would you like some breakfast?"

My stomach knots. I want nothing more than to be escorted back to my cell. I don't want to sit here and watch Dr. Sullivan and Dr. Harvey eat breakfast. My heart hammers in my ears, and I swear it's loud enough for the doctors to hear.

Dr. Harvey clears his throat. "Dr. Sullivan asked you a question, Emily. It's okay to speak now."

I keep my eyes trained on my trembling hands. "Yes, thank

you." It's the expected response for someone who hasn't eaten food since last night. I'm guessing it'll also mean I'm going to be in this room for a while.

Dr. Sullivan saunters to the couch opposite me and sets the plate of muffins and two cups of coffee on the table between us. I draw my eyes up enough to watch Dr. Sullivan flip through a stack of papers on a clipboard.

Dr. Harvey sits next to me, setting his own cup of coffee on the table. He reaches for my arms and removes my cuffs, but I keep my hands in my lap. I don't attempt to grab for the muffin I don't really want. Instead, I rub my wrists.

Dr. Sullivan clicks her pen. "You must be wondering why we brought you here."

I twist my lips to the side. "I'm more interested in why you're keeping me here."

I glance from Dr. Harvey, who's sipping his coffee, to Dr. Sullivan, who now studies my facial expressions like I'm merely a subject of her experiments. She pushes her gold-framed glasses up into her brown hair, a shade lighter than Hunter's, treating them like a headband.

Dr. Sullivan taps her pen against her chin. "Well, dear, what did you expect would happen?"

"I didn't do anything wrong," I say, glaring.

She smirks. "The reports say otherwise."

I roll my eyes. I can't help it. "Dr. Harvey said you were going to perform some tests." I can't sit here and argue about why I'm here. I know the real reason why I'm here.

"We will get to that as soon as you answer a few questions," she says, shifting on the couch.

I peer at Dr. Harvey, who stares into his half-empty cup of coffee and purse my lips. Straightening my shoulders, I don't give in to my desire to sulk. To groan under her scrutiny or relent and answer whatever she wants. Because no matter what I say, it'll never get me out of here. "Then I guess you can take me back to my cell. I don't answer questions for anyone."

Dr. Harvey clears his throat. "What about Agent Hunter?"

I shrug. "What about him?"

Dr. Sullivan sighs and stands up. "Dr. Harvey is insinuating that you answer questions for Agent Hunter. Must we spell things out?"

I hold my serious expression. I've struck a nerve with Dr. Sullivan. If I keep it up, she might transfer me out of the green zone just to demonstrate her sadistic power. I lick my lips. "Hunter doesn't interrogate me and treat me like I'm less than human."

Dr. Sullivan exhales through her flared nostrils. "Dr. Harvey, please restrain Human 9209 and escort her back to her cell. I need to make a phone call." She shifts her eyes to mine. "I'll be seeing you later."

*Find out what happens next in Edge of Awake, the final installment of the Destined for Dreams series.*

# ACKNOWLEDGEMENTS

AS ALWAYS, I want to thank Jan and Jamie for their input and guidance while writing *Nightmare Reality*. Without you, it would sound like my characters' eyes are literally dropping to the floor so often they'd probably lose them altogether. I'd also like to thank Bev Katz Rosenbaum and Amanda Phillips for their editorial guidance. They not only immensely improved my story but also my writing.

Thank you to the bloggers who spend so much of their time dedicated to helping authors. You are invaluable, and I appreciate what you do from the bottom of my heart.

A special thanks to my family and friends. I'm forever grateful for your support and enthusiasm. I can't thank you all enough.

# About Ginna Moran

GINNA MORAN IS a writer from sunny Southern California. She started writing poetry as a teenager in a spiral notebook that she still has tucked away on her desk today. Her love of writing grew after she graduated high school, and she completed her first unpublished manuscript at age eighteen.

When she realized her love of writing was her life's passion, she studied literature at Mira Costa College in Northern San Diego. Besides writing novels, she was senior editor, content manager, and image coordinator for Crescent House Publishing Inc. for four years.

Aside from Ginna's professional life, she enjoys binge watching television shows, playing pretend with her daughter, and cuddling with her dogs. Some of her favorite things include chocolate, anything that glitters, cheesy jokes, and organizing her bookshelf.

Ginna Moran loves to hear from her readers so visit her online at www.GinnaMoran.com. You can also find her on Facebook, Twitter, Instagram, and Snapchat (@GinnaMoran). To stay up-to-date on new releases, sign up for her newsletter. You'll also gain exclusive access to Breathing Water, a serialized retelling of Diving Under from Carter's point of view.

Ginna Moran is currently hard at work on her next novel.